All I W
For
Christmas

Amy Silver is a writer and freelance journalist, and
has written on everything from the diamond trade to
DIY dog grooming. She lives in London and has a
penchant for vintage clothes and champagne cocktails.
This is her second novel.

ESSEX CC LIBRARIES

30130 167513547

Also by Amy Silver

Confessions of a Reluctant Recessionista

All I Want For Christmas

AMY SILVER

arrow books

Published by Arrow Books in 2010

2 4 6 8 10 9 7 5 3 1

Copyright © Amy Silver, 2010

Amy Silver has asserted her right under the Copyright, Designs and Patents Act, 1988, to be identified as the author of this work.

This book is a work of fiction. Names and characters are the product of the author's imagination and any resemblance to actual persons, living or dead, is entirely coincidental.

This book is sold subject to the condition that it shall not, by way of trade or otherwise, be lent, resold, hired out, or otherwise circulated without the publisher's prior consent in any form of binding or cover other than that in which it is published and without a similar condition including this condition being imposed on the subsequent purchaser.

First published in Great Britain in 2010 by
Arrow Books
The Random House Group Limited
20 Vauxhall Bridge Road, London, SW1V 2SA

www.rbooks.co.uk

Addresses for companies within The Random House Group Limited can be found at: www.randomhouse.co.uk/offices.htm

The Random House Group Limited Reg. No. 954009

A CIP catalogue record for this book
is available from the British Library

ISBN 978 0 0995 5322 9

The Random House Group Limited supports The Forest Stewardship Council (FSC), the leading international forest certification organisation. All our titles that are printed on Greenpeace approved FSC certified paper carry the FSC logo. Our paper procurement policy can be found at
www.rbooks.co.uk/environment

Mixed Sources

Product group from well-managed forests and other controlled sources
www.fsc.org Cert no. TT-COC-2139
© 1996 Forest Stewardship Council

FSC

Typeset in Palatino by Palimpsest Book Production Limited, Falkirk, Stirlingshire

Printed and bound in Great Britain by
CPI Cox & Wyman, Reading, RG1 8EX

Acknowledgements

Thanks to Lizzy Kremer and Gillian Holmes.

Tuesday 14 December

4.45 p.m.
Bea

Terry and I were having an argument about garlic. Actually, that's not quite right: we were having an discussion, a perfectly genial one, about pesto, specifically regarding garlic's place (or not) in a pesto recipe. Terry claimed every Italian recipe book he'd ever seen advocated the use of garlic in pesto sauce. He may well have been right, but I learned the hard way, from my Italian mother-in-law, that garlic *has no place in pesto*.

'There's no need for it,' I insisted. 'It's a delicate sauce, the garlic overpowers the flavour of the basil.'

'It adds complexity,' Terry objected. Terry, who owns the antiques shop just across the road from my café, is a stubborn man, notoriously difficult in negotiation.

'Listen,' I said, ignoring the queue of customers standing behind Terry, some of whom were becoming increasingly agitated the longer this conversation went

1

on. 'You take fresh basil leaves, and you crush them in a pestle and mortar. Don't chop! Crush.'

'I just stick it in a food processor,' Terry said.

'Heresy!' called out Sophia, the elderly lady standing a few places back in the queue. Her family originally hails from somewhere near Naples and she's on my side.

'Do you know why pesto is called pesto?' I asked Terry. 'It comes from *pestare*, "to pound". You crush the basil along with pine nuts and coarse salt.'

'Some people say cashews are a perfectly good substitute for pine nuts,' Terry said.

'You're just trying to wind me up now, aren't you?'

'Oh, for God's sake, how long does it take to get served in here?' Our friendly discussion was interrupted by a loud interjection from a tall, thin young woman who was standing directly behind Terry in the (admittedly rather lengthy) queue, regarding me with an expression of utter contempt. I'd seen her in the café before; I'd seen her quite often, in fact, although apart from taking her orders we had never had any interaction.

'What can I get you?' I asked her, giving her my most winning, customer-appeasing smile. She was a regular, after all. Couldn't afford to chase custom away. The tall girl wasn't listening though, she was answering her mobile phone. My hackles began to rise.

'What can I get you?' I asked again. She held out

2

her hand to me, commanding me to be quiet. I moved on to the next person in line. 'Yes, sorry, what would you like?' I asked. But the tall girl was ready to order now.

'Latte, very skinny – that's skimmed milk *not* semi-skimmed – and very hot,' she barked at me before returning to the conversation on her mobile phone. I took at deep breath and began to prepare her order.

I like my customers. Most of them, anyway. I have plenty of regulars who recognise that this is not a high-street chain, this is not Starbucks. This is the Honey Pot, Italian deli-slash-café, a place in which the serving staff (usually me, the owner, and Kathy, my number two) have conversations with our clientele. Sometimes those conversations last more than thirty seconds. Most of my customers understand that. Some of them – that tall girl talking on her mobile phone, for example – might find the service at breakneck speed that Starbucks offers more to their liking. They come back here, though, for the coffee. And the cakes and the pasta and the unbelievably good pesto that we import from Italy.

And we must be doing something right, because despite being a little off the beaten track – a quiet tree-lined road a few minutes from the Crouch Hill – we still manage to do very good business. Sometimes we do a little too well. That afternoon, that Tuesday, had started out fairly typically: a good stream of customers, most of our eight tables busy; it had been perfectly manageable. But come five o'clock, the December drizzle that had persisted for the last couple of days turned to a downpour, and from downpour to deluge. All of a sudden it seemed as if half of London had taken refuge in my café. There was a queue of customers snaking from my end of the counter, past the stairs that led up to the café's kitchen and right round to the opposite side of the room, and not a single table free.

The noise level was rising, and with it, my blood pressure.

'You got any of those sausages in red wine, Bea?' Danny, one of my regulars, was asking, half shouting to make himself heard over the din. 'Only the wife loves those, and she's been in an awful mood the past couple of days. Christmas shopping. She gets herself in such a state about it all.'

'I know how she feels,' I said, ladling spicy boar sausages into a Tupperware tub as fast as I could.

'Cappuccino,' the man after Danny snapped at me, without being asked.

'Coming up,' I replied. When I turned back, Terry was standing in front of me again. 'I really don't have time to get into the pesto argument again,' I pleaded with him.

'It's not that – I was wondering if I could put one of these up?' He held up some flyers. Something about puppies.

'Sure, of course. Over there – in the corner.' I pointed

to our noticeboard, which rests on a shelf against the wall. 'If you can find a space, go ahead.'

'Large, black, decaf,' someone was saying to me. 'And do you have any of those biscotti I got last time?'

'Which ones were those?'

'Oh, you know, the ones in the red tin?'

I didn't know. I do not have the memory of an elephant. Behind me, there was a crash. Kathy was bending over, swearing quietly as she picked up the pieces of a plate she'd dropped. 'Fucking mayhem in here.'

At the table nearest the counter, a child started to cry.

I took a deep breath. *Cut off the aubergine's spiky green cap. Peel the aubergine and cut into cubes. Put the cubes in a colander and sprinkle them with salt. Lots of salt. Let the aubergine steep for an hour. Scoop up the cubes, rinse them in cold water, wrap them in a tea towel and twist it to squeeze out the moisture . . .*

Some people count to ten. Some people play with worry beads. I recite recipes, like mantras. Whenever I feel like killing someone, when I feel like strangling someone with my bare hands or clubbing them over the head with an axe, I think of a recipe. I repeat it to myself, as calmly as possible. I think about the preparation, about the processes involved, about the dicing and grinding and seasoning; I think about the look of the food, the textures, the aromas. It calms me.

That afternoon, I was thinking of a Sicilian aubergine and ricotta sauce, just like the one we'd eaten at the trattoria on the beach front in San Vito Lo Capo three summers ago.

Put the vegetable oil into a large frying pan, place the frying pan on a medium to high heat. Add the aubergine cubes, but not all at once. They need to fit loosely into the pan, so do them in batches. When the cubes feel tender to the prod of a fork, they're done. Take them out and put them on kitchen paper to drain. Pour off the vegetable oil. Wipe the pan clean, pour in some olive oil and add the sliced onions.

Three summers ago? Four summers ago? Jesus, when was that? I couldn't remember. I could barely remember what I'd had for breakfast, if I'd had breakfast at all. Everything was becoming a blur. It wasn't just that the deli was so packed, it wasn't just the rising noise levels, it wasn't just that I'd had around three hours, sleep the night before. It wasn't simply the fact that it had been raining, miserable, bleak, freezing cold rain for three whole days (*always rain in London, never snow*, that's what he used to say), or that the list of things I needed to get done before Christmas, the imaginary list, the one in my head that I still hadn't got around to writing down, kept growing longer and longer and nothing ever got done.

No, there was something else. All of a sudden, everything was irritating. That tall, skinny girl, the one who had been so rude earlier, the one who had been talking non-stop on her mobile phone ever since she'd sat down in defiance of the large 'No Mobile Phones' sign hanging prominently on the wall directly in front of her: she was incredibly irritating. The immaculately dressed and coiffed yummy mummies with their triple buggies clogging up the aisles; the young men who shouted their coffee orders because they couldn't be bothered to turn off their iPods for thirty seconds; the exaggerated, eye-rolling exasperation of the teenage girls who had to wait more than a minute for their double tall skinny no foam extra dry lattes: all these things made me wish that I had an AK-47 stashed under the counter.

Even Sam was irritating. Sam, my friend and neighbour, waving cheerily at me as he hurried past with a new girl on his arm, another day, another blonde, another romantic disaster in the making, he was inexplicably infuriating. Usually I found his endless stream of women a source of amusement, but for some reason it was starting to piss me off.

I took a deep breath. *Sauté the onions until golden. Add the chopped garlic and stir. After a few seconds, add the tomatoes (tinned, plum, cut into strips). Cook for ten minutes. Add the aubergine. Season. Cook for a couple of minutes more. Cook and drain the pasta. Add grated Romano cheese, ricotta and basil leaves. Mix all the ingredients into the pasta, toss and serve, with parmesan on the side.*

7

That was a good sauce. A simple, delicious sauce. I hadn't made that sauce in ages. I should do. I should make it soon. But not tonight. Tonight was not a night for chopping and sautéing, it was a beans-on-toast kind of night. I was dog-tired, dead on my feet, desperate to throw everyone out, to close up and clean up, to stagger upstairs and cuddle up on the sofa with Luca while watching something pleasantly mind-numbing on TV.

But I was feeling guilty, too, because some part of me didn't want to do that at all, some part of me wanted to ring my mother and say, 'Actually, Mum, why don't you just keep him there with you tonight?' and then I could open a bottle of red wine and down the entire thing in forty-five minutes and then open another.

'You with us, Bea?' Kathy gave me a sharp poke in the ribs. I looked down to notice that the coffee I'd been pouring was overflowing on to the floor. 'What's up with you today?' she asked crossly.

'Sorry,' I mumbled. Kathy, a stout cockney with a fearsome temper, is often mistaken for my boss, despite the fact that she's actually my assistant manager. I was about to explain that I was just exhausted because I hadn't had much sleep the night before when the real commotion started. There was a scream from outside, and then a lot of shouting and swearing and people milling around, and then I could see a girl, sitting on the edge of the pavement,

8

a trickle of blood running down the side of her face.

9.20 p.m.
Olivia

When the doorbell rang, Olivia's heart sank. This had to be bad news. What else could it be, after the day she'd had? She had endured a miserable time at work. She had spent the first half of her lunch hour fighting with the vicious Hamleys Christmas crowds in a failed attempt to get her hands on the TeenVamp (TM) doll and the second half trying on party dresses cut to fit rail-thin Amazon women. This had been followed by more office-based misery. Then, on her way home, she'd been run down by a cycle courier. And to top it all, somewhere in the midst of all this mayhem, she had managed to steal someone's purse.

The hellishness had started that morning with a summons to see Margie, the editor-in-chief of *Style* magazine, the number-one women's glossy on the news stand today and Olivia's employer. Margie's opening gambit – 'Close the door, would you?' – was sufficiently menacing for Olivia to know she was in trouble. Olivia did as she was told and stood in front of her editor's desk. Margie looked from her computer screen to the December issue of *Style*, opened to the page of Olivia's beauty column, and then back to her screen. She sighed.

'Have a seat,' she said. Olivia sat. Margie looked up at her and gave her a cold, thin-lipped smile. 'We've had a complaint, *another* complaint, about your column.' Olivia swallowed hard. 'It's about the Jakob Roth Soy Growth Factor Xtreme Serum. What did you say about it?' She scanned the article. 'Ah yes. "Nasty, greasy and foul smelling . . . Like slapping salad cream on your face . . . You would be better off nipping down to Tesco and buying their own-brand moisturiser for a fraction of the price . . .".' Margie sighed again. She placed her elbows on the desk, tucked her hands underneath her chin and fixed her employee with a look of concern. 'As I'm sure you can imagine, Olivia, the people at Jakob Roth are not exactly turning cartwheels over your comments. In fact, they are most annoyed. And I have to say I don't blame them.'

Resisting the temptation to point out that Margie had read – or at least should have read – the column before it went to press, Olivia stuck to her guns. 'It gave me a rash, Margie,' she pointed out. 'You saw it. I had spots for three days.'

'Mmmm . . . And you're sure that was the cream, are you? Not something you ate? I've seen you shovelling down Pringles at your desk, you know. They're terribly greasy. It might have been something else. The detergent you use to wash your sheets perhaps? Can you really say without any hint of doubt that your dermatological problems were caused by that cream?'

'Well, if they weren't it was a bit of a coincidence—' Olivia started to say, but her editor cut her off.

'It could have been a coincidence. Marvellous.' She gave a low, mirthless laugh. 'Olivia, I know that because of your, ah, *situation*, you may feel inured from the economic realities that face so many of us . . .'

'That is simply not true—' Olivia spluttered, but Margie cut her off again.

'Let me finish. We are operating in an incredibly tough market. An impossible market. We are competing with the internet and cheap weeklies as well as our established competitors. Circulation is down. Advertising revenue is down. Do you have any idea how many full-page advertisements Jakob Roth took in *Style* last year? No? They took twelve. One per issue. Do you know how many Tesco took? You do, don't you? That's right, they didn't take any, because Tesco don't advertise their own-brand moisturiser in magazines that charge up to forty grand for a full-page ad.' Olivia cast her eyes downwards, her eyes fixed on the hem of her skirt which, she had noticed, was starting to unravel. Margie went on. 'Do you know how many pages Jakob Roth have booked for next year? Yes, once again, they've booked twelve. Only now I have a letter from their chief executive threatening to pull all of those advertisements – nearly half a million pounds' worth of advertisements – because of *your* ill-advised remarks.'

Margie was no longer calm. Angry red blotches had

begun to appear on her cheeks. She reached for the jug of iced water on the table next to her desk and poured herself a glass, her hands trembling slightly as she did. She took a sip of water, breathed in deeply and looked directly at Olivia. 'We need to find a way to put this right. Jakob Roth has a new fragrance, L'Amour Propre, it's being released for Valentine's Day. You will write about it in the February issue and you will not just write about it, you will *rave* about it. I don't care if it smells like pig swill.' She turned back to her computer, waving a hand at Olivia to dismiss her. But her editor wasn't finished; as Olivia opened the door, Margie screeched, for all the office to hear: 'This is *Style* magazine, Olivia. This is not the *Guardian*, this is not fucking *Panorama*. This is a top-of-the-range magazine for the kind of woman who would not be seen dead buying beauty products in Tesco!'

Back at her desk, Olivia checked her emails.

From: zarahobbes@style.com
Subject: Three Martini lunch?
I told you that Tesco comment was going to land you in the shit. Let's go to Joe Allen for a steak and get pissed.
Zx

Across the open plan office, Zara, Olivia's workplace sister-in-arms was grinning at her, miming knocking back drinks. Olivia hit reply.

From: oliviaheywood@style.com
Subject: Re: Three Martini lunch?
In an alternate universe maybe. Back here in reality, this is the list of things I have to do in my one-hour lunch break:

Buy tickets to Mamma Mia for the Kinsella clan
Pick up dry cleaning
Find presents for Shannon, Erin and Carey
Buy a dress for the Luxe Cosmetics party

Maybe tomorrow I'll have time to eat . . .
Liv
Xx

From: zarahobbes@style.com
Subject: Cruel and unusual
Christ, that is brutal. No one should *ever* have to buy tickets for Mamma Mia.
Zx

Getting the tickets was in fact the easiest part of Olivia's lunch break. Picking up the dry cleaning was painless, too. Trying to find Christmas presents for her boyfriend's three pre-teen nieces, on the other hand, was proving something of a challenge.

The good news was that the pre-teen nieces had very clear ideas of what they wanted for Christmas. The bad news was that the items they wanted appeared to be on the wish-lists of virtually every young girl in the country, and so were almost impossible to get hold of. On this, Olivia's fifth attempt to find the incredibly sought-after vampire doll (what was it with pre-teens and vampires nowadays?) that Erin, the middle niece, had requested, Olivia's enthusiasm for the task was waning.

Under normal circumstances, Olivia liked Christmas. She enjoyed Christmas shopping. She came from a large family (two older brothers, one younger sister, countless cousins, aunts and uncles) and she had great memories of enormous clan gatherings at the house in the Bahamas, of Christmas lunches which lasted from midday until nine o'clock in the evening, croquet games that began in a spirit of friendly competition and ended in sibling-on-sibling violence.

Olivia embraced the Christmas spirit. But Christmas shopping for her boyfriend's entire family, some of whom she had never met, was a severe test of her faith.

'You've no one to blame but yourself,' Zara pointed out helpfully when Olivia returned, late, frazzled and empty-handed save for a triple-pack ham and cheese sandwich she'd purchased on the way back to the office. 'After all, it was your idiotic idea to forgo Christmas in a paradise and offer to host the entire Kinsella clan in London instead.'

This was true. When Kieran mentioned that his mother, who was usually left to do all the Christmas planning, cooking and organisation, had decided to go on strike that year, Olivia had decided, in a fit of goodwill, to offer to host Christmas in London for his family instead.

'It'll give me chance to get to know everyone better,' she'd said, already picturing in her mind the somewhat Dickensian Christmas ideal, complete with snow falling thickly outside and angelic, ruddy-faced children sitting around the perfect tree. She hadn't really thought about the reality of her boyfriend's large family cooped up in her flat for days on end while it pissed with rain outside.

'Actually, it's not the entire clan,' she said to Zara. 'His grandparents aren't coming. Granddad's got a dodgy hip or something. He reckons he won't be able to get up the aeroplane steps.'

'Thank Christ for small mercies.'

The two of them were standing in the office kitchen, Zara making herself her umpteenth cup of coffee of the day while Olivia hastily wolfed down her sandwiches.

'I know, so now I only have to deal with Kieran's parents, his three brothers plus two wives and a girlfriend, two nephews, three nieces and – though this is yet to be confirmed – a basset hound.'

They were interrupted by the arrival of Margie, who had come into the kitchen to fetch her specially prepared macrobiotic udon noodle and vegetable salad from the fridge.

'Good God, Olivia,' she spluttered, picking up the

now empty triple ham and cheese wrapper. 'Please don't tell me you just ate this entire thing?' Olivia nodded sheepishly, gulping down the final mouthful. 'Have you looked at the fat content of this? Twenty grams! There are more than seven hundred calories in this pack! You shouldn't be eating more than fourteen hundred in a full day.'

'Well, I think the recommendation is actually more like two thousand, but—'

'Nonsense. They say that, but that's only for very active people. Or very fat people. This,' she said, proudly holding out her tub of salad, 'has less than a gram of fat in it!'

'Amazing,' Olivia and Zara chimed in unison.

'Isn't it? Actually, Olivia, that reminds me. I might have a little assignment for you. Come along!' She marched out of the kitchen, salad in hand and Olivia in tow, cutting her way through the maze of desks to the centre of the room where, just in between the subs desks and the art department, sat the Freebie Desk.

Olivia's pulse quickened.

The Freebie Desk at *Style* was a hallowed place. It was here that all the goodies, from the lowliest of lip glosses to the most coveted of Balenciaga handbags, were deposited before being divvied up between writers to review and, in some cases, to keep. As far as clothes, shoes and bags went, most of the really expensive stuff had to be returned to the designers, but they still got to keep quite a bit – 'they' usually being Margie, her deputy editor and the fashion girls who fit the sample sizes. In her three years at *Style*, Olivia had come away with a ton of beauty products (she was beauty editor, after all), but in terms of the most desirable loot, all she'd managed to get her hands on was a DKNY clutch and a Burberry key fob.

As they approached the desk, Olivia craned her neck, trying to spot what delights might be on offer. The beauty products for the next issue had already been distributed, so it had to be something else. Lingerie, perhaps? After all, the February issue was all about Valentine's Day. Or maybe . . . oh God, she could barely stand it . . . that bright pink silk dress from Marc Jacobs's spring line?

'Here you go!' Margie said brightly, holding in her hand a small, plain-looking white box. 'I thought you could give these a try?' Olivia opened the box. Inside was a plastic bottle with the word 'EEZYTRIM' printed on its side in large lettering. Diet pills. Olivia felt sure she could hear snickering from the hipsters on the art desk. She felt her cheeks colouring; for a horrible moment she thought she was going to cry. Margie, oblivious to her discomfort, was picking her way through a selection of Missoni scarves. 'I was going to have Suzie do us a feature on them, but that yoga retreat last month seems to have done for the last of her excess baggage. Why don't you give it a try? We could have something like . . . "Give your man a little bit less to hold on to this Valentine's Day ..." Something along those lines.'

'That sounds like a great idea, Margie,' Olivia said sadly. 'Thanks very much.'

Olivia left the office just before six, ignoring the raised eyebrows of colleagues who would not dream of turning off their computers a minute before seven, determined to put the day's misery behind her. She wrapped herself up in her dark blue trench and set off towards the tube, oblivious to the admiring glances of the two security men on the door of the building. Margie could say what she liked, but there was no doubt that the average red-blooded male would regard the idea that Olivia, diminutive, blonde and curvy, with peaches-and-cream skin and enormous blue eyes, should do anything to change her appearance as insane.

Olivia had a reason for ducking out early and it wasn't just to put an end to her miserable day. She wanted to swing by the Honey Pot, her local deli, to pick up something suitably comforting (and fattening, Eezytrim be damned) for dinner, and then get home to get on with Christmas-present wrapping, phase one (of four). She needed to get her own family's presents done that evening ready to be FedExed to the Bahamas the following day if she was going to stand any chance of her nearest and dearest actually have something to unwrap on Christmas morning.

The journey home went perfectly smoothly – as

smoothly as it could in torrential rain – until she was just five minutes from home, crossing Albany Street on her way to the Honey Pot. She was just about to step up off the zebra crossing and on to the pavement when around the corner came a Lycra-clad dervish going hell for leather down the hill and swerving ever so slightly too late to avoid a collision. He crashed into Olivia, who went flying, knocking her head on the pavement as she fell.

Everything went black for a fraction of a second and then she was aware of two things: a cranium-splitting headache and the fact that someone was shouting. As she struggled into a sitting position, Olivia was amazed to realise that the cyclist, the maniac who had crashed into her, was standing over her, red-faced and screaming expletives.

'What the fucking hell is wrong with you?' he yelled. 'You could have got me killed!'

Olivia gawped at him, incredulous. She was searching for a suitably scathing reply when a man, dressed in what looked to the casual observer to be a very expensive suit, said, 'What a ridiculous thing to say! I think you'll find that the young lady was crossing the road in the correct place. You, on the other hand, were going much too fast and riding quite recklessly.'

The psychotic cyclist fixed the suit wearer with a murderous glare. 'Fuck off, you ponce!' he snapped, before returning his gaze to Olivia. 'And you, you fat cow, watch where you're going in future.' And with that he hopped back on to his bike and sped off down the hill, cursing loudly as he went.

Still sitting on the pavement, Olivia burst into tears.

'Don't cry,' Suit Wearer said, stiffly proffering a handkerchief. 'You're not badly hurt, are you?'

'And you're certainly not fat either,' another voice said. Olivia looked up to see a tall, chestnut-haired woman standing over her, holding out her hand. 'Come on, come into the café, have a cup of tea and we'll get you cleaned up.'

The Honey Pot café, which was not a particularly large place, was packed. The windows were dripping with condensation; shopping bags and baby buggies blocked the aisles. Olivia's good Samaritan, who introduced herself as Bea, ushered her through the chaos to a table in the corner – the largest in the café – where a tall, thin, dark-haired girl in a suit sat alone, speaking in an exaggerated whisper into her mobile phone.

'D'you mind?' Olivia's Samaritan asked, pulling out a chair for Olivia to sit in before the girl had a chance to object. Olivia sat down and started to sort through her over-sized handbag, checking the contents for damage. Finding none, she placed the bag on the floor next to her chair and dabbed at her temple with a paper serviette.

'It doesn't look too bad,' Bea said, giving the cut a cursory inspection before turning her attention to the girl on her mobile phone. Bea rapped her knuckles on the table to get the girl's attention and pointed to the

'No Mobile Phones' sign. The girl ignored her and carried on talking. Bea tried again. 'No mobile phones!' she said loudly, gesticulating at the sign. The tall girl rolled her eyes, sighed dramatically and got to her feet, tripping over Olivia's bag as she barged past her. She bumped the table with her hip, sending salt and pepper shakers flying.

'Oh, for Christ's sake,' the tall girl hissed angrily, as though this were in some way Olivia or Bea's fault. She stormed out of the café to continue her conversation, slamming the door as she went.

'God, people are horrible at Christmas,' Bea said. 'Hang on minute, I'll just get you that cup of tea.'

It wasn't until Olivia got home that she realised she had somebody else's purse in her handbag. She was just sitting down to a dinner of tortellini with Swiss chard, prosciutto and ricotta when her mobile rang, and when she delved into her bag to find it, she discovered a purse. A rather elegant, expensive-looking Alexander McQueen purse. A purse that did not belong to her.

Feeling guilty and intrusive, she opened it and inspected its contents. There was about forty pounds plus change in cash, a couple of receipts (£14.50 for drinks at the Compass, N1 and £39.99 for a top from Urban Outfitters), a dry-cleaning slip (one coat, two skirts, to be collected on Thursday), a passport-sized photograph of a man (forty-something, handsome, dark-haired), a scrap of paper covered in a barely legible scrawl, three credit cards in the name of Miss Chloe Masters, and a condom.

Olivia scrutinised the scrap of paper, hoping to find a telephone number, but there was none. It took her a while, but eventually she managed to decipher the handwriting: it appeared to be a food diary.

Monday

½ grapefruit
2 espressos
1 banana
Peppermint tea
Salad – leaves, avocado, crayfish
2 slices rye bread with cottage cheese
Baked salmon with steamed veg
4 glasses red wine

'Typical,' Olivia muttered to herself as she polished off the remains of the deliciously calorific pasta she had picked up from the Honey Pot, 'I would nick the purse of a food fascist.' There was nothing in the purse which gave a contact number or address for Miss Chloe Masters, so she decided she'd just have to hand it into the police the following day – she was planning to go and speak to them about that insane courier anyway.

So there it was. That was Tuesday. Olivia had managed to piss off her boss, fallen further behind in her hideously hectic Christmas schedule, narrowly escaped death by cyclist and become a thief. So when, just before ten, her doorbell rang, she naturally assumed that something had to be wrong. It had to be bad news.

It wasn't. It was Kieran, devilishly handsome in the houndstooth coat she had bought for him for his birthday, sporting an enigmatic smile.

'You're a welcome sight,' Olivia said, giving him a kiss. 'I thought you had to work late. What a completely lovely surprise.' She stepped back to allow him in, but he didn't move. 'What is it?' she asked. 'Aren't you coming in?'

'In a minute. First I want to give you something.'

'Presents? Already? Ooh, are we doing the whole twelve days of Christmas thing?' Olivia asked excitedly. 'Do I get a partridge in a pear tree?'

'Actually, Liv, you godless heathen, I think you'll find that the twelve days of Christmas start on Christmas Day and end on Epiphany.'

'So it's not a partridge then? That's probably a good thing. I mean, I could probably cope with a partridge, but then tomorrow it would be turtle doves and then French hens, followed by all those calling birds . . . Where would I keep them all? And what comes after calling birds?'

'Oh do shut up, will you?' he laughed, pulling her closer and kissing her on the mouth. 'I'm trying to do something here.' And from his pocket he pulled out a little black box. Olivia stopped breathing. She was suddenly acutely aware that for the first time in three days it had stopped raining, and that in the perfectly clear sky hung a large, yellow moon. It was quiet; there were no police sirens or swearing feral youths to break the spell. It was the perfect moment. It was ridiculously perfect, it was Hollywood perfect. Kieran flicked open the box.

'Marry me, Liv?'

11.45 p.m.
Chloe

Chloe's post-coital buzz lasted exactly the length of time it took to smoke a cigarette, and then she was pissed off again.

'I loved that purse,' she said, viciously grinding the cigarette butt into the little silver ashtray on her bedside table. 'I got it on sale. And now is the worst possible time to have to cancel all my cards, isn't it? It's like, two weeks until Christmas. Just so fucking annoying.' She picked up her black silk camisole from where it had been flung on the floor in the disrobing frenzy and pulled it over her head. 'I don't even know if I'll get replacement cards in time. You'll have to pay for everything when we go to Venice.'

'Yeah, course,' Michael said distractedly, rummaging through the bedclothes.

'What the fuck are you doing?' Chloe demanded. 'Because you certainly aren't listening to me.'

'I'm looking for my sock . . . and I *am* listening. You loved the purse, you bought it on sale, I have to pay for Venice . . . *Voilà!*' He sat back triumphantly, holding one black sock in the air. Chloe was unimpressed. 'Oh come on, babe. Cheer up. I'll get you a beautiful new purse for Christmas, and you don't have to worry about the cards, I'll take care of everything. I promise . . .'

'You promise, you promise. You're always promising.' Her lower lip plumped out.

'That's not fair, Chloe. Please, let's not start all this again. There's not a lot I can do right now, is there? Not just before Christmas, it wouldn't be fair.'

'Oh, right, because *this*, what's going on now, that's fair? Fair on whom exactly?'

'Chloe . . .'

'Whatever.' She dismissed him with a wave of her hand. 'Go on, go and get in the shower. It's almost midnight, you need to get going.'

Chloe poured them each another glass of wine which they drank while he was dressing to leave.

'When did you have it last, anyway? Your purse I mean.'

'That's the weird thing. I could have sworn I had it in the Honey Pot. I was sure I'd taken it out ready to pay for the coffee. Then you called and I got distracted and when I went up to the counter to pay I didn't have it. And the annoying thing is that it was all her fault.'

'Whose?'

'Oh, that dreadful haggard witch who runs the place. You know, you've seen her, looks like she hasn't had a decent haircut or a good shag in months.'

Michael laughed. 'How is it her fault?'

'She made me leave the table, she kept banging on about her no-mobile-phone policy. No mobile phones! It's the twenty-first century for God's sake. Someone must have taken it while I was outside. And when I said so, she was completely bloody unhelpful. She just told me to report it to the police. Miserable old cow. I told her exactly what I thought of her and her sodding awful café.'

'I thought you loved that place?'

'Well, yeah, I do,' Chloe grumbled. 'But I won't be going back for a while. A week at least.'

Chloe lay against the pillows, stretching her long legs out in front of her. Michael, perched on the edge of the bed, took this as a sign to give her a foot rub. 'It's a nice life you have anyway, babe, sitting around in coffee shops at six in the evening. Bet you're glad you ditched corporate law . . .' She kicked him, only half-affectionately.

'The only reason I was in a coffee shop at that time is because that moron Fitzwilliam sent me to pick up some papers from one of *his* clients who didn't even turn up for the meeting, and there was no way I was going back into the office after that.'

'He sent you to pick up papers? Who does he think you are, his secretary?'

'Treats me like one, the wanker. And I *do* miss corporate law. Especially at the moment. Family law's hideous this time of year, insanely busy. We have to get the decks cleared before January.'

'Why's that?'

Chloe looked at him as though he was stupid. '*You* of all people should know,' she said, lighting another cigarette. 'January's our busiest time of year. It's divorce season.'

Wednesday 15 December

5.37 a.m.
Olivia

Olivia was sitting at the kitchen table, making a list. Olivia was an accomplished list-maker. She didn't just jot down notes (buy milk, pay gas bill) on a scrap of paper. Oh no, Olivia had a small, dark green leather notebook, a constant fixture in her handbag, in which lists were made. Her lists fell into various categories and sub-divisions. At the front of the book were the straightforward, daily 'To Do' lists. If one of those things to do happened to be shopping, then the first list could be cross-referenced with the shopping lists at the back (also divided into categories: food, cosmetics, clothes, and so on). There were also monthly 'To Do' lists, as well as longer-term lists made up of more significant goals. And then there were the special occasion lists, such as the 'Xmas 2010' list. This had begun with an overall schedule and was then divided into specific days: today, for example, was X-10. Ten days to go until Christmas.

Usually so focused, Olivia was finding list-making more difficult than usual that morning, her eye drawn, as so often it was, to the small but perfectly formed square cut diamond (ethical, natch) on platinum adorning the fourth finger of her left hand. It was just so pretty. It was a distraction. Guiltily, she slipped it off her finger and dropped it into her dressing-gown pocket.

She felt better. Normal. The engagement just didn't feel real yet; it would take some getting used to. It would feel real once she told someone. So far, she hadn't told anyone, there hadn't been time. Kieran proposed, she said yes, they opened a bottle of champagne and went straight to bed to celebrate *à deux*. The memory of it made her smile. It actually made her blush a little.

'Oh bloody hell,' she muttered to herself. 'Focus.'

She went back to the daily 'To Do' list.

15/12
8 a.m. Flower shop on Lyham Street
8.30 Honey Pot to thank Bea
9 a.m. Police station, report cyclist, hand in purse
9.30 Editorial meeting
11 a.m. Make calls for Botox feature
1 p.m. Engagement calls: Mum, Nikki, Katya

They had decided the previous evening to hold off on telling anyone about the engagement until 1 p.m.

because Olivia wanted her family to be the first to be told, and they wouldn't be having breakfast in the Bahamas until 1 p.m. London time. In fact, that was probably a little early to call, but Olivia didn't think they'd mind being woken up for that kind of news. After telling her family, Olivia had decided to tell her two best friends from school (Nikki and Katya) on the phone. Everyone else would have to make do with an email.

2 p.m. Compose and send engagement announcement email
2.30 Write Botox feature
4 p.m. Ideas for Valentine beauty special

She was interrupted by Kieran, who appeared, shirtless, dishevelled and bleary-eyed, in the kitchen doorway. 'What on earth are you doing up at this hour? It's not even six.'

'I've got so much to do . . . I just thought I'd get an early start this morning.'

'How's your injury?' he asked, crossing the room to give her a kiss on the head. 'Hey!' he said, grabbing her left hand. 'Where's it gone?'

'Oh shit . . .' Olivia fished around for the ring in her pocket and slipped it back on.

'Changed your mind, have you?' He turned his back on her and went over to the counter to turn on the coffee maker.

'Don't be ridiculous it's just . . . it was distracting me. It's so, so beautiful.' She got up from the table and slipped her arms around his waist, kissing the tiny freckles in between his shoulder blades. He ignored her and carried on making coffee. 'Don't be cross, Kieran, I love it. It's so . . . '

'Beautiful, I know.' He turned around and kissed her. 'Go on, go back to your list-making, you mad cow, and bring me a coffee when it's ready, will you?'

'I love you, you know,' Olivia said, burying her face in his chest. 'More than humanly possible.'

'Logic fail.'

'Exactly, a love that defies reason, that triumphs over logic . . .'

Kieran started laughing. 'There's a lot about you that defies reason, Liv. I'm going back to bed – and if I don't have coffee in fifteen minutes I'm going to take that ring back and give it to someone who'll actually wear it.'

'You'll have to pry it off my cold, dead fingers,' she said, grabbing hold of him and kissing him again. He slipped his hands underneath her robe, one eyebrow raised suggestively. 'Oh, sod the list and sod the coffee.' Olivia giggled. 'Let's go back to bed.'

Clutching a bunch of flowers in one hand and an umbrella in the other, a bottle of red wine tucked underneath her arm and her mobile phone jammed between ear and shoulder, Olivia tottered along

Albany Street, mentally cursing her decision to wear the boots with the four-inch heels.

'Zara, I'm going to be late,' she barked at her friend's answer phone. 'Can you tell Margie that I was in an accident last night and that I have to go to the police station this morning? True story, I'll fill you in later.'

This was true in the sense that it had happened, although it was not of course why she was going to be late for work. Blissed-out post-engagement sex was the real reason, but somehow she had the feeling that wouldn't fly with Margie. She found herself wondering when was the last time Margie, late forties and unmarried, had had sex. Fortunately she didn't have a lot of time to dwell on that thought, because she'd arrived at the Honey Pot.

Bea was behind the counter, cleaning the coffee machine.

'Good morning!' Olivia said brightly. She dropped her umbrella on the floor and held out the flowers and the wine. 'I just wanted to thank you for yesterday.'

'You really didn't need to do that,' Bea said. 'Wow, that's pretty,' she said, taking hold of Olivia's hand as she accepted the flowers. 'I didn't notice that yesterday.'

'Oh yes. I'm engaged!' Olivia said with a giggle. It sounded so weird to say it out loud. Officially, she wasn't meant to tell anyone before she told her mother but since Bea had noticed . . . well, she could hardly deny it now, could she?

'That's wonderful,' Bea said. 'Congratulations.'

She looked as though she'd been crying.

9.30 a.m.
Bea

I knew it had to happen sometime. I had been on an even keel for such a long time, and I'd been weaning myself off the Prozac for a few months now (I was now down to a very low dose), so it was inevitable that something had to give eventually, and why not now? It was bound to be now, with Christmas coming up, and the anniversary. Still, the force of it took me by surprise.

Lack of sleep was probably playing a part, too. I'd been up three times in the night with Luca, the last time just after four, and then he woke up again at six. For a good fifteen minutes after I first heard the muffled cries signalling he was awake, I ignored him. But gradually his pleas for attention grew louder and louder until I just couldn't stand it any longer, and I gave in.

(Did I give in too easily? I wasn't sure. I should ask my mother about that.)

We breakfasted together, Luca on mashed bananas and a bit of yoghurt while I had a cup of very strong coffee. The trouble began when I decided to get him interested in a bit of kiwi fruit – I was starting to get a little worried about his growing banana-dependence – but he point blank refused to try it, and when I tried

34

to force the issue he spat it out at me. And I was just saying to him, 'You're exactly like your father, he hates kiwi fruit, too,' when I burst into tears and I just couldn't stop. I cried and cried and poor Luca was horrified and then he started howling as well, and the two of us just sat there, him with mashed banana on his face and me with regurgitated kiwi on my shirt, and we must have cried for about fifteen minutes.

So not, all in all, the greatest start to the day. Plus, the breakfast debacle meant that I was late into the shower, and I didn't have time to do the washing up, and the flat's just a bloody tip now, the laundry basket's been overflowing since Sunday and I still haven't got round to doing any washing, so you can just imagine. And there's a pile of unopened mail on the kitchen table which has been growing since I don't know when and I don't know when I'm going to have the time to do everything.

And Christmas, oh God, Christmas. Christmas could *not* be a total disaster this year. Christmas this year had to be perfect. So what if Luca was only fifteen months old? He was an advanced child, he might just remember this one. So there were presents to buy; I had my eye on a very noisy fire engine (which I'd no doubt live to regret) and a 'My First Cooking Set' (no gender stereotyping from me), just for starters. More important than the presents though, much more important than the presents, was the food. I hadn't finalised my menu, but I had in mind a pumpkin velouté with Parmesan toast to start. I hadn't decided which bird I wanted to roast yet (I was tempted to go with chicken, unless I could get my hands on a couple of decent guinea fowl. Definitely not turkey), but there was going to be caramelised radicchio to accompany it, as well as some onions stuffed with pancetta and porcini, and since I loathe Christmas pudding and I'm sure Luca would, too, I was thinking of doing a bread and butter pudding, only with panettone instead of normal bread, which would be delicious.

Just exactly when I was going to get time to cook all this was something I hadn't figured out, and, if I'm honest, just thinking about it at all made me feel panicky and out of control. So I did what I do: I scooped my little boy up in my arms and I walked around my living room, whispering the recipe for panettone bread and butter pudding into his ear.

Luca seemed to like the idea, because he stopped crying and giggled every time I said 'panettone'. I got him washed and wrestled him into the little sailor suit Mum bought him from Petit Bateau which I like, though I'm pretty sure he doesn't, and the doorbell went. I assumed that Mum was early to pick him up, so I ran downstairs in my too-short robe, which used to be quite sexy back in the days when I had the legs for it but which now reveals way too much flesh, my eyes all red and my face all puffy and my hair looking as if I'd been dragged repeatedly through a hedge, and I opened the door and it was Sam. The effort it took me not to burst into tears again was Herculean. He just smiled at me as though I looked perfectly normal and said, 'Any chance I could borrow a hairdryer?'

Just like yesterday, I was completely, inexplicably furious with him and I stormed off upstairs to fetch one, swearing like a trooper, though he didn't seem to notice because when I came back down to give it to him, he just said, 'Ta, Bea. I'll bring it back as soon as she's done with it.'

I remember the days when I used to blow dry my hair every morning. I remember the days when I used to go to the hairdresser more than once a year, when I used to scrub and exfoliate and paint my nails. I used to be thin. I used to be one of those women, one of the ones that really annoy me now, who was effortlessly skinny, who ate whatever she liked and never did any exercise, unless you count dancing all night and having lots of sex. These days I feel . . . chunky. Not voluptuous or curvy. Chunky. And the truly irritating thing is that I'm too young to have gone to seed. I'm thirty-two, for God's sake. I'm not fifty.

Back upstairs I sat Luca down in front of the TV (I know, very bad mother) and made a start on the washing-up mountain. To prevent myself from smashing every single piece of dirty crockery in the flat, I started thinking about a fresh pear tart. A fresh pear tart would also be good after Christmas dinner.

Beat two eggs and a little milk in a bowl, I told myself. *Add sugar and tiny pinch of salt. Mix in the flour. Peel some pears – conference ones are best – scoop out the core and slice them thinly. Add them to the cake batter and distribute as evenly as possible. Smear a cake tin with butter and sprinkle with breadcrumbs . . .*

It always works. Well, almost always. I was feeling almost human by the time I'd got to the baking bit, and then the doorbell rang again.

This time, it was Mum. 'Bea, sweetheart,' she said, gathering my son up in her arms as we did our usual morning switch-over, 'you look dreadful.'

'Cheers, Mum, that helps.'

'Don't be silly, I'm just saying. You look tired. You know what you need?'

'Apart from a couple of litres of bourbon, a handful of Valium and a week off?'

'Don't joke about things like that, darling. No, you need to get some exercise. You used to be so *active*. You should take Luca down to the pool sometime. I bet he'll love swimming. Just like his dad.'

The first time I met Luca's dad, he almost landed in my drink. I was on holiday in Italy, on the Riviera in a place called Lerici. I'd gone with three girlfriends. We planned to hike the cliffs of the Cinque Terre in our first three days there and then spend the next four drinking and clubbing and generally misbehaving. It was our first day, and we'd driven down to the beach. There were thousands and thousands of people there, which was completely weird because it wasn't even high season, it was late September, so we couldn't understand what the hell was going on. It turned out we'd arrived on the day of the annual triathlon, so we fought our way through the crowds and managed to secure ourselves ringside seats: a table in a little café on the marina with a view on one side of the swimmers, and on the other of the runners and cyclists as they came hurtling or stumbling past, depending on their stage of the race and their level of fitness.

It was quite a sight. Among the participants, overwhelmingly male, mostly in their twenties and thirties, almost all clad in Lycra, were some truly magnificent examples of the male form. My friends and I spent the entire afternoon drinking delicious Bellinis, made with fresh, ripe peaches, shamelessly ogling the seemingly endless stream of beautiful, tanned boys passing by our table.

We'd been there a couple of hours, and were reaching the stage when the most of the fitter runners were approaching the end of the race, and they weren't just jogging along either, they were sprinting to the finish. We were sitting there, noisily and boozily cheering them on, when my friend Sally, who was a tiny, skinny little thing with the lowest alcohol tolerance of the four of us, decided to get up to go to the loo. Only she managed to knock her handbag off the back of her chair, get her feet tangled up in the straps and fall headlong into the path of the runners, the nearest of whom leaped to his right to avoid stamping on her and ended up face down, lying across our table, his head virtually in my lap.

Despite sending our drinks flying, the runner was unhurt. He picked himself up off the table, dusted himself down, said, '*Mi dispiace, signorine*. I am terribly sorry. I will buy you a round of drinks on my return.' Then he helped Sally to her feet and sprinted off down the road as though nothing had happened.

'I think I'm going to marry that man,' Sally said, swaying slightly as she watched him disappear into the crowd, and I said:

'Not if I marry him first.'

I was thinking about that afternoon, possibly one of the happiest of my entire life, when Olivia, the girl who'd been knocked over by the cyclist the day before, turned up with a beautiful bunch of flowers for me and then announced her engagement. And I barely even had time to congratulate her before that bitch turned up and really ruined my day.

11 a.m.
Chloe

Chloe was on her fourth cup of coffee of the morning, but she still felt like a zombie. Her pulse was racing and yet she felt sluggish, her limbs weighed down, as though she were underwater or swimming through mud. The light seemed too bright and every sound too loud, and she wondered if it was possible to die of insomnia? She Googled it. Yes, death from sleep deprivation *was* possible. No humans were known to have died from lack of sleep, but in the 1980s a particularly sadistic researcher at the University of Chicago experimented on rats and found that after thirty-two days of total sleep deprivation, all the rats died.

She didn't know how long it had been since she'd slept properly, but it was longer than thirty-two days, that was for sure. Still, she was hardier than the average rat. Chloe was hard as nails. When she did finally succumb to lack of sleep, she knew what they would put on her tombstone: *Chloe Masters, unbelievable bitch.*

Chloe had returned to the Honey Pot that morning before she came into work in the faint hope that someone might have handed her purse in to the proprietor. Unbelievably, the dopey cow who'd got run over the day before was the one who'd taken it (by mistake, allegedly) and she was there at that very moment, wittering on about her engagement and showing off a very sad little ring.

Chloe was not overly impressed. 'For fuck's sake,' she grumbled, snatching the purse from Olivia's fingers. 'Someone might have told me it'd been found. I've cancelled all my cards now, haven't I?'

'I'm so sorry,' Olivia said sweetly, 'but I didn't know it was yours until just a minute ago. I think it may have fallen into my handbag when you—'

'When I what?' Chloe demanded. 'Don't try and blame this on me.'

'What the hell is wrong with you?' Bea snapped suddenly. Olivia looked startled until she realised that Bea was in fact talking to Chloe, who just looked mildly surprised, as though she wasn't used to people answering back. 'Olivia was just going down to the police station to hand this in – she didn't know it was yours. And you don't even have the good grace to thank her. No bloody manners at all. But then I realised that yesterday when you were unbelievably bloody rude to me.' Chloe opened her mouth to say something but Bea didn't give her a chance. 'Just take your bloody purse, check that we haven't stolen anything, then get out of my café and don't come back.'

But Chloe didn't leave. She sank down into the nearest chair and covered her face with her hands. 'Oh God oh God oh God,' she moaned. Olivia, looking stricken, sat down next to her and put an arm around her slender shoulders.

'Don't,' she said. 'Don't cry. We didn't mean to upset you.'

'Speak for yourself,' Bea muttered under her breath, but she must have been feeling bad too, because she retreated behind the counter to make Chloe a cup of tea.

'Everything's just such a mess,' Chloe said. She accepted the cup of tea from Bea, took a sip and handed it back. 'You don't have Earl Grey, do you?' she asked. 'With a slice of lemon?'

Bea flashed her a murderous smile and said, 'No problem.'

With a cup of Earl Grey at her elbow, Chloe apologised. 'I'm just having the most fucking awful time,' she said, looking at Olivia with large, beseeching brown eyes. 'I'm *so* tired. I haven't slept in . . . for ever.'

'Kids keeping you up?' Olivia asked politely.

'God no,' she replied, wrinkling her nose in distaste at the very thought. 'No, it's just . . . I have a very stressful job. I'm a lawyer. I'm under a lot of pressure. And then there's this whole thing with my boyfriend . . .'

'You're having problems?' Olivia prompted, resting her hand on Chloe's and then withdrawing it almost immediately, concerned that flaunting her engagement ring might be rubbing salt in the wounds of a girl with man trouble.

'Not exactly, it's just Christmas, you know.'

'He wants you to spend it with his loathsome family?' Bea ventured. Chloe laughed surprisingly loudly at that.

'No! It's just that I've planned this whole perfect thing: we're going to Venice for four days, leaving on the twentieth, coming back on Christmas Eve, staying in this unbelievable palazzo; I've got us opera tickets and booked dinner at Cipriani . . . the full works.'

'Sounds amazing,' Olivia breathed enviously, wishing for a second that Kieran's idea of a great holiday was less camping in Scotland and more fabulous Venetian palazzo.

'So what's the problem?' Bea asked, but before Chloe could reply, they were interrupted by customers: an attractive couple, one of whom was, rather incongruously, holding a hairdryer.

'Hello!' the man called out cheerily. Chloe and Olivia sized him up appreciatively, a fact not lost on the leggy blonde hanging off his arm.

'Hi, Sam,' Bea replied, getting to her feet and retreating once more behind the counter. 'Coffee?'

'Please.'

'Skinny for me,' the girl said. 'And no foam. Can't stand foam.'

'Thanks for the loan of the hairdryer,' Sam said.

'Not very powerful, is it? When did you get it? Nineteen eighty-three?' the girl asked. Bea ignored her. She handed the coffees to Sam who accepted them with a wink and grin.

'How's Luca? He with his gran today?'

'Yeah,' Bea said. 'And he's well, thanks for asking.'

'Now *that* is a nice looking man,' Chloe said once Sam and his girlfriend were out of earshot. 'Shame about the girl. She looks like she's on smack.'

'You're charming, you are, you know that?' Bea said.

Chloe sipped her tea demurely. 'Anyway,' Bea went on. 'You were saying: Venice?'

'Yes, so I have everything planned, and we've been talking about this for months, and I just can't understand why now, all of a sudden, he seems reluctant to go. Now, just days before we're due to leave, he's started saying that he's not sure he can get away after all, that he's not sure she'll believe that he has to work right up until Christmas—'

'He's not sure *who* will believe him?' Bea asked, her voice suddenly icy.

'His wife. And it's ridiculous, because corporate lawyers often have to work right up until Christmas – there's no reason why she shouldn't believe him. And it's not like he's going to miss Christmas itself. He'll still be there with her and the kids on the day. He promised me that we'd have a bit of time away together. I honestly don't know what I'll do if he cancels on me now, I've been planning this for ages . . .' Chloe's voice tailed off; a lone tear rolled down her porcelain cheek. Olivia sat back a little in her chair.

Bea got to her feet. 'Well, cry me a fucking river,' she said. 'I just can't believe this. You're sitting here, snivelling at us about how tough your life is because the married man you're shagging won't leave his wife and his children just before Christmas so he can go to the sodding opera with you in Venice? Seriously? Are you mentally ill?'

'Well, I—' Chloe started, genuinely indignant.

'Get out!' Bea shouted, storming back behind the counter. 'Get out of my café. And maybe next time you're planning your perfect fairytale Christmas break, you should think about doing it with a man who isn't somebody else's husband, you unbelievable bitch.'

It was all very unfair, Chloe thought as she flicked listlessly through the papers on her desk. She had no one to talk to. She couldn't tell her sisters. They had never been close. And she certainly couldn't tell her mum. Her mum would not be happy that the man Chloe had told her so much about happened to have a wife and children that she'd never mentioned. And for some reason she just didn't seem to make any girlfriends these days. She'd always had them at school. Now she was having an awful time and all anybody ever did was judge her.

Trying to forget the morning's unpleasantness, she scanned the preliminary correspondence on the Miller divorce. The file had been left on her desk with a handwritten note from her boss, Maurice Fitzwilliam, which read, 'Discuss over lunch?' Maurice, who was almost fifty and married with two kids, was incapable of holding a conversation with her without staring at her tits. Whenever they worked together on anything he always wanted to discuss the case over lunch or a coffee or a drink, never just in conference room B. It was very tiresome. But there was no getting away from it: she was going to be spending a lot of time with Maurice in the coming days and weeks – the Miller split did not look likely to be a clean one.

The Millers had started proceedings early. Not early in their marriage – they'd been together for sixteen years – early in that most people wait until after Christmas, until after the kids have gone back to university and the in-laws have departed, to file proceedings. But Mrs Miller clearly couldn't stand the idea of yet another Yuletide spent slaving over a hot stove while her investment banker husband went to the office and got up to God knows what with his personal assistant. In her shoes, Chloe wouldn't have stood for it either, but on the other hand, Chloe could see things from Mr Miller's point of view. She had, of course, never met Mr Miller, but she had met his wife. An intelligent, attractive woman run slightly to fat since having children, Mrs Miller had an MBA from a very decent European business school, she spoke French and German and had, a very long time ago, been chief financial officer of a medium-sized business. And now she stayed at home and ferried the kids to school and back, she organised charity events and school fêtes. She had, Chloe imagined, very little of interest to say over the dinner table in the evening. No wonder Mr Miller had gone somewhere else looking for a bit of excitement. The woman he'd married had all but disappeared. She'd been devoured by a less-than-svelte replacement. Just like Michael's wife.

2.15 p.m.

Olivia

Olivia was not wearing her engagement ring. She had not phoned her mother. She hadn't phoned Nikki or Katya, nor had she sent out the general engagement emails. She had not told her colleagues the exciting news. She had spent her entire lunch hour sitting at her desk, not eating, not working, not really doing anything. She was thinking about that morning, in the café, with Bea and Chloe, and wondering whether into every marriage wandered a woman like Chloe Masters.

Olivia Googled divorce statistics. She discovered that 136,026 people were divorced in the UK in 2008.

Kieran would never fall for a woman like Chloe Masters. Tall and thin and elegant she might be, but he could never be attracted to someone so obviously mean-spirited. Cheating wasn't in Kieran's nature anyway. Olivia had nothing to worry about.

She Googled infidelity figures. More difficult to pin down, these, since the Office of National Statistics didn't keep track of who was cheating on whom. Fifty per cent of married men, one study said. Sixty-four per cent, another study claimed. Olivia thought about the fact that whenever they went to the local pub, the eyes of the extremely attractive Eastern European barmaid lit up when she saw Kieran, about how the barmaid always sized her up a little quizzically as though wondering: What on earth is he doing with *her*?

Her mobile phone rang. She didn't recognise the number, but she picked up anyway.

'Livvie!' a girl's voice shrieked on the other end of the line. 'Congratulations! I am *so* happy for you!'

'Thank you,' Olivia said, desperately trying to place the voice, 'that's so sweet of you to call. How are you doing?'

'Oh fine, you know, uni hellish, boyfriend a pig.' It was Tamsin. Kieran's best friend's girlfriend's sister. Kieran's best friend's girlfriend's sister knew that she was engaged and her own mother did not. 'Have you set a date yet?' Tamsin asked.

Olivia's work phone started to ring.

'I'll have to ring you back Tamsin,' she said. She picked up the other phone. It was Kieran.

'How did they take it?' He sounded so excited.

'There must be something wrong with the phone lines there,' Olivia lied. 'I haven't been able to get through.' Olivia never lied to Kieran. She never had any need to.

'That's a shame. My mother's going mental, I can tell you. She'll be on the phone to you shortly, I'm sure. I think you might have a time keeping her out of the wedding preparations . . . What did Zara say? Is she angling for maid of honour yet?'

Olivia swallowed hard. 'I haven't actually told her yet, Kieran. I wanted to tell my mum first, like we said.'

'Sure, of course.' He sounded disappointed again.

'Well, I'll let you get on. Give your mum and dad another try, yeah?'

Olivia took a deep breath and dialled her parents' number. Her mum answered on the third ring, sounding sleepy.

'Hellish hot here at the moment,' she said. 'It's so hard to get a good night's sleep. I bet it's lovely and bright and crisp in London, isn't it? I'm actually feeling quite jealous of you staying there this year.' Olivia rolled her eyes. Only her mother could make Christmas in the Bahamas sound like a trial.

'Actually it's grey and miserable, Mum. It's been raining for days.'

'Have you changed your mind about coming out then?' Olivia could hear the note of hope in her mother's voice and she felt a lump in her throat.

'No, Mum, I haven't,' she said, her eyes filling with tears, 'that's not why I called . . .' She was starting to cry.

'Livvie, Livvie, what on earth's wrong? Have you fought with Kieran?'

'No, Mum, quite the opposite. He's asked me to marry him.' Olivia was full-on sobbing now. 'And I said yes.'

Half an hour later, Olivia put the phone down. She'd spoken to her mum (who cried), her dad (who cried a little but denied it), her younger sister (who shrieked hysterically) and one of her brothers (who asked where the stag do was going to be). She phoned her best friend from school, Nikki, and her best friend from university, Katya (who both cried), and then she sent Zara an email.

From: oliviaheywood@style.com
To: zarahobbes@style.com
Subject: Meet you on the balcony . . .
. . . for a fag break?

The reply came back in seconds.

From: zarahobbes@style.com
Subject: Meet you on the balcony . . .
Since when do you smoke, Olivia?

From: oliviaheywood@style.com
Subject: Meet you on the balcony . . .
. . . so that you can admire my engagement ring then?

By the time Olivia looked up, Zara was already running, as fast as she could in sky-high heels, towards the exit.

8.30 p.m.
Bea
When I was a child, my mother insisted that we make our own Christmas decorations. By the time I got to about nine or ten, this used to annoy me no end, since she and I (Dad never joined in) would spend hours

sitting at the dining-room table gluing bits of tinsel or glitter to pieces of coloured cardboard and the decorations would come out looking totally crap because neither of us had any artistic talent to speak of. I remember being horribly embarrassed when my best friend came round, because her mother used to buy beautiful and no doubt incredibly expensive decorations from Harrods (a new set each year) and their tree looked as if it belonged in a shop window, whereas ours looked as if someone had thrown a lot of multi-coloured junk at it and some of it had stuck.

Now that I was a mother myself, I could see the point, though. It wasn't about aesthetics, it was about bonding, and in any case, Luca was too young to be embarrassed by the crapness of our tree. So after my mother brought him home that evening, he and I spent a most enjoyable and incredibly messy hour creating our own baubles (ping pong balls smeared in paint and rolled in glitter), as well as a delightful, lurid orange tree-topping angel.

It took me almost as long to clean Luca up as it had to make the decorations in the first place, but it was totally worth it, if only for the fact that we managed to go for almost two hours of playing and bathing without him asking for his gaga, which is what he calls my mother. That's progress. Plus, when he did ask for her, as I was putting him to bed, I managed to stop myself from bursting into tears. That's progress, too.

I was in the throes of making my second assault on the washing-up backlog when the doorbell rang. It was Sam again.

'I was just wondering who you were planning to vote for at the by-election?' he asked when I opened the door. 'Because if you haven't made up your mind, I'd like to draw your attention to what is possibly the most pressing, and overlooked, issue of the day.'

'And what would that be?'

'The ice rink! Says here that not only have the Labour Party led us into an illegal war, not only did they steer our economy into the deepest recession since the dawn of time, but they have thrown the future of the local ice rink into jeopardy!'

He waved a flyer in my face. It was from the Liberal Democrats and it did indeed claim, as a manifesto pledge, that a Lib Dem candidate would 'seek to secure the future of the ice rink'.

'Can you believe this shit?' Sam asked me. 'This is what we're supposed to get excited about?'

Sam does this all the time. He cuts funny stories out of the local newspaper or takes pictures of absurd notices on his mobile phone and brings them to me to share. I think he's lonely. He hasn't lived in London for all that long. When he was married, he lived in Bath or Bristol, somewhere like that. After his divorce he moved to London and took over the shop next door to mine; he sells plants, gardening tools, stuff like that. But his main income comes from garden design – apparently he's a pretty talented landscaper. This not only provides him with extra cash, it also gives him ample opportunity to meet women. He's forever hooking up with the more glamorous singletons (and the occasional bored housewife) who seek his advice. They seem to find him irresistible. I suppose it's due to some combination of charm, which he has in spades, and the fact that he spends a lot of his time hanging around in their gardens with his shirt off.

The women never seem to last though, and I don't think he has a lot of friends in London. So in the end, he just has me.

Sam was hovering on the doorstep waving the flyer around.

'Do you want to come in?' I asked.

'Nah, you're all right. I just wanted to apologise for this morning really. I shouldn't just drop round like that, not at that hour . . .'

'It's fine, Sam,' I lied, embarrassed now because he clearly had noticed that I was upset. 'Why don't you come in for a drink?'

Upstairs, I opened the bottle of red that Olivia had brought that morning. Sam admired the tree. (Along with his penchant for bringing me amusing scraps from his day-to-day existence, this is another thing I love about Sam. When he comes into my flat and it's a total tip, as it usually is, he never notices on the mess. He comments on the picture Luca has drawn which I've stuck on the kitchen wall, or on the fact that the plant he gave me three weeks previously is still, despite very long odds, alive. He notices the good stuff.)

He noticed the angel. 'I *love* the angel,' he said. 'It's very footballers' wives, y'know, with the orange tan? Very of the moment. Perhaps I should borrow Luca this weekend – he could help me out with my decorations. I don't seem to have anything at all. Lost them in the divorce.'

I handed him a glass of wine, and poured another for myself. 'I don't mean to pry,' I said, 'but is there anything you didn't lose in the divorce, Sam? From what I can make out, she got the house, everything in the house and the car. Did she have a really good lawyer or did you just have a really rubbish one?'

He grinned ruefully. 'Honestly, the only things I wanted were Reggie and my tools.' Reggie was Sam's dog, an ageing lurcher who spent most of time curled up in an old white armchair in Sam's shop window. 'Oh, and I wanted her, of course. But she wasn't up for grabs. Not by me, in any case. Not any more.'

I noticed that his glass was already empty, so I topped him up.

'Are you hungry?' I asked, getting to my feet. 'I can't be bothered to cook, but I do have some rather delicious leftovers in the fridge . . . Sausages and porcini mushrooms in a rich tomato sauce?'

'Bea, I live on pot noodles. I'm forty-one years old

and I live on pot noodles. Sausages and porcini mush-rooms in tomato sauce sounds like heaven to me.'

We ate the sausages with a French stick and a hastily assembled salad.

'This is bloody great,' Sam said to me. 'You've got to teach me how to make this sometime. I don't cook anything these days, y'know? I used to, but I need to follow recipes and I don't seem to have any cookery books any more.' He laughed. 'Lost them in the divorce.' I poured him another glass of wine. He didn't seem to notice that I had not yet touched mine.

'So you won't be cooking Christmas dinner, then?' I asked him.

'No, we're going skiing,' he said.

'We?'

'Me and Chiara. The girl from this morning?'

'The one with the hairdryer.'

'Yeah.' He looked a bit embarrassed. 'She's a little high maintenance. She went mental when I told her I didn't have one. Why would she think I had one?' he asked, quite reasonably, pointing to his closely shaven head. 'She also made Reggie sleep down-stairs "because he smelt of dog". What else would he smell of? I'm not entirely sure I can see this one lasting.'

I laughed. 'No, neither can I. Where on earth do you find these women?'

'Chiara has a very chi-chi little place in Chelsea with a garden about three feet by four that needed landscaping,' he said with a wry little smile. 'I think Daddy has money. She's a sweet girl, just a bit . . .'

Stupid, I thought, but I didn't say it. 'Blonde?'

'Now, now.'

'I'm joking, Sam,' I said (although I wasn't). 'I'm sure she's lovely.'

'Well, lovely might be pushing it. I don't know, Bea. It's not entirely my fault, you know? The ones I want, the really good ones, they never seem to want me back.'

'So you have to content yourself with beautiful blondes. It's a tragedy.'

There was a whimper from the bedroom. I went to check on Luca. He was making noises in his sleep, his cheek flushed and pink. I checked the room temperature. It seemed fine, but he looked hot to me. I removed his top blanket. Then I put it back again. I wondered whether I should ring my mother, just to check if twenty-one degrees really was OK. Perhaps he was getting a fever? I gently touched his forehead. He seemed cool enough.

As I stood there fretting, wishing I was better at these things, that I had the instincts for it, Sam appeared behind me in the doorway. He had the almost-empty bottle of red in his hand.

'Everything OK?' he asked in a whisper. He was peering at the framed picture on the dresser next to the doorway; it's the only photograph of Marco in the house.

'Fine,' I said and quickly ushered him from the room.

Back in the living room Sam collapsed on to the sofa and put his feet up on the coffee table. 'How old were you when you got married?' he asked, squinting slightly at the dregs of the wine in his glass.

'Twenty-eight. You?'

'Twenty-three! Way too young.'

'Is that why it went wrong, do you think? Because you married too young? You didn't wait long enough for the right person?'

'No. Well, not for me, anyway. At least . . . I thought I found the right person. I thought she was perfect for me. Only now she's married to someone else and when I see them together, which isn't very often, I realise that he's perfect for her. And I just keep on looking, and no one measures up. Which in itself is odd because she never treated me very well. It's like I said, you know? The ones I fall for never fall for me. Or they do fall, but they just get back up again.'

He got to his feet and swayed into the kitchen.

'That's it, Sam,' I said. 'There's nothing else to drink in the house.'

'What? Not even cooking sherry?' he laughed. 'Sorry. I'm pissed. I had a couple of pints before I came over . . .' I steered him gently in the direction of the door. He slipped his hand around my shoulders.

'What about you Bea? Don't you get tired of being all on your own?'

'I'm not alone, Sam,' I said. 'I have Luca,' and with that I said goodnight.

23.45 p.m.
Chloe

Chloe went to the gym on her way home. She did forty-five minutes on the treadmill at eight miles per hour, followed by a quick round of weights. She went home, showered and washed her hair, ate a salad and watched the news at ten. At ten thirty she took off her tracksuit and put on the new Myla knickers and corset set she'd bought during her lunch hour. She took a bottle of Laurent Perrier Rosé out of the fridge and popped it into an ice bucket. She lit some candles and slung a black silk blindfold and a couple of scarves over the headboard. Then she lay back on her pillows and read the notes Fitzwilliam had left her on the Miller case. She fell asleep for thirty-two minutes.

She woke, shivering and stiff-necked, to the sound of her mobile buzzing on the night-stand. It was a text from Michael.

Can't make it. Becky unwell. So, so sorry. M x

Chloe blew out the candles and climbed into bed. Her stomach felt as though it were full of acid, there was a lump like a peach pit in her throat and yet she couldn't cry. She readjusted her pillows. Several times. She felt exhausted, yet at the same time defeated, because she knew sleep was not coming. She sat up in bed, lit a cigarette and went back to her work, but she just kept reading the same lines, over and over again, without taking anything in. Her thoughts kept returning to that morning at the Honey Pot, to the expression on Bea's face when she called her a bitch; there had been a hatred there that was almost visceral. And, probably, understandable. Bea had a child and yet there was no man around; perhaps he'd gone off with someone else. So she *would* hate the other woman, wouldn't she?

Chloe didn't know anything about Bea, she didn't know anything about her marriage, but then Bea didn't know anything about her, or about Michael. She was in no position to judge. If she heard the things Michael said, about how *stultifying* it all was, the endless conversations about car pools and bathroom tiles and whether they should go to Cornwall or Devon for half-term. If she knew about that she might start to understand the attraction Michael felt for an equal. She might understand that he didn't just want a wife who made the dinner and picked up the dry cleaning, he wanted a woman who could talk politics and law and art, who drafted contracts for multi-million-dollar mergers, who was going to make partner by the time she was thirty *and* who looked good in her underwear.

The acid continued to boil in her stomach, a toxic combination of anger and loneliness and the awful, persistent suspicion that on those nights when Michael didn't come to her, on the nights he went straight home from work, he probably made love to his wife.

Thursday 16 December

5 a.m.
Chloe

Chloe gave up trying to sleep. She slipped out of bed and put on her running clothes, which she had laid out on the armchair in the corner of her bedroom the night before. She made herself a small espresso (studies have shown that consumption of caffeine before exercise boosts weight loss), downed it in a single gulp, grabbed her iPod and set off into the freezing darkness of north London.

Running in the dark didn't scare her. She enjoyed being out in London at this time, a London populated solely by cats and foxes and the odd minicab driver, sitting in his car, listening to Five Live, waiting to drive someone to the airport. No one bothered her at this time of day; there were no men in white vans to give their unsolicited opinions on her form; no dawdling school children blocking the pavements; she didn't even have to stop for red lights. The few people who were out and about at that time were usually on

61

their way to work, the only exceptions being drunken revellers on their way home from the night before, and if any of those ever gave her any trouble, she was pretty sure she could outrun them.

Her habitual route took her past Stroud Green to Finsbury Park. She usually completed two or three rounds of the park before heading home, but that morning she just kept going. She headed out of the park and all the way up Crouch Hill, along Park Road and all the way to Alexandra Park, which she rounded once before eventually heading homeward.

She checked her Garmin. She'd run over eight miles. Eight hundred calories down and it wasn't seven o'clock yet. Well, that might go some way towards offsetting the alcohol consumption from the forthcoming evening's Christmas party, anyway. She accelerated at the very thought.

The most direct route home took her immediately past the Honey Pot. She thought for a moment about taking a detour, but she'd already been out for over an hour and she needed to pick out an outfit to wear that evening before she went into work. She couldn't afford to be late again. As she headed along Albany Street towards the café, the sun was just coming up. Chloe quickened her pace. There was a lorry parked outside; someone was offloading something. And then, from the open doorway, emerged Bea, hair scraped back into a pony tail, sleeves rolled up, ready to receive a delivery. Chloe thought about crossing the road to avoid her. Then she changed her mind.

She ran straight up to Bea, yanking her headphones out of ears as she did so. 'Oi!' she called out. 'I'd like to have a word with you.'

'What a delightful surprise at this time of the morning,' Bea said, grappling with a box of lettuces. She turned her back on Chloe and marched into the shop. Chloe followed her.

'We're closed,' Bea said, 'and even if we weren't, you aren't welcome here. I thought I made that clear yesterday morning.'

'Well, ever since yesterday morning I've been thinking about the way you treated me.'

'How *I* treated *you*?' Bea was staring at her, astonished.

Chloe launched into the speech she had been giving in her head as she pounded the streets of London.

'I'm terribly sorry that your husband left you,' she said. Bea took a step towards her and for a moment she thought she might slap her. 'He did, didn't he? He ran off with someone else. Younger, was she? I'm sure that makes you very bitter, and I'm sure whoever did it *was* an unbelievable bitch.'

Bea stepped back again, folded her arms and leaned against the deli counter. The delivery men ferrying vegetables to and from the van stopped for a second, clearly wondering how this was going to pan out. One sharp look from Chloe sent them back to work.

'But actually, I'm not a bitch. Well, maybe I am sometimes, but I didn't plan any of this. I didn't set out to wreck anyone's home or ruin anyone's marriage. You know what happened to me? I had to work late. For weeks and weeks, for months on end, I was working on a case, and the guy who was working on the case with me, my boss, was a married man called Michael. And while staying at the office until three o'clock in the morning wouldn't usually be my idea of a good time, Michael and I got on so well, we had so much in common, we enjoyed each other's company so much, that after a while, staying late in the office wasn't even a chore. I would have moved into the fucking office if it had meant I could be with him. I fell in love with him. And he fell in love with me. He doesn't love his wife any more. He stopped loving her before he even met me. Don't you think it might just be possible that it would be better, not just for me and for him but for his wife and his children too, if he left sooner rather than later?'

Chloe didn't wait for Bea to reply, she put her head-phones back on and turned to leave. As she got to the door she turned back again.

'He promised me that he would leave her. He prom-ised me he would do it months ago, and I've been waiting and waiting and it just hasn't happened. So I knew that I wouldn't be able to spend Christmas with the man I love, I knew I would be spending it alone, again. But I thought that just maybe I might have a few days with him, our own private Christmas, and now I don't even think that's going to happen, so maybe I am just a little bit bloody disappointed about that.'

Feeling a bit better, she jogged off down the road, heading home.

8.30 a.m.
Bea

Caramelised radicchio, I said to myself. *With grated pine nuts.* It was one of the side dishes I was thinking about making for Luica's and my Christmas feast. Not that very minute, of course. At that very minute I was doing my level best to serve the always impatient morning punters while at the same time keeping Luca, who was sitting in his pushchair behind the counter, sufficiently entertained to prevent him from yelling the place down. My mother, who was supposed to pick him up at eight, was running late and I was starting to feel those homicidal feelings bubble up again. I turned my back on my queuing customers and busied myself with the coffee machine.

Halve the radicchio, I said quietly. *Dust the cut side with icing sugar, season with salt and pepper. Melt some butter in a non-stick sauté pan. Once it's foaming, place the radicchio cut-side down into the pan and cook over a high heat . . .*

'It's a sign of madness, you know,' a voice said

behind me. Sam was leaning over the counter pulling faces at Luca. 'Talking to yourself.'

'Yes, well, I think we're all well aware I went bonkers years ago. Coffee for you?'

'Could you make it a strong one? Got a bit of a head after last night. Sorry if I was a pain in the arse—'

'Not at all,' I cut him off. For some reason I really didn't want to think about last night.

'I must have been a bit of a bore at least. Your mum not around today?'

'Running late,' I said, handing him a triple-shot latte.

'Let me take the young man for a minute then. Get him off your hands. We'll be next door sorting seed packets if you need us.'

'You're an angel, Sam,' I said, flipping up the hatch so that Sam could come back behind the counter to collect Luca.

'It's not a problem,' he said, and he winked at me, and for some ludicrous reason I blushed. I turned my back and busied myself with the coffee machine again.

The coffee machine was the first thing we bought when we secured the lease for the place. The previous tenants, who'd run a greasy spoon, had a Magimix coffee maker, which they left behind and which I thought would do just fine for the first few years at least, but Marco had the thing on a skip within minutes of getting the keys to the place.

'*That* is not an espresso machine,' he kept saying. 'It is a kettle. A glorified kettle.'

He wanted to have a Gaggia (it had to be a Gaggia) shipped over from Italy, but I pointed out that you could actually buy them in England, a fact which seemed to astound him.

'So why would anyone have any other sort of machine?' he asked.

'Because Gaggias cost thousands, Marco. Not everyone cares about coffee that much.'

He shook his head sadly, the way he often did when he discovered yet another thing about the English that was strange and inexplicable.

I didn't think I cared about coffee that much, but when I laid eyes on the deep red Gaggia Deco Auto Flow, I fell in love. It cost a fortune, more money that we should have ever contemplated spending on a coffee machine, but Marco promised it would last for ever. (Not that *that* meant anything, of course; Marco promised a lot of things would last for ever.)

We opened the Honey Pot in May 2007, just over a year after we got married. The name was Marco's idea, because it was my dream, and because I was Bea, his honey Bea. I actually didn't like the name. It certainly didn't scream Italian deli-slash-coffee shop, but Marco was adamant. I don't mind it so much now, it's grown on me.

I always loved the place. We came across it by accident. Opening our own deli was something we had talked vaguely about doing, at some unspecified time in the future; we weren't thinking about doing it right away. We'd come to Crouch Hill to look at a flat; we'd been living in a horrible one-bedroom flat just off the Holloway Road since Marco moved over from Italy and we were both desperate to move. Thanks to a promotion for Marco, who was working for a chemicals firm, and a raise for me at the catering company I was slaving away for, we were finally in a position to do so.

We liked the area right away; it had that London village feel, a community within a community. The flat we'd come to see was a bit of a disappointment, but we decided to take a stroll around, popping into estate agents as we came across them to leave our details. Then we came across Albany Street, a perfect little tree-lined street populated by independent shops: a butcher, a bakery; no candlestick maker, but no Boots and no Starbucks and no WHSmith either. There was a book-shop and a little French restaurant, an antiques dealer and a decent curry house, a proper pub and a boutique selling beautiful but incredibly expensive clothes. And right smack-bang in the middle of all this was a greasy spoon owned by a middle-aged couple who'd decided to sell up and move to the Costa del Sol.

This was in February. We opened the Honey Pot in May and ran it together for a year and a half. And then Marco was gone. I wanted to shut the place down, I was in no state to run it on my own, but my mother persuaded me not to. She advertised for a manager and recruited Kathy who ran the place while I was away, and stayed on after I was ready to come back. She was an invaluable second-in-command, and ran the place all by herself on Fridays and every other Sunday and on the (all-too-frequent) days when I couldn't handle things.

I left the café in Kathy's capable hands when Mum finally did arrive, just after nine thirty, and we went next door to fetch Luca.

'So lovely to see you, Sam,' my mother said, giving him a kiss, which seemed a bit inappropriate since she'd only met him a couple of times. 'Don't you look well? Doesn't he look well, Bea?' she asked, giving me a wink. I hate it when she does this – and she always does this, she has done ever since I was about twelve. If I'm not already in a relationship she tries ever so unsubtly to push me into the arms of whatever male might be on hand. 'What are you up to for Christmas, Sam? Any plans? If not, you should spend it with Bea.' Oh, for God's sake. 'She's refusing to come up to Edinburgh with me – I'll be spending it with my new beau, Christopher.' She winked again, at Sam this time. 'I don't think Bea really approves of him . . .'

'That's not true,' I protested. And it wasn't, I thought Christopher was remarkably normal for one of Mum's boyfriends. 'I just want to spend Christmas with Luca, here at home. It's our first Christmas together and

I want it to be just right. In any case, Sam does have plans, don't you?'

Sam mumbled something inaudible. There was an awkward moment of silence brought to an end, mercifully, by Luca, who started to gabble something unintelligible which, of course, my mother understood.

'We're going to the park today,' she said, picking Luca up and putting him into the pushchair. 'Feeding the ducks is his favourite pastime, isn't it, sweetie?' He gurgled at her happily, a sharp little knife to my heart.

I waved them off and was about to return to work when Sam said, 'What did you mean, Bea, your first Christmas with Luca? What happened last year?'

'Nothing,' I said. 'I was a bit unwell last year, that's all. I was in bed most of the time, so I couldn't really enjoy it.'

That wasn't the truth. Not the whole truth anyway, but I couldn't tell him the whole truth, could I? I couldn't tell him that I didn't see my son last Christmas, that I barely saw my son for the first eight or nine months of his life because I wasn't really in a fit state to look after an infant, not when I was drinking the best part of a bottle of Jack Daniel's before lunch.

12 noon
Olivia

Olivia and Zara went to Joe Allen for lunch. Zara ordered grilled tuna with pak choi, Olivia opted for slow roast pork with candied sweet potatoes and apple sauce.

'Diet starts tomorrow,' she said, looking a little embarrassed.

'Bugger that, Liv,' Zara said. 'You look great.'

'Margie doesn't seem to think so.'

'Who gives a shit what Margie thinks? She's your boss, not your life coach. If I were you I'd chuck those pills in the bin and just claim to have lost ten pounds. It's not like she's actually going to check, is it? She's not going to put you on the scales.'

'Wouldn't put it past her,' Olivia mumbled. 'In any case, I can't just lie . . .'

'Of course you can! Most of the stuff we write in the magazine is totally made up, why should this feature be any different?'

'Ah, journalistic integrity,' Olivia said with a grin as they clinked wine glasses. 'Seriously though, don't you ever get tired of it? God, if you'd told me five years ago that aged thirty I'd be writing about anti-ageing creams and sodding eyeliner I think I'd have shot myself. I was supposed to be in somewhere exotic by now, covering war and famine, getting shot at by other people.'

'I don't know, Liv. Somehow I just can't see you as the war correspondent type. I don't know why . . . must be something to do with the Miu Miu handbag and the Marni boots? Oh yes, and the pathological fear of insects, spiders, snakes, frogs, jellyfish . . .' Zara was interrupted by the arrival of the waiter with their food.

71

'OK, I admit, my whole Kate Adie fantasy was a bit overblown,' Olivia said. 'But I thought that at least I'd be doing something more *substantial* by now. When Kieran gets home from work, he can look back on his day and think: Today I made sure that a few hundred more kids in Sierra Leone will get the diphtheria vaccine this month. When I get home, I think: Oh great, I persuaded a few hundred more women to buy some overpriced sludge to slap on their thighs which will have no impact on their cellulite whatsoever. Score!'

'Hey, I just spent the entire morning writing a story debating whether the armlet is the new glove. Not everyone can be Kieran, you know. Some of us are just shallow.'

'He is a saint, isn't he?'

'Bullshit,' Zara replied through a mouthful of tuna. 'Saints don't look like that. Saints are suppose to inspire godliness, or devotion, or something chaste like that. Not unbridled lust. Kieran's not a saint, he's just . . . perfect. He reminds me a bit of Zac Goldsmith, y'know? Looks-wise, I mean, not in the sense of being a tax-evading Tory wanker. Do Kieran's brothers resemble him at all, by the way?'

Olivia giggled. 'They do, actually. Especially Conor, the youngest one.'

'The unmarried one?'

'He has a girlfriend, Zara.'

'Yeah, yeah. But you'll hook me up anyway, won't you? At least introduce me. Invite me to at least one of the fifteen different Christmas events you're planning?'

'Mmmm,' Olivia murmured, retrieving from her handbag her dark green leather notebook, 'I'll just have a look. OK . . . everyone's arriving on Sunday. So we're just going to stay in that night. I'm cooking. Dinner for ten adults and five kids.'

'Christ almighty,' Zara said, taking a swig of her wine.

'I know, I'm trying not to think about it. On the Monday, Kieran and I are still working, so everyone is going to be left to their own devices during the day. Then I have three parties in the evening – we've got the Luxe party and that PR thing, and then I've got a Christmas party with actual friends to go to after that – so Kieran is taking all the boys out on the lash. Not sure what the girls will be doing.'

'Wifely things, probably,' Zara said with a wry little smile.

'Piss off. Anyway. Tuesday is London sightseeing followed by dinner and *Mamma Mia*. That's going to be a particularly dark day. Wednesday we have a day at leisure, followed by a drinks party at my place in the evening. Why don't you come to that? We're thinking of making it a sort-of engagement party – close friends only, of course.'

'That sounds perfect.' They clinked glasses to seal the deal. 'Oh crap, Liv, it's quarter to three already, we'd better head back to the office before Margie has an aneurysm.'

Outside, the rain had started to come down in earnest. Huddling beneath a single umbrella, Olivia and Zara negotiated their way through the crowds of Christmas shoppers as best they could given the twin handicaps of high heels and three glasses of wine at lunch. By the time they got back to the office, they were both soaked.

'There you are!' Margie called out to them as they took off coats and wrung out scarves. She was standing next to the head of the art department, scrutinising a layout for the main fashion spread. 'We were about to send out a search party.'

Zara scuttled off to her desk, head bowed, Olivia was not given the option.

'I hear you're getting hitched, Ms Heywood? Is that true? Let's see the rock.'

Her heart sinking to her boots, Olivia approached her boss and reluctantly held out her left hand. Margie popped her glasses on to her nose and peered at the ring. 'Very nice,' she said, to Olivia's amazement. She'd been convinced that Margie would use this as yet another opportunity to put her down. 'Did you choose that?'

'No, he did it all by himself.'

'Impressive. Have you set a date yet?'

'No, no. It's a recent development. We haven't really talked about anything yet.'

'Well, I think it's wonderful. And such good timing. We can put your first "Diary of a Bride-To-Be" column in the February issue – which is all about love, love, love, of course.'

'Oh, Margie . . . I really don't know . . .' Olivia had a bad feeling about this, a very bad feeling, the kind of feeling one might get when one realised one's plane was being hijacked.

'I think it's perfect. You can cover dresses and venues, you can try out different looks, report on the hottest honeymoon destinations, detail your weight-loss goals, all that sort of thing. The bridal market is huge, Olivia, and while we're never going to compete with the specialist bridal titles, we can cannibalise at least a section of their market . . .'

Cannibalising brides, Olivia thought. Now that's a lovely image.

7.15 p.m.
Chloe

Unable to decide what to wear that morning, Chloe had taken three possible party dresses to work: boring Little Black Dress, daring, backless electric blue mini or fashion-forward sequinned beige silk. Since there were no fashionistas at work to appreciate the silk one and no men around that she felt the need to impress with the backless blue, she opted for the boring LBD.

In the ladies' loos, she slipped into the dress and zipped herself up. Appraising herself in the mirror she decided that the dress didn't look as good as she thought it had when she'd bought it a couple of months ago. They never do though, do they? There was something about the fit that wasn't quite right. Apparently she wasn't the only one who thought so: at the other end of the mirror, the other two female junior partners, Karen and Rebecca, were sizing her up with ill-disguised disapproval.

'It looks weird, doesn't it?' Chloe asked them.

'It's a bit big for you,' Karen replied. 'You should have got a smaller size.'

'It's a size eight,' Chloe replied, turning around to check out her rear end in the mirror.

'Show-off,' Rebecca muttered.

Chloe ignored her. She took her hair down and then put it up again. 'Up or down?' she asked the others.

'Down,' they replied in unison.

'If you wear it up you can see your collarbones sticking out,' Rebecca said.

Chloe's mobile rang. It was Michael.

'Missed you last night,' she said.

'Yeah . . . um . . . sorry about that.'

'That's OK. How's Becky?'

'Yeah, she's OK . . .' He sounded tentative, nervous.

'What's up?' Chloe asked, but her heart was sinking like a stone; she knew what was coming.

'Chloe, it's just not going to happen. I can't go away now. She's got her bloody parents coming for Christmas, *and* she's invited my sister and her husband and their entire brood and for some unfathomable reason she's invited them all to come up three days before Christmas, which makes no bloody sense at all. I can't get away, I can't lie to them all . . . It's just too many people. Too many lies. I'm sorry, Chloe, I'm so sorry.'

Chloe didn't say anything.

'Chloe, please. Say something. After New Year, babe, after New Year, I promise you . . .'

Chloe ended the call, went into a cubicle and sat down on the loo seat. She was damned if she was going to let Karen and Rebecca see her cry.

The office party was taking place at a hotel just off Chancery Lane. Drinks in the bar followed by dinner and, for those who lasted the pace, further drinks and the possibility of dancing at a private members' club just around the corner. Chloe had never had any intention of going dancing with her colleagues, but after speaking to Michael she wondered whether she would last until dessert.

At the hotel, she headed straight for the bar, ordered two gin and tonics, took them into the corner and drank them both. She was just pondering the calorie content when Maurice Fitzwilliam and his toady-in-chief, Greg Stocker, appeared at her side.

'Don't you scrub up well?' Greg said, grinning to reveal teeth yellowed by ten years of twenty Marlboro a day. Chloe made a mental note to book a trip to the hygienist.

'Pretty girl like you shouldn't be standing in the

corner all by yourself, Chloe,' Maurice said. 'And with an empty glass! What can I get you to drink?'

'I'll have a gin and tonic, thanks, Maurice,' Chloe replied.

'Coming right up. Is that slimline, Chloe? I know you like to watch your figure.' He was trying to be charming. It was painful.

'We all like to watch your figure, Chloe,' Greg murmured as Maurice disappeared off to the bar.

'Oh, do fuck off, Greg,' Chloe said, before calling out to her boss: 'Could you make that a double?'

At dinner, Chloe found herself seated in between Maurice and Clive Mortimer-Harvey, one of the senior partners at the firm. The first course was a foie gras and lentil terrine.

'I do love a bit of foie gras,' Clive said to Chloe, 'although one does have to feel rather sorry for geese.'

'Absolutely,' Chloe said. She didn't give a crap about the geese, although she was slightly concerned about the calorie content. It was pure fat, wasn't it? She signalled to the waiter to bring her more wine.

'In my younger days, I represented quite a few of them, you know,' Clive was saying.

'Geese?'

Clive chortled, spraying the plate in front of him with a fine brown mist. Chloe pushed her plate to one side.

'Animal-rights bods,' Clive said. 'I worked for Carter Samuels in the eighties. I spent quite a lot of my time defending the great unwashed. Activists charged with breach of the peace, criminal damage, that sort of thing . . .' Chloe took another swig of her wine. As Clive launched into a detailed description of one such case, Chloe turned her attention elsewhere.

Across the table, Rebecca was telling Greg about the present she had bought her fiancé for Christmas.

'It's a Tissot trekking watch,' she said. 'You know, with a compass, and an altimeter. For mountain climbing. They're very expensive. But my fiancé's very keen to get into mountain climbing.'

Chloe had met Rebecca's fiancé. He was a short, bespectacled actuary. She was finding it difficult to picture him scaling Everest.

'Last year, when we were on holiday in Carcassonne, my fiancé was saying how much he'd like to climb Mont Perdu,' Rebecca was saying. Chloe was tempted to suggest a drinking game: you have to empty your glass every time Rebecca says 'my fiancé'.

Fearing she might throw something across the table if she had to listen to any more of Rebecca's inanities, Chloe tried to interest herself in whatever her boss was talking about. Not an easy feat, since he was talking about trust law.

'Very complex these days,' he was saying to Karen. 'Lot of legislative changes in recent years. Keeping your cash out of the hands of the taxman is an even trickier business these days. Still, got to keep on top of it – I've just got a new client who wants a trust set up by the end of the year. Can you believe they bring this to us now, at Christmas? Still, can't turn down the business. Very rich Russians,' he said, giving her a wink. 'Probably gangsters.'

'Nothing like a bit of national stereotyping,' Chloe muttered.

'What was that you said?' Maurice asked her, irritated.

'Oh nothing. I was going to say that I can help you out with that client if you like. Turns out I'm not going away next week after all, so I can work right up until Christmas if you need me to.' If she wasn't going to be with Michael, she may as well be in the office. Sitting at home in her flat would just be too depressing.

'Well, that's marvellous, Chloe.' Maurice beamed at her. 'That'll be a great help. I could really use you next week.' He was resting his arm on the back of her chair. She felt his fingers graze her spine. 'I'll try not to work you too hard. We'll have a bit of fun too, won't we?'

Chloe tugged at the silver chain around her neck. It seemed too tight; it was choking her. The room was stuffy and airless. Greg, opposite her, had patches of perspiration under his arms. Chloe felt ill.

'Would you excuse me?' she said, scraping her chair back across the stone floor so that everyone turned to look at her.

'Are you all right, Chloe?' Maurice asked. She ignored him, grabbed her handbag and headed outside on to a balcony overlooking a small quadrangle. She lit a cigarette. As the nicotine hit her bloodstream she thought she might faint; apart from a mouthful or two of foie gras she hadn't eaten all day and now she couldn't remember how many drinks she'd had. She checked her phone. There was a text message from Michael.

I'm so sorry. We'll be together next year. Promise. M

She called his number. The phone rang thee times before it was answered.

'Michael's phone,' a woman's voice said. Chloe hung up.

For the main course they were having medallions of pork with a mushroom and cream sauce. Chloe cut into her first medallion and took a small bite. She could taste the fat in the sauce. She placed her knife and fork on her plate and chewed slowly, hoping that she wasn't going to throw up. Maurice was asking people what they were doing for Christmas.

'I'm spending it with my fiancé,' Rebecca said, 'in Yorkshire. My fiancé's family has a lovely place on the edge of the moors.' Clive was having a 'big family do' at 'the place in Sussex'. Greg, who was single and likely to remain so for a very long time, Chloe imagined, was spending Christmas with his parents in Birmingham. Maurice and the wife were taking the kids to Florida, 'a special treat'.

'How about you, Chloe?' Maurice asked. 'What are you up to?'

'Oh, you know, the usual,' Chloe replied, making a grab for her wine glass and instead knocking it over.

'Steady,' Greg said with a sneer. 'Had a bit too much, have we?'

'Well, 'tis the fucking season,' Chloe replied loudly. An uneasy silence descended over the table. 'Isn't it? 'Tis the season to be jolly, or merry, or something. Peace on earth, goodwill to all men, all that crap. 'Tis season to buy charity singles in aid of starving children in countries you'd sooner kill yourself than visit . . .'

'Chloe,' Maurice said, gently placing a hand on her arm, 'are you feeling all right?'

Chloe turned to face him, giving him an exaggerated wink. 'It's the season for shagging your boss at the office party, isn't it? The time to load up your credit cards to breaking point, to gorge yourself to the point of nausea on food you wouldn't dream of eating at any other time of year. Christmas: it's the season of suicides and family arguments, booze-fuelled domestic violence, binge drinking, sixteen-car pile-ups on the M1 . . .' She raised her glass. No one shared her toast.

'I'll be spending Christmas with my boyfriend,' Karen announced in a desperate attempt to alleviate the awkwardness. 'He lives in Croydon.'

Chloe started to laugh. She got up from the table and weaved her way out of the restaurant.

In the taxi on the way home, her phone beeped, signalling that someone had left her a message.

Desperately hoping that it would be Michael (maybe he had told her after all?), she rang her voicemail.

'Hi, sweetheart, it's Mum.' Her heart sank. 'I've been meaning to call you for days but I've been frantic with Christmas things. How about you? Is Venice all organised? Give me a call soon.'

The flat was absolutely freezing when she got home. She touched the radiator in the hall; it was cold.

'Oh, for God's sake,' she muttered, kicking her shoes off as she staggered into the kitchen. The light on the boiler was off. She turned the electricity off and on again and pushed the restart button several times. The light remained off, the radiators stone cold. Shivering, Chloe returned to the hallway and retrieved every blanket she could find from the closet. Then she dragged herself to bed, pausing for a moment to admire the elegant, grey glass vase from the Conran Shop that Michael had given her for their three-month anniversary. She took it from the mantelpiece in the living room and hurled it as hard as she could, smashing it against the opposite wall.

Friday 17 December

8.25 a.m.
Bea

I felt better on Friday. I felt it as soon as I woke up. The past couple of days I'd been irritable and miserable, but it was a glitch. I knew it, I felt sure of it; it wasn't a long-term thing, it wasn't the start of another descent into despair, it was just a couple of bad days.

I slipped out of bed and padded quietly into Luca's bedroom, which is adjacent to mine. He was still fast asleep (at quarter past six! Result!). I sat down in the armchair next to his window, which looks out on to the street. Gently, I opened the blind. Sometime during the night it stopped raining, and although it was still dark, the air was clear and you could tell that it was going to be brighter day. I sat there for a good twenty minutes before he started to stir; I was there to take him into my arms as soon as he woke. He seemed to like that; there was none of the usual bad temper we usually get when he first wakes. He just smiled at me.

He was actually pleased to see me. I felt ridiculously grateful.

After breakfast we went downstairs together and he dozed contentedly in his buggy while I started decorating the café. I wasn't due to work that day – Kathy ran the place on Fridays – but if I didn't get make a start on the Christmas decorations soon, we'd be putting them up around the time they were due to be taken down.

I was standing on a stool, pinning red tinsel to the shelf above the coffee machine, when I heard a knock on the door. 'I'm not open yet,' I yelled, not turning around.

'I can see that,' a voice yelled back. 'But I've run out of coffee. Please! It's an emergency.'

I turned round to see Sam shivering on my doorstep wearing tracksuit bottoms, a thin grey jumper and flip flops. I clambered down and unlocked the front door. 'What on earth are you doing? It's about minus three out there.'

'I was desperate for a caffeine fix,' he said, rubbing his hands together and blowing on them, 'I completely forgot to buy coffee yesterday.' He sat down, cross legged, on the floor in front of Luca's chair. He pulled faces at him while I put on the coffee.

We drank our cappuccinos together. Sam shared an apple Danish with Luca, which wasn't a very good idea because he'd only just had breakfast, but the pair of them looked so disappointed when I told them that that I relented. I always give in too easily.

'So, skiing's been cancelled,' Sam announced with a rueful smile.

'I'm sorry, why's that?'

'Well . . . Chiara – you know, the high-maintenance one? She rang last night. She got a better offer, apparently. Her ex, who does something important in the City, wants her back. He's offering a week in a luxury chalet in Vail, I'm offering three nights in a hotel in Trois Vallées. No contest apparently.'

'Sam, I'm sorry, that's awful,' I said, trying to ignore the fact that deep down I wasn't sorry at all. 'You know I'm holding a waifs and strays party on Christmas night, don't you? You know, for those of my customers who don't have anywhere special to go for Christmas. I think quite a few people will be dropping by. There'll be loads to eat. Why don't you come along to that?

But Sam wasn't really listening to me any more, he was looking at the door, where a curvy blonde was peering through the glass, immaculate in jeans and boots and a beautifully cut red coat, a large pair of sunglasses perched on top of her head. It was Olivia.

'You've got a customer, Bea,' Sam said. He was virtually drooling. I got up to let her in.

Sam got to his feet and held out his hand. 'Hello again,' he said, flashing her a smile. 'You were here the other day, weren't you? I'm Sam. I live next door.'

'Very nice to meet you,' Olivia said.

'Olivia's getting married,' I blurted out. They both looked at me in surprise.

'Congratulations,' Sam said. 'When's the big day?'

'Oh, we haven't got that far yet. This is all new. I've actually got the day off today so I was thinking of doing a little bit of preliminary dress-hunting. I'm not looking to buy anything yet, I just want to see what's out there.'

'You don't have the idea of the perfect dress in mind then?' I asked her.

'Not at all. I've never been particularly . . . *bridal*, you know?'

'Oh, I know. I was the same way.' I handed her a latte. 'You should have something to eat,' I suggested. 'You need to fortify yourself. Bridal shops can be frightening places.'

'I'd recommend the apple Danishes,' Sam said. Olivia regarded the pastries with barely disguised lust.

'I'd better not,' she said eventually, 'I'm supposed to be starting a diet today.'

'Why on earth would *you* want to go on a diet?' Sam asked, genuinely incredulous. 'In any case, you can't go on a diet now. It's Christmas.' Olivia relented and took a Danish.

There was a blast of cold air from outside as Kathy bundled in, wrapped up in a huge puffa jacket. 'Bea, love, what have you opened up for? It's your day off. I'm not late, am I?' she asked, frowning at her watch.

'Not at all, I was just doing a bit of decorating and had a couple of early punters, that's all.'

Kathy took off her coat and took up her place behind

the counter, eyeing the bits of red tinsel pinned to the top shelf with disdain. 'Call those decorations?'

'Well, I *was* interrupted.'

'Oh yes,' Kathy said, giving Sam a curt nod. Kathy hadn't been keen on Sam since he'd briefly dated her niece. She looked Olivia up and down. 'You're the latest one, are you?' she asked.

'The latest . . . ?' Olivia looked confused.

'Olivia's just a friend,' I said. Sam blushed.

'I probably ought to get going,' he said. 'It was nice to meet you, Olivia. Good luck with the dress shopping.' He was halfway to the door when he turned to me and smiled, and said: 'I'd love to come to your party, Bea. Thanks very much for asking.'

My stomach gave a little flip: excitement, or nervousness, or something else I couldn't quite place but vaguely remembered feeling. I didn't want to think about it, so I offered Olivia another pastry. 'Try a bit of torta di ricotta,' I suggested.

Guiltily, Olivia accepted. 'God, that's fantastic,' she said, through a mouthful of cake. 'Where do you get this stuff? You don't make it all, do you?'

'Not all of it, although I did make that one. I cook a lot of the savoury stuff, the pasta dishes, that sort of thing. Most of the pastries and cakes are ordered in though. We used to make a lot more ourselves, but now that it's just me . . .' On cue, Luca started to grizzle. I picked him up and sat him on my lap. Olivia reached out and took his chubby fingers in hers.

He smiled at her coyly. Like Sam, he also has a thing for blondes.

'It can't be easy.'

'It isn't.' For a moment neither of us said anything. I knew what she was going to say, and I didn't want to talk about it, but I couldn't think of anything else to say right at that moment and, inevitably, she asked: 'When you say "we", you mean . . . ?'

'Me and my husband, Marco. We started the place together. But, as you can see, he isn't around any more.'

'I'm sorry. How long were you married for?'

'Not very long,' I said. 'Two years, eight months and fourteen days.'

11.15 a.m.
Olivia

In an attempt to get in touch with her inner bride, Olivia had booked a bridal consultation at Harvey Nichols. She was directed on arrival to the personal shopping area where she was confronted by an terrifyingly thin South African woman called Marlene, who had a severe haircut and lips which drew back to reveal enormous teeth.

'All the better to eat me with,' Olivia muttered to herself nervously. She was ushered into a small room containing nothing but a couple of chairs and a rail full of frothy white dresses. Olivia was suddenly terrified.

'Glass of champagne?' Marlene offered.

'God yes,' Olivia replied, a little too eagerly.

Marlene smiled at her. 'Nothing to be nervous about, my darling,' she said. 'We're just going to have a little chat, and then we can look at some dresses. The first thing we need to decide is what sort of bride you want to be. When you picture yourself walking down the aisle with the man of your dreams, are you wearing a classic romantic gown, a Lady Di dress? Are you a modern bride? Are you Gwen Stefani in Galliano? Or do you see yourself more in the sexy bride mode? You know, like Stephanie Seymour in the Guns 'n' Roses video?' Olivia downed her champagne in one.

She came away from her bridal consultation feeling that she had been something of a disappointment to Marlene. She had no idea what sort of bride she wanted to be, she had not set a wedding-dress budget, she had not determined what her ideal wedding-day measurements might be. The experience had not been particularly enlightening. She had learned (*a*) that wedding dresses are phenomenally expensive and (*b*) that most of them looked exactly the same, but then she pretty much knew that anyway. On the plus side, she had three glasses of champagne out of the deal, so it hadn't been a total loss.

On her way down from the fourth floor, Olivia took a brief detour into the shoe department, where she was marvelling at the price tag on a pair of Fendi suede sandals when she heard a loud and familiar voice behind her.

'I asked for these in a size six, a SIX! These are a five. Jesus Christ, how hard can it be to read a number on the side of a bloody box. That is basically what your job entails, isn't it?' Over on the other side of the shoe section, sitting amongst a pile of shopping bags, sat Chloe, berating a terrified shop assistant. For a moment, Olivia was tempted to slink away unnoticed, but the look on the beleaguered assistant's face was so desperate, she took pity on him and decided to intervene.

'Hello, Chloe!' she called out cheerfully. 'Doing a bit of shopping, I see?'

Chloe looked at her blankly.

'It's Olivia. We met at the Honey Pot. I took your purse by mistake.'

'Oh right,' Chloe said miserably. 'Someone else who hates me. Fantastic.'

Olivia wasn't sure if her judgement had been impaired by all that champagne or if the haunted pallor of Chloe's demeanour simply inspired pity, but she decided to invite her for lunch. They went to the restaurant on the fifth floor where Chloe picked at a Caesar salad while Olivia wolfed down her steak sandwich with shiitake mushroom relish.

'So, you've got the day off today?' Olivia asked politely.

'I called in sick,' Chloe replied miserably, sinking lower into her seat. 'This is the first time I've ever called in sick, do you know that?'

'Bloody hell, that is impressive. I can't even count the number of times I've pulled a sickie. If this is your first one, then you're well overdue.'

'Yes, well, you're older than me, so I imagine you've had more opportunities,' Chloe remarked. 'What is it that you do? PR?'

'I'm a journalist. For *Style* magazine.'

'Well, there you go then. Journalists. No one notices if they don't turn up for work, do they?'

'Well they do actually—' Olivia started to say, but Chloe interrupted her.

'So what are you doing shopping in the middle of the day then? Did you call in sick too?'

'No, I had the day off. I came in for . . .' Olivia could hardly bear to say it, '. . . a bridal consultation.'

Chloe laughed. 'Jesus. Really? What was that like? Did you get to try on loads of hideous meringues with metre-long trains?'

'We didn't even get to that stage. We just talked about the sort of bride I wanted to be, and I didn't know, so it was kind of a short conversation.'

Chloe was pensive for a second. 'I think if I were ever to get married, which I won't, but if I were, I'd just get some lovely couture thing that you could wear more than once. I mean, why spend a fortune on something you're only ever going to wear once?'

'Because it's supposed to be unique, a one-off, the most fabulous thing you'll ever wear. It's not supposed to be something you're going to throw on for New Year's Eve parties a couple of years down the line.'

Chloe shrugged, unconvinced.

They ate in uncomfortable silence for a minute or two. Eventually, Olivia asked, 'So why did you call in sick, if it's something you never do?'

Chloe pushed her plate to one side, propped her elbows on the table and covered her eyes with her hands.

'Oh God . . .' she moaned, 'I can hardly bear to think about it.'

Chloe told her the whole sorry tale: Michael's U-turn on the Venice trip, the bitches in the loo virtually calling her anorexic, the excessive alcohol consumption, the painful outburst at dinner.

'I couldn't face everyone today,' she moaned, 'but in fact I'm just making the whole thing worse because now everyone *knows* that I was too humiliated to face them all and that's just going to add a whole extra layer to the level of humiliation I'm going to have to deal with on Monday. Fuck, I wish I was rich. I swear if I was rich, I'd quit my job today. I'd go back to corporate law. I hate family law anyway. Don't you wish you were rich?'

Olivia shrugged non-committally. She thought it might be foolish to admit to Chloe that she in fact was rich. Not a confession to make at this point, not with Chloe in a delicate state of mind. Instead, Olivia asked her why she didn't like family law.

'It's all about marriage and children, that's why. I don't see the point of marriage and I can't stand children. I'm not cut out for it at all.'

'OK . . .' Olivia said, racking her brains for an alternative topic, since this one didn't seem to be heading in a particularly happy direction either.

'Why are *you* getting married?' Chloe asked, before Olivia could come up with anything. 'Are you religious?'

'No, I'm not.'

'Is your other half religious?'

'In theory, he's Catholic, but he's lapsed. Very lapsed. Lapsed into complete and total atheism, if I'm honest, but—'

'So what's the point? And please don't tell me it's because you want to declare your love to the world, because honestly, the world does not care. The world is too busy dealing with war and famine, earthquakes and global warming. The world doesn't give a shit that you're in love.'

'I think it's more about sharing something with your friends and family, showing them you're committed.'

'That you should be committed, more like. I think I'm going to have a glass of wine. Want one?'

Olivia nodded, relieved that the marriage topic was off the table. Turned out it wasn't.

'I just don't understand how people do it, not now, not when the possibility of living until you're a hundred is a realistic one. Can you honestly say that you'll never, over the course of the next seventy years, want to be with anyone else? It's completely fucking ludicrous.'

'Not for everyone . . .' Olivia said, although there was a part of her, a part she was doing her damnedest to ignore, that thought Chloe might have a point. 'In any case, they do say – *studies* say that married people live happier and healthier lives than unmarried ones, so in general I do think it's a good thing—'

'Not true,' Chloe interrupted. 'Married *men* are happier and healthier than unmarried ones. Married women are not. Married woman are more likely to be drunk, obese or just batshit insane. Honestly. They never highlight *that* in the *Daily Mail*, though, do they?' Olivia was not convinced that Chloe was right about that, but she was too frightened to argue. Chloe gazed morosely into her wine glass. 'Still, I'm guessing you won't be alone at Christmas, will you?'

3.30 p.m.
Bea

I took Luca to Finsbury Park in the afternoon to feed the ducks. According to my mother, this is his favourite pastime. She ought to know. It was a freezing cold day, but the sun was doing its best to break through the clouds, and at least it had stopped raining. I wrapped Luca up in the little sheepskin coat his *nonna* had sent him for his birthday and bundled him into the buggy. By the time we got to the park I was starting to regret the decision to leave the warm confines of our flat; a bitter wind was howling around my ears and my hands, despite being encased in gloves, had turned to ice. Luca seemed cheerfully oblivious, and the moment he realised where we were I knew there was no turning back. To get his hopes up only to dash them would have dire consequences.

'Wak wak wak,' he yelled at me happily, 'wak wak wak.'

'Yes, that's right, sweetie, quack quack quack,' I replied through chattering teeth.

We'd worked our way through a quarter of a loaf of bread when a young woman doing her best to control three children under the age of five approached. They greeted Luca with unbridled enthusiasm. I didn't recall having ever seen them before.

'You must be Luca's nanny!' the woman said to me. 'We usually see him here with his grandma, but we haven't been around so much lately. He's grown so much!'

I stood there, speechless, a smile I didn't mean plastered to my face. 'Actually . . . I'm his mother. I'm Bea.'

'Oh . . .' The woman looked horribly and suitably embarrassed. 'I didn't realise . . . As I said, I haven't seen Mrs Chadwick – your mother, I mean – for ages . . .'

'Of course. I was unwell for a bit, but I'm looking after him now. I mean, my mother still has him four days a week because I work but most of the time he's with me.' I was babbling stupidly. 'We're doing well now, aren't we, sweetheart?' I picked Luca up out of his buggy to give him a cuddle and prove to the total stranger that I was a fantastic mother with an incredibly happy child. Luca, snatched away from his ducks, started to cry. 'He's a bit cold,' I said. 'We ought to be getting home.'

Motherhood was never going to be an easy thing for me. I wasn't a natural with babies. Back in the days when I worked in an office (a miserable ten-month stint labouring in the regional headquarters of a multi-national corporation), I used to hide behind the photocopier when the new mums, back for a quick visit after maternity leave, would bring their offspring for all and sundry (read: the women in the office) to coo over. I just didn't get the baby thing. I liked other people's kids well enough, but only in small doses. Until I met Marco, I wasn't even sure that I wanted kids of my own at all, but he was determined, and determined Marco was not to be denied. The more time we spent with his family (three sisters, all older, all incredibly fertile), the more I started to embrace the idea. I loved the long, long Sunday lunches at the local restaurant, four generations of the same family sitting at the table, everyone talking at once, the children eating the same dishes as the adults, part of the same conversation, no kiddie menus, no segregation. I could picture us, our family, fitting into that.

I was prepared for that. I hadn't been prepared to find myself doing it alone.

But we were coping. What I had said to the stranger at the park wasn't a lie: we were doing OK. It was true that Luca didn't light up when he saw me the way he did when he saw his gaga, and that sometimes at night he cried to be comforted by her. It was true that there wasn't a day or night that went by that I didn't wonder how much damage I'd done to him, before and after he was born; there wasn't a day when I wondered whether he'd ever love me the way other little boys loved their mums. But I was trying. I was trying to make it all up to him and we were making progress. We were on the right track, or at the very least headed in the general direction of the right track. So the very last thing in the world I needed right then was to see *her*, the woman who took Marco away from us.

4.15 p.m.
Olivia

Olivia left her lunch with Chloe feeling about as un-bridal as it was possible to feel. She needed to do something about it. She needed to do something wifely, or at least wedding-related. And then she had a brainwave. Maybe it was the memory of that morning's torta di ricotta, or maybe it was the fact that she and Kieran went there almost every Sunday morning, (it was the place where they had coffee and read the papers, a place they always felt completely at home), Olivia wasn't sure, but on the tube on the way home from Knightsbridge, it hit her: she could get the Honey Pot to cater the wedding. She wasn't even sure that they did catering, but it was worth suggesting. If she actually managed to organise something for the wedding it would signal her commitment to the whole thing, to herself as much as to anyone else. And there was something incredibly fitting about it: Bea had been there for her on the awful day that turned out to be the perfect one; Bea was the first person she'd told about the engagement. Plus there was something about Bea that she warmed to, and she knew that if they got to know each other better, they would be friends. She decided she'd stop by the café on the way home.

She crossed the road carefully (who knew what maniac cyclists might be out and about?) and made her way along the street towards the Honey Pot. Bea was standing outside the café, her son in her arms, talking to a tall woman dressed all in black. For a moment, Olivia thought that they were laughing about something. And then she got closer and she realised that Bea wasn't laughing, she was sobbing, and the woman in black was saying something to her, apparently trying to comfort her, but Bea kept pushing her away. Olivia quickened her pace, and then she heard Bea shouting.

'Get away from me! How dare you come here? How dare you come here? You took him, from me, from my son! You took my husband away from me. What the fuck makes you think I would ever want to talk to you?'

Olivia stopped in her tracks for a second; she didn't know whether to intervene or not. What was the protocol when witnessing a confrontation between the wronged wife and the mistress? For one horrible, sick moment, Olivia was tempted to film the whole awful scene on her mobile phone. One look at this sort of raw anguish might make the likes of Chloe think twice before sleeping with someone else's husband again.

Of course she didn't do that, but as Bea continued to scream and sob, Olivia decided that she must do something, but as she approached the two women, who were now being watched by half the street, Sam appeared. He stepped between Bea and her tormentor, gently pushing the woman in black away.

'Go on now, you need to leave,' he said, his voice low and calm. 'You're upsetting her, you're upsetting the boy, you need to go now.'

Then he turned to Bea and put his arm around her and ushered her away, into the shop next door to the Honey Pot. For a moment, the woman in black stood completely still, watching them go. Then she turned to leave; she was walking towards Olivia, and Olivia saw that she, too, was crying.

4.15 p.m.
Bea
It took me a moment to realise who she was. She looked different. Thinner and much older. When I did realise

101

that it was her, when she held out her hand to introduce herself (to introduce herself!), I just couldn't believe it was happening to me. I couldn't believe that she was standing there on the doorstep of my café, *our* café, expecting me to shake her hand.

After that, I don't know what I said to her. I think I just shouted at her to go away. I don't know what she said to me either, her lips were moving but I couldn't hear anything except for the screaming in my head. Luca started crying and I picked him up and the next thing I knew Sam was standing between us, between me and her, telling her to go. He took me up to his flat and gave me a cup of tea and bounced Luca up and down on his hip until he stopped crying. He didn't once ask me what was going on.

Everyone tells you that there will be moments like this, when you know for sure that you aren't going to hang on. I've been waiting for my moment to come, and in a way I was relieved that it had; I was ready to embrace it. I couldn't see straight, I couldn't think straight, and no amount of recipe recitation was going to help me now. I needed something much more powerful than that.

I asked Sam whether he could look after Luca for a bit, and he said that he could. I walked downstairs and out of the door, along Albany Street to the crossroads; I just kept going. It was starting to get dark and the wind was still whipping along, but I didn't feel the cold any longer.

I wasn't aware that I had gone very far, but I must have done, because I found myself standing outside the off licence on Palace Road, which is a good two miles from home. I know it well though, because in the bad old days I found myself seeking out ever more distant corner shops and off licences. It gets embarrassing to go to the same ones every day, to be regarded not with judgement, but with surprise, or even concern, by the hard-working (and probably teetotal) young men on the opposite side of the counter.

I went into the off licence and asked for a bottle of Jack Daniel's, a packet of twenty Marlboro Lights and a cigarette lighter. I walked a little further along the road and into Priory Park, where I found a bench, sat down and lit a cigarette.

I scrolled through the contacts in my telephone, pausing briefly at my mother's number. I scrolled down a little further. I dialled my sponsor's number. Her phone went straight to voicemail. Typical. The bottle of Jack Daniel's was wedged between my feet, burning a hole in its carrier bag. I lit another cigarette.

When I first met Marco, we both smoked. It was one of the many things which surprised me about him. You don't expect someone like him, a biochemist and food-obsessive in the peak of physical fitness, to smoke cigarettes. But he did. The day of the triathlon, true to his word, he returned to the café to buy us all a drink. He ordered another round of peach Bellinis for us and a beer for himself, then he leaned back in his chair and stretched out his arms.

'Beautiful day, no?' he asked. He was looking straight at me; he had the most dazzling smile I'd ever seen. Then he leaned forward, as though he was about to whisper something to me, a secret perhaps, and he asked: 'May I?' pointing at the packet of cigarettes on the table. As I handed him the packet his fingers touched mine and it sounds like the most ridiculous thing in the world, but there was a jolt, like electricity. We sat there all afternoon, he and I, until the last cigarette in the packet was gone.

While my friends went off in search of other bars and other men, Marco and I went for a walk on the beach. The crowds had dispersed by now and the sun was starting to set, and if you have ever seen the sun set over the Gulf of Poets, a place which inspired Byron and Shelley, you'll understand that it was almost unbearably romantic. At the opposite end of the beach we found a restaurant where we ate trofiette with green beans and pesto followed by the most heavenly pannacotta with raspberries, and I knew for sure that I'd found him – the one. Completely unexpectedly, and without looking for him, I had found the love of my life. I was twenty-three years old.

I took the bottle out of the carrier bag. My stomach turned over in anticipation, or fear, I wasn't sure which. What I did know was that I was just seconds away from that lovely rush you get when the first drink hits your bloodstream. It was close enough to touch. My trembling hand was on the screw top, ready to twist, and then I heard it, faint at first but growing louder. Somewhere, in the darkness up ahead or maybe in the apartment block that loomed over the east side of the park, a baby was crying. I got to my feet straight away, jolted out of misery into something like panic; more than anything on earth – and certainly more than I wanted a drink – I wanted to be at home with my boy in my arms. I left the bottle of JD and the rest of the cigarettes under the bench (I hoped it might serve as an early Christmas present to someone in greater need than I, but it would probably just be necked by a bunch of teenagers).

I ran most of the way home. Sam greeted me at his door with a sleeping Luca in his arms and an anxious expression on his face.

'Bea, where were you? You've been gone for two hours,' he whispered. 'I was starting to panic.'

As gently as I could, I took my son from him and held his deliciously warm, limp form to my chest. 'I'm sorry,' I said, breathing Luca in, 'you had my number, you could have called.'

'I've been calling you,' he hissed at me. 'I called you a dozen times.'

I slipped my phone out of my pocket. He was right, or almost right: eleven missed calls, eight from Sam, two from Ellen, my sponsor, and one from Olivia.

'I'm sorry,' I said again. 'Thank you for watching him. I'm taking him home now.'

'Bea, please . . . at least tell me what's going on?'

I left him standing on his doorstep, knowing the second I turned my back on him that I owed him an apology.

At that point, I can honestly say that I didn't care. All I wanted to do was get home with Luca, where the two of us could be safe and warm and shut away from cars and noise and people in general, but especially from *her*. I woke Luca to feed him, which irritated him no end, but after a short battle I managed to get him to eat his dinner. Then I put him down on my bed and lay next to him in the dark, listening to occasional grizzling turning to shallow breaths, and then deeper ones, as he fell into sleep.

In my pocket, my phone buzzed. There was a text from Sam. *You ok? Don't want to bother you but I'm worried. xS*

I moved Luca from my bed to his cot and, after checking that he really was still asleep, I slipped out of his room and into the living room. I dialled Sam, who picked up on the first ring.

'Have you eaten?' I asked him. 'I can make you something if you like. You can have . . .' I opened the fridge to check what I had in. 'I've got a couple of steaks here, I could just do those with a mushroom sauce and some salad? Or if that doesn't suit, we can just raid the deli fridge. There's loads of stuff downstairs.'

'A steak sounds fantastic. I'll be round in ten minutes.'

I rang Kathy and got her voicemail. 'Kathy, I know I told you I only needed Saturday and Sunday off, but I was wondering if you could possibly cope until Christmas without me? I hate to do this to you now but . . . something happened. I'll call you tomorrow, I'm sure we can arrange cover one way or another.'

True to his word, Sam was at my door within ten minutes, clutching a bottle of red in his hand. Upstairs, he sat at my kitchen counter while I chopped up some wild mushrooms for the sauce. He opened the bottle and poured us each a glass.

'I don't actually drink, you know,' I told him with a smile.

'What? Not at all? We've been for a drink before.'

'We have, but I've always stuck to orange juice.'

'You've always had to get back to Luca . . .' The light was dawning on him. 'But the other night? You had wine the other night.'

'I poured myself a glass to keep you company. It makes people uncomfortable if they're drinking and you're not.'

'Right.' He swilled the wine around his glass, looking disconcerted. 'But you don't mind if I . . . ? Because I don't have to, you know.'

'It doesn't bother me at all, Sam. Hell, an hour ago I'd have been happy to join you. In fact, you'd have had to fight me just to get the bottle out of my hand.'

There was a long, less than comfortable silence before we both spoke at once.

'If you ever . . .'

'I owe you . . .'

We both stopped, and I started to laugh. He just looked miserable.

'I owe you an explanation, about what happened here tonight and about why things are the way they are with me. I owe you an apology, too. We've been friends for a while now, and I probably should have explained all this ages ago. It's just . . . it's hard for me to talk about it.'

'You don't owe me anything, Bea,' he said softly. He reached over the kitchen counter and took my hand. 'But if you want to talk about it . . .'

'I think it's time.'

I told him about Marco. I started with the story about the triathlon in Lerici. I told him about the year which followed that, in which I travelled to Italy once a month and he travelled to London once a month and we were both bloody miserable because we never had enough time together. I told him about how, through a lengthy process of cajoling, promising and threatening, I managed to persuade him to move to London.

'The deal was, he would come to London for a few years, then we would reassess, and if he wasn't happy, I would have to try Italy for a while. I would actually have been very happy to try Italy, although I never did get around to learning much Italian. His English was pretty much perfect, so there wasn't much incentive.'

'So when was this?'

'That was . . . 2003. A couple of years after we met. We got married in 2006, and the year after that we opened the Honey Pot.'

'The Honey Pot because you're . . .'

'Because I'm Bea.'

'Very cute.'

'Yeah, I thought it was corny, but he persuaded me.' The tears came all of a sudden. I tried to blame the onions, but Sam wasn't having any of it. He fetched me a Kleenex.

'Bea, if you don't want to talk about this . . .'

'No, it's OK,' I sniffed. 'I want to. I never tell anyone. I've literally never told anyone the story. I mean, my mother knows, because she was there, but my friends . . . I lost touch with everyone. To be honest, I'd lost touch with a lot of them even before Marco went. I think they were all so surprised to see me married, to see me embracing this incredibly traditional thing. I hadn't been all that traditional up to that point.'

'What were you like?' Sam asked with a smile.

'Oh God, I was just this total party girl.' Sam's smile grew wider. 'Honestly! Hard to believe now, I know, but it's true. Until I met Marco, it was all clubs and drugs and festivals, I never stuck with anyone – any man, I mean – for longer than a few weeks. And my friends were a bit like that, too. So they found it a bit hard to take when I suddenly shacked up with this rather cerebral Italian and then, even worse, married him. I think they thought that I was losing something of myself, but I wasn't, not at all, I never felt like I was compromising myself for him.'

I stirred the sauce around the pan. 'How do you like your steak? Rare? Bloody? Still moving around?'

'Rare's great, thank you.'

We sat at the kitchen table and tucked into our steaks. We ate in virtual silence – I was surprised to find, after the emotional ravages of the past couple of hours, that I was ravenous – and Sam always seems to love whatever I make for him (I like to think it's because I'm a decent cook; it may simply be that my cuisine bears up well in comparison to the crap he usually eats).

We made small talk for a while: he complimented the food; I promised to give him the recipe for the sauce. He poured himself more wine. I made a cup of fennel tea. We sat down on the sofa, next to each other. It felt intimate, and odd, and I was about to say that I really needed a shower and to go to bed, I was about to ask if we could do this whole confessional thing another time when he asked, 'Who was she, Bea? The woman at the door earlier?'

There wasn't going to be any escaping this, not now.

'She', I said, taking a deep breath, 'was Lucy. She's the one who was driving the car.'

'The car?'

'The car that hit him. It'll be two years on Tuesday.'

'The weather had been vile. Truly, utterly vile. Relentless, freezing rain, a bit like this year in fact. I wasn't feeling well – I'd been suffering from some sort of stomach bug for a couple of days – so I hadn't been working in the shop. Marco had been coping all on his own at one of the most stressful times of year, and he was gloriously cheerful about it, which was driving me mad. Actually, he was just in an incredibly good mood because we were due to leave for Italy on the twenty-second, to spend Christmas with his family, and he was incredibly excited about it.

'He'd spent ages shopping for presents. He'd spent a fortune: a Wii Fit for his sister, Xboxes for the nephews, a Hannah Montana Malibu Beach House for his favourite niece. He'd bought clothes, CDs, even a Nigella Lawson cookbook for his mother in an attempt to prove to her than English people did, on occasion, make decent food. The flat was full of this stuff, which he'd spent hours wrapping (really badly, most of it needed rewrapping by me) and we'd had to buy an extra suitcase just to lug it all over.

'It was such a big deal for him, because it was the first Christmas that he and I were going to spend with his family as a married couple. Our first Christmas as husband and wife was spent on a belated honeymoon in Costa Rica; and the following year we had –

highly controversially – decided to spend it with my mum. His mother was furious about it. She didn't talk to him for weeks. Christmas in Italy is a big thing – I mean, it's a big thing everywhere, I know, but in Italy it's not about presents, it's about family. Family and food, two things that Marco held very dear.

'He came up from the café around eight thirty. He'd stayed open an extra hour because we'd had tonnes of orders for special Christmas goodies: panettone and almond biscotti and things like that. He was making fun of how grumpy everyone was, asking me why the English had this knack of turning a joyous occasion into a complete trial, and he was really irritating me because I was feeling rotten. I asked him to go to the late-night pharmacy on Mason Street to pick up some painkillers for me. It was completely unfair, he'd been on his feet all day and I'd just been lying on the sofa, watching TV. I wasn't that ill, just feeling under the weather. I could easily have gone myself. I should have gone myself.'

I was feeling tearful again, so I got up to fetch myself a tissue. When I sat back down, Sam put his arm around my shoulders, pulled me closer to him. His jumper smelt of wood smoke, like bonfire night. I sat up straighter, pulling away from him.

'He didn't complain, of course, he was happy to go. He was determined that I should be better by the time we left for Italy. He said as much before he left. "I want you to be perfect for Genoa, even more perfect than usual." And off he went. I was dozing on the sofa in front of the TV and suddenly I noticed that he'd been gone half an hour. The chemist – well, you know – it's five minutes' walk from here. I was *furious*. I was absolutely bloody furious because I was convinced that he'd bumped into Stan – you don't know him, he used to run the hardware store just across from the chemist; it's closed now. Anyway, I was sure that Marco had bumped into Stan and that they'd decided to go for a sneaky pint, and I was absolutely livid because I was feeling like shit and I wanted him to come home and take care of me.

'I rang his phone, which I immediately heard ringing in the bedroom – he'd left it behind. That made me even more annoyed, because I was then convinced he'd left it on purpose so that I wouldn't be able to drag him out of the pub. So I hauled myself off the sofa – I didn't even get dressed properly, I just put my coat on over my tracksuit bottoms and grubby sweat shirt – and I headed down the road towards the Fox, which is where I was sure they'd be. I didn't get that far though, because there were police stopping people going up the road, and there was an ambulance parked on the corner. I immediately felt guilty because I knew then that Marco was on the scene, he'd be helping out. I knew he would be. I was about to turn around and go home when I saw Stan. He was standing talking to one of the police officers; he looked awful, ashen-faced. He caught sight of me, and then . . . Well. He started walking towards me with this look on his face. I can't describe it. That's when I knew.

'I don't really remember much of what happened after that. Stan was there, and a policewoman; she was trying to pick me up off the pavement, but I wouldn't stand up. I couldn't. It's a cliché, isn't it, to say people collapse in grief? But it's true, that's what it was like. I just fell down.

'They let me ride with him in the ambulance. I sat at his side and held his hand, felt it getting colder. The paramedic told me that they had tried to revive him on the scene, but that the injuries to his head and neck were fatal, he probably wouldn't have felt anything, it would have been over, they said, almost instantly.

'My mother came to the hospital to pick me up. She took me back to her place. One of the doctors at the hospital had given me a sedative, so I went straight to sleep. When I woke up in the morning I thought I'd dreamt it. That's one of the worst things, you know? Every time you wake from sleep, you have a moment or two when you think it was a nightmare, and then you have to go through it again and accept it again, and again and again and again. It's been two years now, and there are still mornings when I wake up and roll over, when I stretch out my hand to his side of the bed and I wonder, just for a fraction of a second, where he's gone.'

I got up from the sofa to make us a cup of tea. Sam followed me into the kitchen. He put his arms around me and held me until I stopped crying, which must have been a while.

'I wish you'd told me,' he said softly.

'I know. I didn't deal with it, you know? I never dealt with it properly. After the accident, there was a trial, and then there was Luca, and then I just . . . fell apart. It wasn't until after Luca was born that I let myself fall apart.'

Sam took my hand and led me back to the sofa. We sipped our tea in silence for a bit. Then he asked,

'Why did she come here? That woman . . . Lucy, was it?'

'Yes, Lucy. She came to apologise to me.' I started laughing. 'It's funny, isn't it?'

'Not really, no,' Sam said. 'Why on earth would she come now? Almost on the anniversary, just before Christmas? It's not funny at all, it's cruel.'

'I don't know,' I replied with a shrug. 'It probably seemed appropriate to her. Plus, she hasn't really had the opportunity to come and talk to me before now. She got an eighteen-month sentence for "causing death while under the influence of drink", so I imagine she hasn't been out of prison that long.'

'Christ, she was drunk when she hit him?'

'She was, although not very drunk. She'd been to an office party, she'd had three glasses of wine.' I paused to wipe away more tears. 'In a very strange sort of way,

115

I feel sorry for her. She had three glasses of wine and she ended three lives, his and mine and her own. Because I'm sure it's ruined her life, too.'

'That's ridiculous, Bea, you shouldn't have to feel sorry for her . . .' He pulled me closer to him and wiped the tears from my cheeks. He pushed the hair out of my face, saying, 'And your life isn't ruined, it's not over, you're young and you're beautiful and kind and you've got this wonderful little boy . . .' And then he stopped talking because I was kissing him.

Saturday 18 December

7.15 a.m.
Bea

The moment I opened my eyes, I knew something was wrong. First of all, I could smell coffee brewing. And second, it was after seven and I hadn't heard a peep out of Luca. Then I remembered the night before, that kiss, the one that lasted way too long and felt way too good and my heart gave a little leap. Oh God oh God oh God. He was still here.

He'd said, You shouldn't be alone, and I'd said, I can't do that, Sam, and he'd said, No I don't mean like that, and he offered to spend the night on the sofa and I said yes. Fuck. Why in God's name had I said yes?

I grabbed my dressing gown (the floor-length one this time) from the back of the bedroom door and flung it on. Sam was in the kitchen, pouring coffee, Luca balanced on one hip.

'Oh, you're awake,' he said when he heard me come in. 'We thought we'd give you a lie-in since you don't have to work today. Didn't we, my man?'

'Well, you shouldn't have,' I said, taking Luca from him. 'I have stuff to do today.'

'Oh . . . well. OK. Sorry.'

'It's fine, but . . . You should probably go, Sam. As I said, I have stuff to do today.'

'Bea, about what happened—'

'Honestly, Sam,' I said, cutting him off. 'I need to get Luca ready, I need to get ready, I have loads to do.' He put a cup of coffee down on the table in front of me. 'Well, you have that then. I'll be on my way.' He stepped towards me to give me a kiss, but I took a step back and he ended up just reaching out his hand to ruffle the blond fuzz on Luca's head. 'All right then, Bea,' he said, a little bemused. 'Maybe I'll see you later on.'

I did have loads of things to do, it was true. I had to get Luca breakfasted and ready, I had to shower and wash my hair, I had to clean up the flat, and I had to get to Heathrow by eleven thirty to pick up Elina, Luca's *nonna*, Marco's mum.

Of course, I hadn't told Sam that.

10.30 a.m.
Chloe

Mid-morning on a freezing Saturday, Chloe found herself hanging around the corner of Stratford Street and Abingdon Road, reading the headlines of the newspapers in the rack outside the newsagent. She wasn't really particularly interested in the newspaper headlines, this was just cover. She was really keeping

118

an eye on the handsome royal-blue door of number 54 Stratford Street.

She had been there once. Two months ago, Michael's wife had taken the children to stay at her mother's place in the countryside somewhere for half-term. Michael had too much work to do and couldn't get away, so he stayed behind. On the Wednesday night, he'd realised, just as he was leaving the office, that he needed some papers that he'd left on his desk at home. He'd had a long day, and he didn't want to have to travel all the way from Chancery Lane to Kensington and back up to north London, so he'd asked Chloe to meet him at the house.

It was a beautiful house, a lovely three-storey Georgian town house a few streets from Kensington Gardens, with an enormous kitchen in the basement, a bright, airy study on the top floor and lots of authentic modern artworks on the walls. Michael's wife was one of those posh women who studied art history at university and worked in an auction house until she was married. It was a grown-up's house, a family home, complete with clutter and toys and shopping lists stuck to the fridge with colourful magnets. Being inside that house filled Chloe with an odd combination of envy, disdain and guilt.

And now here she was, lurking outside it, one eye on the blue door adorned with a perfectly tasteful Christmas wreath, complete with cinnamon sticks and clementines, waiting for a glimpse of her lover. It was official. She had become a stalker.

She was about to leave when the door was flung open and two little girls came bundling down the stairs, shrieking excitedly.

'Be careful on the stairs,' a woman's voice was yelling. 'Don't run! Becky! Eva! Wait there!' Chloe picked up a newspaper and held it up in front of her face. Realising that she had picked up a copy of the *Daily Mail*, she quickly replaced it and grabbed a copy of the *Independent* instead. Michael's wife, Harriet, emerged from the house, alone. Michael wasn't with her. Harriet shut the door, locked it behind her and rushed down the stairs after her children, roughly grabbing them both and loudly insisting they stand still while she buttoned their coats. Chloe replaced the newspaper on the stand. It was unlikely that she'd be recognised; she and Harriet had only met once, before the affair had started. It was a little over a year ago, at the office Christmas party.

'Can I help you?' Chloe's stalking was interrupted by the appearance of the newsagent's owner in the doorway of his shop. 'This isn't a library, you know. If you want to read the papers, you have to buy one.'

'I'm still choosing,' Chloe huffed at him. 'I'll buy one when I'm ready.' Shaking his head, the newsagent turned around and went back into his shop.

Chloe noticed that Harriet and her children were making their way towards her. She pulled her hood up over her head. As they approached, Chloe glanced slyly over at them. Harriet was almost unrecognisable as the svelte, well-groomed woman she'd met at the party twelve months ago. That night she'd been dressed in an unadventurous but nevertheless stylish midnight-blue shift, her blond hair swept up on to her head. Chloe remembered noticing her; she'd looked quite glamorous that evening, she stood out from the other stay-at-home wives. Today, she looked a mess in too-tight jeans and a shapeless coat, her hair pulled back into a ponytail at the nape of her neck. It struck Chloe that seeing her love rival in this state should have made her feel good, it should have made her feel triumphant, but it didn't.

One of the girls, the older child, was skipping a couple of steps in front of her mother and sister, but Harriet was struggling with the other one, who kept stopping, holding out her arms, imploring her mother to pick her up.

'Please, Becky, I need you to walk. I can't carry you now,' Chloe could hear Harriet pleading with her; she had a catch in her voice, as though she were about to cry. She looked as exhausted as Chloe felt. Becky shrieked, sat down on the pavement and started to cry. Harriet grabbed her hand and pulled her to her feet, but the child just sat down again, howling now, asking for Daddy.

'He's working, sweetheart,' Harriet was telling her. 'He'll be back this afternoon. We're going to go and see the Christmas lights this evening, remember? And Santa? We might even see Santa!'

'Daddy said he'd take us to see the lights yesterday, but he didn't,' the older child, Eva, said matter of factly.

'I know, darling,' Harriet replied. 'But he had to work late. Tonight we'll go, we'll definitely go tonight. I promise.'

'Daddy promised he'd take us yesterday,' Eva insisted.

Unable to persuade her youngest child to walk, Harriet relented, picking her up with an audible grunt.

'He promised he'd help decorate the tree, too,' Eva was saying as they walked past Chloe.

'I know he did, darling. I know.'

Chloe put down the newspaper and went home to her flat where, thanks to a broken boiler, the temperature inside was barely higher than it was outside. She'd rung four plumbers that morning and none could come until Tuesday at the earliest, so she'd just given up. She felt like giving up on everything.

11.30 a.m.
Bea

Heathrow is not a pleasant place at the best of times. A week before Christmas it closely resembles the fifth circle of hell. And as if a visit to hell weren't bad enough in itself, my little jaunt was made worse by (a) my extraordinarily grumpy child and (b) a raging case of guilt induced by the passionate kiss I'd shared with Sam on the eve of my dead husband's mother's visit.

Thankfully the plane was on time and Elina was one of the first passengers through, pulling a little carry-on-sized suitcase behind her. Seeing us, she gave a little hop into the air, let go of the suitcase and flung her arms out wide.

'*Caro mio!*' She beamed at Luca. 'Look at how big you are!' She took Luca from my arms and kissed him on the nose. Amazingly, he didn't scream blue murder; if anything he seemed happy to be out of my hands. Another knife to the heart. 'And you,' Elina said, holding out her hand to me and kissing me on both cheeks, 'you are beautiful as ever.'

'And you, Elina, are a fantastic liar.' We stood there and hugged for a moment, blocking the Arrivals path. People tutted and tsked as they passed (it's not like *Love Actually* at all, you know, people are just as shitty, just as grumpy, just as rude – if not more so – at Heathrow at Christmas than they are anywhere else). 'It's wonderful to see you,' I said. 'You look so well.'

Both of these things were true. Elina, mother to four children and grandmother to ten, looked not a day over fifty despite being closer to seventy. And although she was never a wonderful mother-in-law (she was initially horrified that her only son was going to marry *una inglese*, and it took her quite a while to get over this), she'd become a good friend.

She was the second person I called from the hospital the night Marco died, after my own mother. I remember sitting on a green plastic chair in an empty corridor, dialling her number and praying she wouldn't answer. She did answer though, and there followed the worst conversation of my entire life. She was in London by midday the following day though, and when, after the funeral was over, I went back to the flat for the first time, she was there with me.

That was one of the worst days, and that's saying something, given that there was a fair amount of competition. Passing the front of the café, darkened and sad with a 'Closed due to a family bereavement' sign hanging on the door, unlocking our front door and going up the stairs into our living room, usually warm and filled with the smells of cooking and coffee, now just cold and stale. And there, scattered around the room and in our bedroom, all the presents he'd bought, some wrapped, some still waiting, the cards he'd scribbled to his nieces and nephews, all the debris of a perfect Christmas planned and ruined. Despite her own grief, the depth of which I could only begin to guess at after I became a mother, Elina was there with me. She helped me sort through the gifts and pack them into a suitcase which she promised to take over when she left.

'Maybe we'll open them next year,' she said to me.

Eight and a half months later, when I was heavily pregnant with Luca and my mother was in hospital for an eye operation, Elina came over to London again. She helped sort through Marco's things, packing up his clothes (most of which are stored in the attic, where she put them because I was too fat to get up there) and sorting through his papers. Elina helped me put together Luca's cot; she bought nappies and blankets and bottles; she got me ready for the birth.

We got stuck in traffic on the M25. Elina didn't seem to care. She kept turning around in her seat, prattling to Luca in Italian.

'Do you play him the tapes that I sent you?' she asked. 'It's important that he can speak his father's language.'

'I do, Elina,' I said, though I hadn't done for a while. 'There's actually a lady who comes into the café every morning who gives private Italian lessons. I was thinking that we could both go, we could both take classes.'

'Humph!' Elina snorted. 'Why don't you just come to Genoa in the holidays, spend some time with your family? We can teach you to speak Italian. You don't have to pay money to some lady to do it. Why don't you come to see us?'

Italian mothers-in-law can go head to head with Jewish ones when it comes to guilt-tripping.

'Next year, Elina,' I said, 'I promise.' I half meant it. I knew it was important to take Luca over to see the family. I just wasn't sure how I would cope being there myself. All of my memories of Italy are golden. I wasn't sure I could stand to go there without him, it might tarnish them.

'We miss you so much, *cara*. We miss you both so much,' Elina said, resting her hand on top of mine.

Elina hadn't approved of me when she first met me. She hadn't approved of me for a long time, in fact. Once she'd accepted me, though, she did it completely. And she forgave without hesitation everything I did after Marco died.

I've always been a drinker. Marco was too, though less so, and in a rather more civilised, European way. But there was wine with dinner every night and we rarely stopped at one bottle. We liked spending afternoons in the pub with our friends; we liked going out for cocktails, just the two of us. I'm sure we both drank too much, we certainly drank more than they tell you to in those government health warnings, but then so do a lot of people I know. It didn't seem problematic. After Marco died though, problematic was an understatement.

It was only problematic for a couple of months, however, because it took me a couple of months to realise that I was pregnant. It finally hit me, some time in early March, that I hadn't had a period in for ever, and that I'd started throwing up in the morning *before* I started drinking all day. It eventually dawned on me that the tummy bug I'd had back before Christmas, the one which had kept me out of work and on the sofa, the one that had made me feel so rotten that I sent Marco out to get pills for me – that had not been a tummy bug. That had been the early stages of pregnancy.

So one of the things I have to live with, and one of the things that Elina forgave me for, was that I risked my child's health by smoking and drinking my way through the first ten weeks of my pregnancy. It got worse, though, because at least when that happened I was in a fog of grief, unaware of what I was doing. What happened later was far worse.

13.30 p.m.
Chloe

'Hello. It's not very classy to do this over the phone, I know, but I don't think I'm likely to see you until after Christmas now, and I need to do this. It's probably even less classy to do this with your answer phone, but there you go. It's over, Michael. And it's not because I'm angry with you about Venice. I'm not. I was, I was very angry and I was hurt, but I'm not any more. Now I'm just sad. I know that you love me, I love you too. I also know you love her, I know you love your children. What we have, which is amazing, it really is, it'll go away, won't it? The passion always does. It'll go away for you and me, in the same way it went away for you and her, and then what happens? I know I've been asking you to leave her for months, but now I don't think I could bear it if you did. I don't want you to. More than that, if you do, you won't be what I wanted in the first place. This probably doesn't make any sense. I'm going to go now.

'Oh, this is Chloe, by the way.'

2.22 p.m.
Olivia

Olivia crossed off her fifth point – make up beds in spare rooms – from her list of the day. Five down, seven to go. She still had to:

Do shopping for Sunday dinner (see shopping list)
Buy fresh flowers to put in hallway and bedrooms

Pick up red dress from dry cleaners for Monday's parties

Call Bea [she'd still not heard from her despite leaving two messages.]

Chase up non-rsvpers for Wednesday's engagement soirée

Check basement flat was cleaned and ready for Kieran's brother and family.

Olivia's flat, while not palatial, was larger than that inhabited by the average London singleton wage slave. There were three double bedrooms, a large living room, separate eat-in kitchen *and* a study, which is in fact more space than most London families live in. It was far too big for one person on their own to live in, although Olivia always refused to rent out the other rooms. ('I need them for when my parents are in town,' she always said, although whenever her parents were in London they tended to stay at the Lanesborough.) In any case, big as Olivia's flat was, she had come to realise that it was still not big enough.

One of the double bedrooms, of course, was hers. Olivia was prepared to sacrifice many things in order to make her future family-in-law's stay enjoyable, but giving up her own room was not one of them. Kieran's parents, Daniel and Sheila, would have the second bedroom. The third would house Richard and Diane and their youngest daughter, Carey. Shannon and

Erin, the elder daughters, would sleep on inflatable mattresses in the study.

As luck would have it, the couple who rented the basement flat in Olivia's building – also owned by Olivia – were away for Christmas and had agreed to allow Kieran's middle brother, Brendon, his wife Suzie and their two boys, Oscar and Danny, to stay there.

This still left the youngest brother, Conor, and his girlfriend. Olivia's original plan had been to put them in a hotel, but Kieran vetoed the idea.

'They'll never let us pay for it, and they can't afford it themselves,' he argued. 'We'll just have to put them up at my place.'

'We can't do that, Kieran,' Olivia had protested. 'Your place is a total shithole. Whatever will they think?'

Kieran's flat, while not exactly a 'total shithole' by most people's standards, was more in line with the sort of property you might expect a single, thirty-something employee of a charitable organisation to inhabit. Just around the corner from Olivia's impressive Victorian maisonette, Kieran lived in a tiny two-bedroom place in a former council block.

'It is *not* a total shithole,' Kieran protested. 'You can barely remember what it looks like anyway. We never stay at my place. I've got some new curtains. And there's a futon in the living room.' Olivia grimaced. 'I can sleep on that, they can have my room. It'll be fine.'

They had agreed that, in theory at least, Kieran should stay at his place while his parents were in town.

'Mum's a bit old fashioned about that kind of thing,' he'd said. In practice, they knew that what would probably happen was that they'd stay up until after his parents had turned in, then they'd go to bed themselves and he'd have to get up early before anyone else was about.

'It's slightly ridiculous, don't you think?' Olivia had said to him. 'This is the twenty-first century and we are adults. Engaged adults.'

'It'll be fun,' he promised her. 'Like a French farce.'

17.45 p.m.
Bea

For the first time in for ever, I didn't have to make dinner. Elina was insistent.

'Your mother is a terrible cook, I know this,' she said, chopping onions with the speed and skill of a sous-chef. Elina is nothing if not direct. 'You need someone to take care of you for a change.'

She asked about my plans for Christmas.

'I'll be spending it here, with Luca,' I told her. 'Just the two of us for Christmas Day. My mother's going to be away.' Elina shook her head sadly at this; I could tell she was about to launch into yet another lengthy plea for us to come to Italy. 'Elina, it's important for me,' I said, before she could get going. 'I didn't have Christmas with him last year. I hate that I missed the first year. I want us to wake up together, in our own home, this Christmas, to open presents under our own tree. Please understand.'

She stopped chopping, took a long, hard look at me and shrugged her shoulders. Just so long as you promise me . . .'

'Next year, Elina. We'll come to Genoa.'

'You and Luca and even your mother if you like,' she said with a small smile. 'And her latest gentleman friend, too.'

Elina, who had decided, after a cursory inspection of the contents of my fridge, to make chicken cacciatora, was browning juicy pieces of chicken over a fierce heat.

'You don't have wine in the house, no?' she asked me. 'We will have to do without. It is not the same, but . . .' She tailed off with a resigned shrug.

'I can get some if you like,' I offered.

Elina simply shook her head.

After Luca was born, I took him home with me, to the flat. That homecoming, the one that for most mothers, most new families, is no doubt one of the happiest of their lives, was horrible for me. I felt isolated, terrified, above all bereft. He cried all the time and I had no idea what to do. I couldn't comfort him. I couldn't cope, and after just two nights, I took Luca to my mother's house. I stayed there for about three weeks. One day, about three o'clock in the morning, I got up, gave Luca a bottle, got myself dressed and packed and left, alone. I drove back home, disconnected my phone, turned off my mobile and started to drink.

I didn't stop for the best part of six months. In the early days, my mother used to come round all the time, banging on the door, begging me to open up. I'd turn the radio up as loud as I could to drown her out. She tried everything, she even persuaded my father, whom she hasn't spoken to in years, to get involved. Nothing worked. During those first six months, I hardly saw Luca at all. Sometimes, my mother would park her car outside in the street and sit there for hours and hours, waiting until I had to leave – to get more cigarettes or more to drink – and then she'd ambush me, with him in her arms, trying to get me to look at him at the very least. I refused. I wanted nothing to do with him, with her, with anyone.

In March, a little over six months after Luca was born, I woke up to a terrible banging on my front door. This had happened before, and I ignored it. It didn't stop. It went on and on and on until eventually, in utter desperation, I hauled myself downstairs. On my doorstep were my mother and Elina. They forced their way past me into my apartment and flat out refused to leave. They cleaned the house, clearing it of all the bottles and all the pills. Then Elina went back to my mother's house to look after Luca, while Mum stayed with me.

For three weeks, Mum supervised everything I did,

refusing to let me out of her sight for a minute. We shopped together and ate together, she searched the bathroom before I went in to take a shower and sat outside until I was finished. Every day, Elina would bring Luca to the flat for an hour or two.

At first, I was too ashamed to look at him, let alone hold him. When eventually I did find the courage to pick him up, he cried until I gave him back to my mother. It was torturous, it was painful. (It was all my fault.) But eventually I learned to soothe him, to feed him, to take care of him. After three weeks, Elina left, leaving Luca with me and Mum, and a month after that, by which time I was seven weeks and three days sober, my mother moved out, leaving us alone.

Neither of them, neither my mum nor Elina, ever got angry with me for what I'd done. They never shouted at me and told me I was stupid, selfish and a terrible mother. They just helped.

Elina stirred the sauce. 'There is no gentleman friend for you, no?' she asked, regarding me slyly out of the corner of her eye. 'No one even to invite for some cake or something on Christmas Day?'

'Actually, I'm throwing a bit of a party in the evening,' I said. 'Downstairs, in the café. A waifs and strays Christmas party.'

'"Waifs and . . . strays?" What are these?'

'It's an idea I had a while ago,' I explained. 'I know quite a few of my customers quite well, and not all of them have plans over Christmas, so I've invited them to come here for some food and a few drinks.'

'Where are their families?' Elina demanded crossly. '*Natale con i tuoi*,' she muttered. Christmas is spent with family.

'Not everyone has family close by, some people have to work over Christmas and can't get away, some people just aren't talking to their parents . . .' Elina tutted angrily at this. 'I have some older customers who are alone at Christmas, too, so it's nice for them to have somewhere to go.'

Elina grunted in reply. 'The English are so strange,' she said finally. 'But it is nice that you do something for the old people.' I knew that would win her over.

I took over the cooking while Elina fed Luca, all the while babbling to him in Italian. Then she put him down and two of us sat down to dinner. We were interrupted, halfway through, by the doorbell.

'Ignore it,' I told her. 'It's probably just antisocial youths selling overpriced dishcloths.' She looked at me blankly. 'Don't worry about it.'

'The English are so strange,' she said again. 'At home, when someone knocks on my door, I open it. Even if they come during dinner. It might be important.'

'It won't be, I can guarantee it.'

The doorbell rang again. Elina got up from the table. 'I'll go,' she said, waving away my protests, 'you stay, eat.'

134

I heard the front door open, I heard voices.

'It's fine, it's fine,' I heard Elina saying. 'She is upstairs. Come inside.' My heart sank. 'We have a visitor,' Elina announced as she arrived at the top of the stairs, Sam following closely behind her. He was dripping wet, it was still raining outside.

'Terrible weather, isn't it?' Elina asked. She knows this is a topic English people enjoy.

'Awful,' Sam agreed. I could feel his eyes on me; I just sat there, staring down at the table.

'Get another plate, Bea,' Elina instructed. She turned to Sam. 'Will you join us for something to eat?'

'I wouldn't want to interrupt your dinner,' Sam said. 'I didn't realise you had company.'

'I do, as you can see,' I said. 'Sam, this is Marco's mum, Elina. Elina, my next-door neighbour, Sam.'

'You aren't interrupting—' Elina started to say, but I cut her off.

'What did you need, Sam?'

'Nothing,' he said, taking a step backwards towards the door. 'I just . . . It was nothing. It was nice to meet you, Elina,' he said, and turned to go.

Elina sat back down at the table and resumed her dinner. We finished our meal in silence. As I got up to clear the plates, she said, 'You used not to be so rude, Beatrice. One thing I always thought about you was that you had impeccable manners. Even when you had too much to drink, you were always polite.' As I said, she's nothing if not direct.

'I wasn't being rude, it was just . . . inconvenient. Him turning up like that in the middle of dinner. He shouldn't do that. He thinks I'm always free, mostly because I am always free, but even so . . . Would you like dessert? I have some rhubarb crumble I made yesterday. It's quite good.'

Elina nodded without saying anything. We ate dessert in silence, too. What had started out a perfectly pleasant evening had soured. Inwardly, I fumed at Sam. It was all his fault.

Except, of course, that it wasn't his fault. He had no idea that I would be eating dinner with my dead husband's mother. He had no idea, because I hadn't told him, despite having had ample opportunity that morning. That morning when, instead of simply explaining why I needed to rush off, I just kicked him out of the flat. After he'd spent the entire previous evening listening to me go on and on about Marco. After *I* had kissed *him*. And now I'd been rude again, rude and unkind.

My dessert, delicious though it may have been, stuck in my throat. I put down my spoon and pushed my plate away.

'I was being rude,' I said quietly. 'I'm sorry. I felt a bit . . . awkward.'

'Why on earth would you feel awkward?' Elina asked. She smiled at me. 'Because you like him, perhaps? You like this man?'

'We're good friends,' I said.

136

'He likes you,' she said. 'I could tell. He looked at you . . .' She tailed off, starting to giggle.

'How did he look at me?'

'Like you are a juicy steak!' She giggled again.

'Don't be ridiculous,' I said crossly, clearing the rest of the dinner things. 'Would you like coffee?'

Elina got to her feet to help me clear away. 'Why do you keep offering me things to eat and drink when I want to talk to you about your friend?'

'There's nothing to talk about,' I snapped, my voice rising a little.

Elina put the dishes down, took my hand and led me into the living room. We sat down on the sofa.

'You are so . . . how do you say it? Touchy about this? Why are you so worried? Do you think that because I am Marco's mother that I would want you to spend the rest of your life in grief, is that it?' I could feel the tears welling up again. I bit my lip. Elina brushed my hair back from my forehead. 'Listen to me, *cara*, I will tell you something. When I met you, I wasn't sure about you. I thought you were a pretty girl who liked to have fun and I liked you, but I thought perhaps you were not so good for a serious man like my son. Plus,' she said with a grin, 'you are not Italian, so that was terrible all by itself.' She put her arm around my shoulders and pulled me closer to her tiny frame. 'But then, when I see you two together, after a while, I know that everything is going to be all right. Marco was not always so serious, you were not always so fun, you mixed well together. I remember when you came for that holiday, when you just were engaged, you remember?'

I remembered it well. Marco asked me to marry him in the north terminal of Gatwick Airport.

We were standing in the check-in queue for the Easyjet flight to Rome. We were going to spend a few days there, take the train to Florence and then hire a car and drive to the Riviera to spend a couple of weeks with Marco's family. I'd met them before, but only during brief, flying visits. I had never had to deal with the entire Marinelli clan en masse, and for a considerable period of time. I wasn't particularly nervous about it. In those days, I never seemed to be nervous about anything. But Marco was, I could tell; he'd been growing increasingly nervous about it as the date grew nearer. His nervousness had resulted in increasing neuroticism, culminating in him asking me, for the fifth time that morning, whether I was sure I had my passport. Fishing it out of my handbag and waving it in his face for emphasis, I snapped, 'Here it is! For God's sake. Why don't we just get to what's really bothering you? You don't think they'll like me, do you?'

The pair of teenage boys standing in front of us in the queue turned around and smirked.

'I do, darling,' Marco said soothingly. 'They love

you. They already do.' He was as unconvincing as I'd ever heard him sound. 'It's just . . . my mother.'

'Well, yes. We know she doesn't like me. I'll be on my best behaviour. I promise.'

'No, no. It isn't that.' He was fidgeting with strap of his watch, a sure sign that something was up. 'I haven't told her,' he said finally. 'About us.'

'Marco, I hate to tell you this, but we've been together for three years now,' I said to him. 'I think your mother might have cottoned on by now.'

He rolled his eyes at me. 'Not *that*. I haven't told her we're living together. It's a big deal for her. It is for a lot of people of her generation in Italy.'

I didn't really know what to say about this. After all, at this point, we had been living together for about six months. I had no idea that every time she phoned and I answered he'd been telling her that I'd just popped round for a bit and he'd being making dinner, and that was why I'd answered the phone.

'I don't believe this!' I spluttered, when words finally came to me. 'How could you not tell me?'

'You're in trouble now, mate,' the spottier of the two teenage boys in front of us said. I resisted the urge to slap him.

'I know, I should have said something, to you and to her. I am going to tell her,' Marco reassured me. 'But I think . . . I think she will be happier about it if

139

you wear this . . .' He held out a closed fist, rotated it upwards and opened out his fingers to reveal a silver ring in his palm. 'Will you marry me, Bea?' he asked.

The teenage boys in front of us gave a small cheer.

'That was a great trip,' I said to Elina, to whom we had never told the real engagement story. She'd heard a ficti-tious – and much more romantic – one, involving roses, champagne and a moonlit ride on the London Eye.

'I never saw a man so happy,' Elina said, smiling at the memory. 'I never thought I could see anyone make him laugh so much. He was always a serious boy at home, hard at work, you know? A bit quiet, with all those women around him, his sisters and me. But then with you . . . He was the one who was at the centre of everything for a change. It was such a gift, you gave me, to make my son so happy.'

She stopped as we both reached for the Kleenex in unison. I should have shares in Kleenex.

'So now, do you honestly think I could wish that your sadness goes on? Not for one moment do I want your unhappiness to be extended. And this is not just for me – I love you, of course I do – but this is for Marco. Marco would not want you to live the rest of your life in this kind of pain. That would be the worst thing in the world for him and you know that.'

We stayed up until three in the morning, talking about Marco's sisters and their children, about Elina's work (despite being almost seventy years old, Elina still managed to work three mornings a week for a Catholic charity which helped house immigrants), and – eventually – about Sam and me.

She asked me when we'd met (March), what I liked about him (aside from his good looks) and whether he had a girlfriend (a complicated question). Finally, she got to the question she really wanted to ask.

'Do you love him, Bea?'

'I'm not sure I can love anyone properly, Elina. Except for Luca, of course. And my mum. And you.'

'Maybe you will surprise yourself,' she said. 'If you could love someone, could you imagine yourself loving him?'

'Maybe.'

11.55 p.m.
Chloe

'Michael, I love you. I don't think you're a very good person, but neither am I. So we're right, you know? For each other? Uh . . . excuse me. I have hiccups. I love you. I mean it. I didn't mean what I said earlier. I was just . . . I don't know. I had something to say but now I can't remember what it was. I love you, Michael. Please call me.'

Sunday 19 December

7.30 a.m.
Chloe

'Michael, it's Chloe. As you may have gathered from the message I left last night, I'd had quite a bit to drink and wasn't thinking straight. I *was* thinking straight when I phoned you earlier, so I stand by that message. The first one. We're all broken up. Sorry about the confusion. I won't be calling you again, and I'd appreciate it if you didn't call me.'

12.15 p.m.
Olivia

Olivia was feeling remarkably calm. The food was bought; the flat was spotless; she was on schedule. Kieran had taken the train to Gatwick to meet the clan who were due to get in at two. Olivia estimated it would take at least an hour for everyone to clear immigration and pick up their bags, and then another hour to get from Gatwick to Crouch Hill. If she was lucky, an hour and a half. So, tea and cakes at four thirty, or drinks and snacks at five? She decided to go with drinks and snacks. They were Irish, after all.

Accommodation sorted; afternoon activities sorted. There remained the issue of cooking dinner for ten adults and five children. Typically, Olivia had it all under control. She'd opted for a low-maintenance starter – a Gorgonzola, pear and walnut salad – which was to be followed by a roast leg of lamb. She was keeping the veg simple: roast potatoes, carrots, peas. Things children would eat. The only tricky part of the meal was the dessert.

Against her better judgement and despite limited cooking skills, Olivia had opted to make a chocolate soufflé. When she had told Kieran about this (she'd consulted with him over the menu on Friday, just to make sure that she wasn't going to prepare anything to which a member of his family either had strong objections or was allergic), he looked a little sceptical.

'It never works on *Masterchef*, Liv,' he said. 'Whenever someone says they're going to make a soufflé, any soufflé, you get that collective sharp intake of breath from John and Greg. Then they go off into a huddle and talk to camera about how it's going to be a disaster. And this is *Masterchef*. Featuring people who can actually cook.' Olivia fixed him with a steely glare. 'I mean . . . have you ever made a soufflé before? Maybe we should go for something a little less ambitious? You know, they'd be perfectly happy with ice cream. I can pick up some of that expensive organic stuff if you like.'

'I'm not giving your family ice cream, Kieran. I'm going to make a soufflé.'

It turned out that you could make the soufflé mixture in advance and just pop it in the oven twenty minutes before serving. So, Olivia reasoned, she'd make the mixture now and even have time to do a test run to make sure she had the technique down.

The first thing she had to do was to prepare the dishes in which the soufflé was to be cooked. The recipe stipulated that each drier should have their own dessert, cooked in its own individual ramekin. Since Olivia didn't have fifteen ramekins (in fact, she was not entirely sure what a ramekin was), she was just going to have to make do with a single, giant soufflé. She greased a pan as instructed and moved on.

Next she had to make something called a *crème pâtissière*, which involved mixing flour, sugar and cornflour. Simple enough. At least, it would have been simple enough if she'd had any cornflour. What the hell was cornflour? Sod it, it was a sort of flour – how different could it be to ordinary flour? She'd just add more flour.

She had a spot of bother separating egg yolks from whites – not as easy as they make it look on *Ready, Steady, Cook*. She was sure she'd had a little plastic spoon which held the yolk while allowing the whites to drain out, but she was damned if she could find it.

After wasting fifteen minutes rooting through kitchen drawers, which for some reason were almost all filled with takeaway menus, rolls of sellotape and novelty egg cups, she decided to attempt the separation manually. Her first four attempts failed, the fifth was successful. The bad news was that she was now short on eggs, She'd have to run down to the shops later.

It was at this point that things started to go awry. The chocolate cream she'd made came out a little lumpy, and its lumpiness was transferred to the *crème pâtissière*, into which it had to be mixed. No matter, she'd just whisk it for a while longer. Olivia whisked and whisked. She whisked until her arm ached. The lumps remained. She placed the bowl down on the counter and moved on.

After that, she had to make something called a ganache. This really was ridiculously complicated. Kieran was right. She wasn't up to this. Still, she wasn't about to admit defeat now. As instructed, she warmed some cream in a pan, removing it before it came to the boil and adding lumps of chocolate. Given that her arm was still aching from all that whisking, she decided to go high-tech and use the electric whisk to blend the chocolate this time. She plugged it in and turned it on, too high. Cream and chocolate splashed up into her face. Blinded by confectionery, she groped around for a tea towel, but as she did so her hand brushed against the bowl of *crème pâtissière*.

The bowl teetered on the brink of the counter. Olivia

made a grab for it. As she did so, her right hand tightened on the handle of the electric whisk, starting it up again. Cream and chocolate spurted up everywhere, the bowl of *crème pâtissière* crashed to the floor, Olivia took a step forward, skidding in the mess and went flying.

The phone rang.

1.15 p.m.
Chloe

There was nothing else for it. Chloe had exhausted every possible activity she could think of. She had been for a long run; she had washed her hair and her clothes; she had tidied the flat; she'd caught up with her correspondence and filing. She had, after all, been up since four in the morning. She had to do something, had to find some way to occupy her time. If she didn't, she might go mad. Either that or call Michael again, which pretty much amounted to the same thing.

She cringed when she thought the call from the previous night, her slurring and hiccuping her way through a declaration of love. Christ. If this was what men reduced you to, they were not worth having around.

Chloe realised that she didn't have anyone to call. Years of workaholism, the past year's all-consuming affair and her naturally spiky personality had combined to ensure that she didn't have a girlfriend to rely on.

147

Thinking about that fact made her feel even more miserable, so she tried not to dwell on it. She flicked on the television. Predictably, there was nothing on. She checked her Sky+: the listing showed a documentary on libel reform and a month's worth of *Grey's Anatomy* episodes. Ten minutes into the first *Grey's*, she turned it off. It was all sex, love and infidelity. She tried the libel documentary. If nothing else, it might get her off to sleep. It didn't. It turned out that as fantastically boring as it was, it wasn't quite boring enough.

All of a sudden, it hit her – she was not friendless! She had, in fact, made a new friend recently: Olivia. All right, so perhaps friend was a bit of a stretch, but they had had lunch together. So she was a bit ditzy and naïve, but Olivia had been kind to her when Bea had been yelling at her in the café. Niceness was not usually a quality Chloe sought out – it tended to go hand in hand with vacuity in her opinion – but kindness was certainly something she could do with more of. She grabbed her bag and flipped open her purse. Tucked inside was Olivia's business card, which she had taken when they'd had lunch the other day. You never knew when a journalist might come in useful. Even a journalist who wrote about the pros and cons of different sorts of bronzer.

She rang Olivia's mobile.

'Hold on!' a voice shrieked when the phone was answered. There was an unpleasant, high-pitched whirring sound in the background, like a chainsaw, or possibly a food mixer. Chloe held the phone away from her ear. 'Just hold on! I'll be with you in—' There was a loud crash and then the phone went dead.

Chloe redialled.

'Can't talk now!' Olivia said as she answered the phone. 'Bit of a crisis.' And the phone went dead again.

In the past, on weekends when she didn't have any work to do and Michael couldn't get away from the family, Chloe used to spend hours in the Honey Pot, reading the papers and people-watching. It kept her distracted. She wondered whether, if she went there that afternoon, Bea would slam the door in her face. Chloe usually found the idea of confrontation exciting – she was a lawyer after all – but that Sunday she didn't quite have the stomach for it.

On the table in the living room, her phone beeped. Her heart racing, her breath held, she picked it up. It was a text from her dentist's office telling her she needed to make an appointment for a check-up. For a second, she thought she might cry. She opened her contacts and scrolled down to 'Michael'. Her finger hovered over his name. She clicked on it. Then she clicked 'Options'. Then she clicked 'Delete'.

There was nothing else for it. Desperate times called for desperate measures. She was going to visit her sisters.

Anna and Beth were happy. They were well adjusted. Their marriages were solid. They had good relationships with both their parents and their in-laws.

They were, in Chloe's opinion, fucking boring, but after the few days she had endured, Chloe was starting to wonder whether fucking boring was preferable to interesting but also bitter and alone.

Anna and Beth lived on the same street in Chiswick, three doors away from each other. They were best friends. In their early twenties, they had shared a flat. When Chloe, the youngest of the three, left university, she half expected to be invited to join the flatshare. No invitation came. The eldest, Anna, a GP, met Matt, an investment banker, when he came to her practice with an ankle sprain picked up on a company paint-ball outing. They married two years later. Beth was a bridesmaid. Chloe was not. When Beth (primary school teacher) married Christopher (also an invest-ment banker, the uncle of one of her charges) a year later, it was Anna, not Chloe, who was chosen as a member of the wedding party.

It had been like that at school, too. Anna and Beth, born barely eighteen months apart, hung around with the same group of pretty, popular girls. Chloe, who was younger than Beth by three years, was always left out. Over the past few years, she had seen her sisters less and less; the last time they had all got together had been for a family gathering in the summer. The talk had been of babies. Anna and Beth were going to try to get pregnant at around the same time, so that their kids could play together. The idea of coordinating attempts to get knocked up made Chloe feel vaguely nauseous, but she probably should not have told them so; they didn't take it well.

She picked up her phone again and considered her options. Which one should she call? Beth. She would call Beth. Beth was less successful than Anna (doctor definitely trumps teacher). Her husband was a slightly less successful investment banker than Anna's husband, so they had less money, a smaller house, Beth had only one pair of Jimmy Choos, Anna had three. The result was that Beth was slightly less smug than Anna. The downside of this was that it did tend to make her marginally bitchier. On second thoughts, perhaps she should call Anna. Because Anna was so incredibly pleased with herself, she could, on occasion, be quite magnanimous in her dealings with her youngest sister. On occasion. On other occasions, she would lord it over her, crowing about her life as though the acquisition of a husband with a six-figure income and a home with four bedrooms in an area with close proximity to good schools was the pinnacle of human achievement.

Chloe rang Beth. Predictably, after all that deliberation, there was no answer, so she had to ring Anna anyway.

'Chloe? I thought you were in Vienna?' Anna said when she picked up the phone.

'Venice,' Chloe said, 'and I haven't left yet.'

Chloe had thought about telling her sister that the trip to Venice was off. She might even manage to elicit some sympathy, provided that she didn't explain the circumstances or let on that Michael was married. However, the downside of letting them know would be that they would tell her parents and she would then almost certainly be press-ganged into travelling to Worcestershire to spend Christmas with the family. While facing Christmas alone wasn't a delightful prospect, it was probably preferable to going home: she wasn't sure she could bear to be around that much jollity and contentment right now. In the end, she decided that she could probably do without her sister's sympathy, since it was bound to come with an accompanying pinch of judgement and condescension, so she would just lied.

'We're going tomorrow,' she said. 'Leaving first thing. So I thought I might come around and see you today, give you your gifts, and the ones for Mum and Dad?'

'Today?' Anna didn't sound thrilled. 'Hang on a minute.' There was a fumbling noise, and then Chloe heard her sister say, 'She wants to come round this afternoon'.

'Who are you talking to?' Chloe asked.

'Beth's here. Look, Chloe, we were thinking of going to the cinema this afternoon. So it's really not that convenient for you to come over.'

'I won't stay long,' Chloe said. 'I have to pack, so I'll just come round for a little while.'

There was a pause, in which she could hear her

sister whispering something, but she couldn't make out what it was. 'No, I'm sorry Chloe but it's just not a good day for us.'

'But it's my last chance to give you your presents . . .' Chloe said, her voice catching in her throat. She was surprised by how hurt she felt.

'Well, next time give me a bit of notice. We can do the present thing after Christmas. I'll call you to set up a convenient time. Have a good time in Vienna.'

'Venice,' Chloe said again, but Anna had already hung up.

Chloe sat on the sofa, blinking back tears. She really didn't know why she was so upset. They'd always been quite cruel. They used to tease her horribly at school, so why was she surprised? And although it would have been nice to have something to unwrap on Christmas Day, it wasn't as though her sisters were the most thoughtful gift-givers. Last year, she'd got a Tiffany silver bracelet with pink sapphires from Anna, exactly the sort of thing that Beth would wear and Chloe never would; and a couple of vouchers from Beth: one for a facial at the Elemis day-spa and a second for the Allan Carr's Easyway to Stop Smoking clinic.

It was just after two and Chloe was back to square one, with no one to talk to and nothing to do. The silence in the flat was deafening. She decided to go out for a walk. There was a light drizzle falling as she left the house; by the time she'd got to the end of her road the sky had darkened. In the distance, thunder rumbled ominously. She thought about turning back, but she couldn't bear the idea of just sitting in the house all afternoon trying not to think about Michael and dreading the following morning when she was going to have to face everyone at the office for the first time since her outburst at the Christmas party.

She wandered aimlessly for a while, trudging along the High Street staring gloomily into the windows of chain stores she had no desire to visit. It was freezing cold and a blister on her foot, which had begun to develop on her run that morning, was now starting to chafe against the hard leather of her boots. She turned back towards home – she had every intention of going home – and yet somehow, five minutes later, she found herself ordering a coffee in the blissful, cosy, convivial warmth of the Honey Pot.

Well, it felt cosy and convivial for a moment or two anyway – until Bea emerged from the kitchen carrying a tray laden with some sort of pastry. She clocked Chloe, sitting in her usual spot in the corner, almost instantly. She put the tray down and marched over, a look of barely suppressed irritation on her face.

'What are you doing here?' Bea asked. 'I thought I'd made it clear you weren't welcome last time I saw you.'

'I didn't have anywhere else to go,' Chloe replied in her smallest voice.

'So you came here?'

'Can't you just ignore me?' Chloe pleaded, looking up at Bea with huge doe eyes. 'I'll just sit here, drink my coffee, I won't talk on my phone, I won't talk to anyone. I don't have anyone to talk to.' She gazed sadly down at the table, tracing patterns with her forefinger in some sugar she'd spilt.

Bea sighed. 'Oh, for God's sake,' she said. 'How do you do that? How do you make people feel sorry for you when you completely don't deserve it?'

Chloe shrugged.

Bea hesitated a second, caught between irritation at the thought that she was being played, and a genuine feeling of sympathy. Even if Chloe was hamming up the tragic-loner act, Bea had a feeling that Chloe probably was, in reality, something of a tragic loner. Bea's good nature got the better of her.

'Would you like some cake?' she offered.

'Oh, no thanks,' Chloe said. 'I'm low-carbing this week.'

'Of course,' Bea said. 'You are *enormously* fat, after all.'

Despite herself, Chloe smiled. 'Thanks,' she said.

Bea pulled up a chair and sat down. 'Can I assume from your miserable face that your Venice trip is off, then?' she asked.

Chloe nodded. 'Did you cancel it or did he?' Bea asked.

'He did.'

'So what are you going to do? You're going to keep waiting for him?'

'I broke up with him yesterday,' Chloe said, swallowing hard to get rid of the lump in her throat. 'Well, I broke up with him the first time yesterday. Then I called him – drunk – to make up last night, and then I broke up with him on the phone again this morning.' She wiped a tear from her cheek.

'You sure you don't want some cake?' Bea asked.

Chloe shook her head sadly. 'I'll have another coffee with some chocolate sprinkles on it, though.'

'That's right,' Bea said. 'Push the boat out.'

Bea got them both another coffee, with sprinkles for Chloe, and brought them back to the table. 'You've done the right thing,' she said. 'Breaking up with him.'

'I know,' Chloe said. Catching the look on Bea's face, she said, 'No, I'm not being arrogant or self-satisfied or something. I know I've done the right thing because I saw his wife yesterday. I saw her with their kids, looking dreadful, having an awful time, trying to explain to her child why Daddy was too busy to take them to see Santa Claus. God, I felt like shit. She just looked . . . tired. So fucking tired.'

For a while, they just sat in silence, sipping their coffee.

'I'm sorry,' Bea said eventually. 'Breaking up with someone you love is hard. I'm sorry.'

'No you're not.'

'Well, I'm glad for his wife, I suppose. Although she doesn't seem to have chosen particularly well, ending up with a man who ducks out of taking his kids to see Father Christmas so he can spend the night with his mistress. But I am sorry for you. I'm sorry you're alone.'

Chloe sighed. 'I'm not that sure that being alone is such a terrible thing. There are actually some really good things about being alone.'

'Such as?'

'Always being able to watch whatever you want on TV,' Chloe said.

'Yeah, but I'm not sure never having to relinquish control of the remote really makes up for the absence of a fulfilling relationship.'

'You can, if you feel like it, sit around in your underwear all day eating ice cream.'

'Do that often, do you?'

'Yeah, OK, maybe I'm not coming up with the best examples, but there are worse things, aren't there? Than being alone, I mean? I think I'd rather be me, alone at Christmas, than Harriet, spending Christmas with a husband that doesn't love her any more and would sooner be somewhere else.'

Bea said nothing to this.

'Sorry,' Chloe said. 'I didn't mean—'

She didn't get time to say what she did or didn't mean because at that moment the door was flung open and Olivia burst into the café, wild-eyed and dishevelled, with something Chloe hoped was chocolate smeared on her neck.

'Thank God,' Olivia said when she saw them. 'Bea, you have to help me.'

3.32 p.m.
Bea

It was a completely bizarre afternoon. Elina was looking after Luca for the day, ostensibly so that I could get some cooking done in the café kitchen, although in reality I'm pretty sure it was because she wanted some one-on-one time with her grandson. I wasn't officially supposed to be working, but I knew that if I didn't do anything at all we were going to run out of stock. And as it turned out, I ended up doing a lot less cooking than I'd hoped thanks to a string of visitors.

The first was Chloe, of all people. I'd just finished making a batch of mince pies, and I brought them out for Kathy to serve and there she was. If it hadn't been for the fact that she'd been sitting by herself at our largest table, I'd probably just have ignored her, but she always does that and it bloody irritates me. Why can't she sit at a small table when she's alone? Does her ego really need four seats to itself? I went over to her and asked her what she was doing here. I think I was kind of spoiling for a fight, but she wasn't up for it. She practically begged me to let her stay and I ended up offering her some cake. There's something about that girl that's annoyingly irresistible.

Anyway, we were having a vaguely interesting

158

conversation – about the pros and cons of living alone – when Olivia came dashing in looking like a madwoman, pleading for help.

'I'm so, *so* sorry to bother you,' she said, 'but I'm in a bit of a fix.'

Hilariously, she'd tried to make a chocolate soufflé for about a hundred people.

'Olivia,' I said when I'd stopped laughing, '*I* can't even make a great chocolate soufflé, and I consider myself to be a halfway decent cook.'

'Yes, all right!' she snapped. I actually jumped – I hadn't seen her get cross before. 'I'm rubbish in the kitchen! I know! Kieran's told me, you're telling me—'

'Calm down,' I said to her.

'I can't bloody calm down,' she wailed. 'They're arriving in half an hour and the flat's a tip and there's no dessert and I look like shit . . .'

'It'll be OK,' I said, pulling out a chair for her. 'I don't have a soufflé, but I can offer you an extremely delicious chocolate amaretti torte. Guaranteed to impress the relatives. I'll just get it for you, then you can go home and clean up. They're bound to be late, anyway. I can't imagine flights are arriving on time in this weather.'

'Thank you,' Olivia whimpered, 'you're a life-saver.'

'Not a problem,' I said, getting to my feet. 'And you don't look like shit, by the way.'

'But you don't look great,' Chloe added. Olivia glared at her. I went to get the cake.

159

By the time I returned from the kitchen with the cake in box, Olivia had sat down and Chloe was wiping chocolate off her neck with a paper napkin. They seemed to be deep in conversation about something, but fell silent as I approached.

'Thank you for doing this, Bea,' Olivia said. 'It's very kind of you.'

'It's really no trouble,' I replied. 'All I'm doing is selling you a cake.' They were both looking at me rather oddly, it was slightly unnerving.

'Well, thank you anyway. Are you all right, by the way?' Olivia asked, cocking her head to one side in that way people do when they ask if you're OK and they're expecting a negative answer.

'I'm fine. Why do you ask? Don't I look all right?'

'No it's just . . . the other day . . .' She didn't get to finish whatever she was about to say because her phone rang.

Ever the model customer, she took the call outside. When she came back in, she looked a good deal more relaxed.

'It was Kieran,' she said. 'You were right. They're going to be late. They're not going to be here until after five now. Maybe as late as six.' She breathed a huge sigh of relief. 'Thank God for the shitty English weather,' she said.

'Would be nice to get some snow though, wouldn't it?' Chloe said, gazing out into the gloom. 'I mean, if you're going to have shit weather, it may as well be interestingly shit, don't you think?'

'Always rain in London, never snow,' I said.

Since Olivia now had an extra hour or so to spare, she decided to stay for a cup of tea and a mince pie. Three mince pies, actually, which Chloe watched her eat with an expression of astonishment on her face.

'Stress always makes me hungry,' Olivia said apologetically. 'I just can't believe I thought it would be a good idea to host Christmas for fifteen people.'

'Fifteen? Bloody hell, that is brave.'

'It could have been worse. They were talking about bringing their basset hound as well. Fortunately they couldn't get a passport for him in time.'

Chloe shrugged. 'At least the dog wouldn't complain about the lack of chocolate soufflé.'

'I'm not really much of a dog person,' Olivia admitted, reaching for a fourth mince pie.

'Oh God, I miss having pets,' Chloe said. 'Our dogs are the best part of my family. I certainly miss them a lot more than I miss my sisters.'

I laughed. 'You don't mean that.'

'I do,' Chloe protested. 'It's sad, really. The two of them get on really well, but I've always felt . . . excluded.'

'What about your parents?' Olivia asked.

'Oh, I got on fine with them. In a superficial sort of way, I suppose. They always seem ever so slightly disappointed in me, though. Anna and Beth are their golden girls.'

For perhaps the first time since I'd met her, I felt a genuine pang of sympathy for Chloe. She really did seem all alone. 'But you are going to spend Christmas with them, aren't you?' I asked her.

'No. Originally I'd planned to stay in London so I could be with Michael on Boxing Day, but that's not happening now. I could go to my parents' place, but I just don't think I could stand it. There's no way I can keep up the pretence that I've just been to Venice, and I can't face telling them the truth.'

'So you'd rather spend Christmas alone?' Olivia looked aghast. Chloe just shrugged. 'I can't imagine that,' Olivia said. 'I love Christmas with my family. There's no stress over there.'

'Over where?' I asked her.

'The Bahamas. That's where my parents live. Well, they spend around half the year there.'

'All right for some,' Chloe muttered.

'We have staff over there,' Olivia carried on, 'and in any case, I'm never really expected to *do* anything, you know? It's just like a big family reunion, the only things we have to do are the fun things, like decorating the tree or deciding which mistletoe locations optimise the chances of getting a kiss from one of our dreamy next-door neighbours when they pop round for egg nog.' Olivia glanced at her watch. 'Shit, I'd better get going,' she said, leaping to her feet and knocking a chair over as she did.

'Steady on,' a voice said behind me. My heart leaped. I turned around and there he was, standing behind me with a bunch of blood-red roses in his hand. Sam.

4.04 p.m.
Chloe

She should have gone straight home, but she didn't feel like it. Despite the darkness, despite a bitterly cold drizzle, a sleet closer to rain than snow, she decided to walk in the opposite direction. After her brave words about the joys of living alone, she had no desire to go home and eat ice cream in her underwear, and she was pretty sure there would be nothing she wanted to watch on TV. There never was.

And, of course, there was the guilt. Guilt always made Chloe want to exercise. Her latest dose of guilt was a result of the hushed conversation she'd had with Olivia in the café. Olivia, apparently, had witnessed a dreadful confrontation between Bea and a woman who, she assumed, was the other woman, the one who had stolen Bea's husband away, the Chloe equivalent in the breakdown of Bea's marriage. Imagining a similar scenario between herself and Harriet made her feel sick. And very, very guilty.

She found herself wandering towards Highbury, along roads she'd never been down before. The pain from her blister was growing and she decided to turn back. Only she wasn't exactly sure where she was. She whipped out her phone and clicked on the map application. 'Server busy', came the response. It wouldn't load.

'Oh, this is perfect,' she whispered to herself. 'Just bloody perfect.'

The sleet was coming down more heavily now. Chloe looked desperately right and left, hoping to spot some landmark which she'd recognise, or even better the comforting yellow glow of a taxi light. There were none in sight. She hobbled miserably on, the pain in her foot quite acute now, her coat soaked through, her fingers numbing in her gloves. And then she spotted it. A little way up the road to her right there was a bookshop with a light on. Somewhere she could stand still for a moment, somewhere dry and hopefully warm. Chloe limped over and pushed open the door.

A bell jangled above the door as she did so, and the lights flickered. The shop was deserted. Completely deserted: there wasn't even anyone serving behind the counter. The room was dark, the only light coming from a lamp next to the cash register, and another on a table on the opposite side of the shop. The place was like some sort of weird combination of a commercial premises and someone's front room.

'Is anyone here?' Chloe called out, a little spooked. There was no reply. Chloe weighed up the pros and cons of haunted bookshop versus death by high heels and decided she'd take her chances with the ghosts.

On a rickety-looking table in the centre of the room, she browsed the week's recommended buys. She picked up a novel entitled *No Fury*; the blurb on the back described it as 'a terrifying tale of murder and revenge, a chilling insight into the twisted mind of a woman scorned'. It sounded perfect. Chloe sat down on a threadbare armchair in the corner of the room, unzipped her boots, tucked her aching feet beneath her and began to read.

She was a few pages in when a disembodied voice asked her, 'What d'you think?'

Chloe jumped to her feet, letting out a yelp of terror.

'I'm up here,' the voice said. She hadn't noticed it in the gloom, but directly above her was a kind of mezzanine, and on it stood a dishevelled blond man holding a stack of books. 'The writing's not fantastic, but it's a cracking plot,' he said. He moved to the end of the mezzanine and climbed down a ladder, balancing the books in one arm while clinging on to the ladder with the other. When he'd reached the ground floor and dumped the books unceremoniously on the counter, he held out his hand. 'Jack Doyle,' he said. 'This is my shop. So, tell me, what do you think so far? Would you like some tea? Do you have sore feet?' Jack didn't wait for the answers to any of these questions. He disappeared through the stacks of books to a room at the back, re-emerging a couple of minutes later with two cups of tea. 'Filthy day, isn't it?'

Chloe was fighting with the zip on her left boot, mindful of the need to be ready to run should Jack Doyle turn out to be an axe murderer instead of a bookshop owner. He didn't look like an axe murderer, although admittedly she'd never met one, so she couldn't be sure. He looked good, actually. Tall, slim build, grey eyes, a slightly weather-beaten look about the face.

'Are you leaving already?' he asked her. 'You haven't had your tea. Leave the boots off until you go, give your feet a rest.'

'Thank you,' Chloe said. He handed her the tea. It wasn't Earl Grey, but she didn't complain.

'You like thrillers, then?' Jack asked her.

'Actually,' Chloe said, 'I haven't read a novel in months. Months and months. I did read *The Life of Pi* when it came out, I remember that.'

'That was published in 2002.'

'Right. So I haven't read a novel for a really long time.'

'If that's the case, I'm not sure *No Fury*'s where I'd start.'

'It was on your recommended table,' Chloe pointed out.

Jack shrugged. 'Recommended is a fluid concept.'

Halfway through their second cup of tea, Jack asked what she'd been doing there. 'It's not a well-frequented road, this,' he said. 'In fact, it's a terrible place for a shop. As you can probably tell.' She had been there over half an hour and there had not been another customer. 'Not much of a Christmas rush, as you can see.'

'I was on my way home,' Chloe said.

'You live around here?'

'Oh no, a mile or so from here. Crouch Hill.'

'But you decided to walk because it was such a nice day?'

'Something like that.'

Gently, Jack prised *No Fury* from her fingers. 'I don't think that's what you need,' he said. He wandered off back into the book stacks. A while later he re-emerged. 'Have you read this?' He held up a copy of *The Shipping News*. Chloe shook her head. 'Much more suited to a girl like you.'

'And what am I like?'

'You're sad. And you're just not quite yourself. You need a pick-me-up, something life-affirming, but I'm guessing that you don't like schmaltzy and you do like challenging. This is perfect.'

'Is it really?' Chloe was alternating between being irritated at his presumptuousness and touched by his kindness.

'Yes it is. You also need to buy a gift for someone. Altruism will always make you feel better. Buy something unexpected for someone. Or buy something for someone unexpected.'

Chloe finished her tea, she made her purchases

(including *No Fury* which she'd started so she thought she might as well finish) and asked Jack to call her a cab. As they pulled away into the foggy London night, she found herself turning round to look back at the shop. The whole experience seemed suddenly surreal; she had to keep checking whether the shop really was there.

4.08 p.m.
Bea

After the girls left, Sam just stood there, holding the flowers, looking at me, not saying anything. I couldn't read his expression, I couldn't tell what he was thinking. I wasn't sure I wanted to find out. I got to my feet.

'I ought to get back to the kitchen,' I said. 'I need to prepare some more dishes for the next few days.' But Sam didn't move; I couldn't get past him.

'I need to talk to you,' he said.

'OK,' I said, sounding a lot more casual than I felt. 'I suppose the cooking can wait a little while longer. Let's sit down. Would you like something to drink?'

'No, not here, Bea. I don't want to talk to you here. I want to talk to you alone.'

I didn't want to be alone with him. Anything could happen if I was alone with him. Christ, I might kiss him again.

'I'm sure no one's going to listen to our conversation here,' I said, peering around us as though looking for spies.

'Oh forget it,' he said, throwing the flowers down on the table in front of me. 'If you can't talk to me seriously, then . . .' He turned to go.

'Sam!' I called out, getting to my feet. 'Don't just walk away.' People were looking at us now, rubbernecking.

'I need to talk to you. Not here, not in a crowded café, all right? If you don't have the time . . .'

'I do,' I said, suddenly more afraid of him walking out than I was of being alone with him. 'Of course I have the time. Let's go upstairs.'

I don't think the walk from the café up the stairs to my flat has ever felt so long. As I got to the top of the staircase I glanced at myself in the little mirror that hangs at the entrance to the flat. I looked like a woman who'd spent most of the day in the kitchen.

'Do you want a tea or something?'

'No thanks.' He was standing at the entrance to the flat, his hands in his pockets, as though unsure of whether he wanted to have this conversation after all.

'Sam? Aren't you going to come in?'

'No, I don't think I will,' he said. 'I just wanted to tell you that I'm in love with you. And I think you know that.' Halfway between the kitchen counter and sofa I froze. I just stood there, looking at him, completely thrown. I'd been expecting something, maybe questions about the way I'd behaved over the past couple of days, possibly even recriminations. I hadn't expected this.

'You do, don't you? You know how I feel.'

I didn't say anything, I couldn't. I knew there was *something* between us. For a while now, even before the kiss, I'd felt something. I think I knew, deep down, that there was some reason, other than just loneliness or convenience, why he always ended up knocking on my door when he wanted someone to talk to. But was it love? I wasn't sure and, until now, I'd tried not to think about it, because thinking about it meant letting go and moving on.

'Bea?' He was waiting for an answer.

'I . . . I . . .' It was going to be a long wait.

'I know that when you kissed me the other night you were in a state, you were upset and emotional. I understand that, I know that kiss didn't necessarily mean anything to you—'

'Sam . . .' I said. Fortunately he cut me off because I had no idea what I was going to say.

'Let me finish. If it meant nothing to you, that's OK. But you needed to tell me that. You can't just cut me out, not talk to me, it's not fair. Not when you know how I feel.'

'I'm sorry,' I said. I took a step towards him, but he stepped back. If he retreated any further he was going to fall down the stairs. 'I know I haven't handled this well. I'm just a bit . . . confused. The thought of being with someone else is still difficult for me.'

'But you *do* feel something for me, don't you?'

'Of course I feel something. You've become my

170

closest friend. Which is why the thought of messing things up between us is terrifying.'

'We won't mess things up. I promise.'

'No, don't promise. Whatever you do, don't promise.'

'OK then.' His face softened, he walked across the room, put his arms around me and squeezed. 'I know this isn't easy for you. I shouldn't be pushing you. I'm sorry.'

'It's OK.'

'I just thought you should know that I'm in love with you. And now I've told you. So I'll leave you alone.'

'I don't want you to leave me alone,' I said, holding on to him as tightly as I could.

'But I think I need to,' he said. 'Just while we both get things sorted in our heads, OK?'

He kissed me on the lips, and on the neck, and then he let me go.

6.05 p.m.
Chloe

She caught sight of him as the cab drew up in front of the house. Michael was standing underneath a tree, sheltering from what was by then torrential rain, waiting for her. She paid the cab driver and walked straight past him up to her front door. She opened it, let herself in and slammed it behind her. She listened to him banging on the door for a good three or four minutes before she relented and opened the door again.

171

'Jesus, Chloe!' he yelled at her when she finally let him in. 'If I die of pneumonia, I'll know who to blame.'

'What do you want?'

'I want to talk to you, obviously. You can't just break up with me over my answer phone. You can't just break up with me, get back together with me and then break up with me again over my answer phone. We've been together for a year, for God's sake. I think I deserve a little more than that.'

Reluctantly, Chloe stepped back to allow him in. He took off his dripping coat in the hallway; she went to fetch a towel.

'Christ, Chloe, it's freezing in here. Are you on an economy drive or something?'

'Boiler's on the fritz,' she replied, throwing the towel at him. 'That's why I'm still wearing my coat.'

'Is someone coming to fix it? You'll freeze to death in here.'

Chloe ignored him. She walked into the kitchen and grabbed a bottle of red wine from rack. She opened it and poured them each a glass. 'Where does *she* think you are?' she asked.

'Work crisis.' Michael passed his hand across his face; he looked exhausted. The temptation to go to him, to put her arms around him, was strong. A few days ago, a few hours ago, it might have been overwhelming. But somehow now it wasn't. She stayed put. 'Listen, Chloe. Please could we just talk about this? I don't want this to be over. I love you. I know that I have to leave her, I will leave her. I want to leave her. We just have to wait a bit longer . . .'

'Until what, Michael? How long do we have to wait? Until your kids are at school? Do you think it will be easier for them then? Will it be easier for her then?'

'Just give me a few more months . . .'

'No. Not a few more months, not a few more days. You say that you want to leave her? The thing is, I'm not sure that *I* want you to. I'm not sure I want to be responsible for that. I don't know that we're worth it.'

She kissed him goodbye at the door. She'd intended a chaste peck on the cheek, but it didn't turn out like that. It was a proper kiss, deep and long, a kiss goodbye.

'You're going to miss me,' Michael said.

'I don't know that I will,' Chloe replied.

'I do. You'll miss me,' he insisted.

'Well, off you go then,' she said. 'Go! How can I miss you if you won't go away?'

9.15 p.m.
Olivia

Olivia downed a glass of wine in the kitchen. She took a deep breath, steeling herself for the return to the fray. Kieran appeared in the doorway.

'You OK, Liv? You look frazzled.'

'Yeah, well, you were right about the soufflé. Fortunately I managed to pull it out of the bag with that chocolate torte,' she said, giving him a wry little smile.

173

He laughed, slipping his hands around her waist. 'Dinner was grand. The roast was brilliant. My mother said it was fantastic and she's none too generous with the praise when it comes to other people's cooking.'

'Just hope nobody spotted the Honey Pot packaging the cake came in,' Olivia said. In fact, she wasn't really worried about dinner at all. Dinner had been fine. It was the conversation over dinner that had given her the fear.

The Kinsellas had finally arrived just after six, which had given her ample time to get back to the flat, wash her hair, dress for dinner and do a final spruce-up of the place. She needn't really have bothered, since five minutes with five children under twelve haring about the place and it looked anything but spruced. Plus, her in-laws to be were not interested in the décor. All conversation was about the wedding.

Well, not just the wedding: over drinks, they talked about the proposal and the engagement; over starters, the hen party, the stag do and the honeymoon; and over the main course, conversation turned to the many, many babies which were envisaged in their future.

'How many are you thinking of having?' Suzie asked, beaming at Kieran and Olivia. She watched lovingly as her youngest, Danny, did his best to shove a piece of roast potato into Olivia's iPod dock.

'Oh, we haven't really thought that far ahead,' Olivia replied.

'But at least three,' Kieran said, giving Olivia a wink.

'You'd better get started soon then,' Diane chipped in. 'You're going to want to wait at least a year or two between each.'

'More wine?' Olivia asked, her voice dangerously shrill. 'No? I think I'll probably have another glass. I think there's another bottle in the kitchen.'

Kieran grabbed her hand as she got to her feet. 'Only joking,' he whispered to her, 'relax.'

She almost broke her neck marching into the kitchen. Someone had spilt something on the floor and she slipped. Orange juice. The children. Obviously. She poured herself a glass of wine and stood there, fuming. She would gladly have stayed in there all night and polished off the bottle, but it wasn't long before Kieran came to get her.

When they returned to the table, the conversation had turned to churches: which were the loveliest churches in which to hold christenings? Olivia couldn't stand it; surely there must be something else to talk about. She knew this might be a sensitive subject, but she no longer cared: she turned to Conor, who was sitting across the table to her left.

'No girlfriend with you, Conor? We were expecting to meet her.' An awkward silence descended over the table.

'We split up actually,' Conor said. 'A few days ago. I meant to call you and let you know, I'm sorry.'

'Oh, that's a shame,' Olivia said. She could sense that he didn't want to talk about it, but in her desperation to steer the conversation towards something other than her fertility, she bumbled on: 'What happened? Is there someone else?'

'Liv,' Kieran admonished her, 'this might not be the best time.'

'Of course not, sorry,' Olivia said, feeling herself blush.

'So,' Diane said after a pause, 'are you hoping for boys or girls?'

10.30 p.m.
Chloe

After Michael left, Chloe boiled the kettle and filled a hot-water bottle and a washing-up tub. She sat on the sofa with her feet in the tub and the hot-water bottle clutched to her chest, enjoying the return of feeling to her extremities. But with physical sensation came a sudden rush of emotion, anger with herself, frustration with her sisters, a deep sense of loss over the end of her affair. She sat there for what seemed like hours, and cried and cried until she had nothing left.

She went to bed, now piled high with every blanket she could get her hands on, and began to read *No Fury*. She opened it to the third page, where she'd left off earlier. There was a slip of paper tucked into the book. On it, written in small, neat lettering, was

a question – 'Could I take you to dinner sometime?'
– and a telephone number. Chloe put the scrap of
paper down on her bedside table and read until
dawn.

Monday 20 December

8 a.m.

Bea

Elina woke me at eight. She didn't just wake me, she shook me awake. 'Beatrice!' she hissed at me, 'you must come now!'

I leaped to my feet, assuming something was wrong with Luca, and with my heart thudding fit to burst my ribs dashed into his room. He was sitting up in his cot, playing with the squeaking plastic duck my mother bought him. He looked up at me and smiled.

'What are you doing?' Elina asked. 'Not there, in here. Come in here.'

On the table in the living room was a parcel wrapped in brown paper. I looked over at Elina. She was standing at the top of the stairs eyeing the parcel suspiciously, as if eager to make a getaway.

'It looks like someone might have left me a Christmas present, Elina,' I said, approaching the table.

'Don't open it!' she whispered. 'This is London. There are bombs here all the time.'

'Not all the time, no,' I said, but my heart was racing just a little. I knew who it would be from. It was from Sam.

I picked up the parcel; my name was scrawled across its front. 'Well,' I said, my heart sinking, 'I'm pretty sure it's not from Osama bin Laden. I don't think he knows my name.' It wasn't from Sam either. It wasn't his handwriting. I reached for a pair of scissors, about to cut the string.

'Perhaps it is from *her*,' Elina said. I dropped the package back down on the table as though stung. The thought of getting something from Lucy was much more terrifying than receiving something from al-Qaeda. Elina picked it up and placed it on the bookshelf in the corner of the room. 'Never mind that now,' she said. 'Let's have breakfast.'

'I'll go and get Luca,' I said, turning away from her.

'Forget about it now, *cara*,' Elina said, mistaking my disappointment for something else. 'Now is not the time to think about it.'

It wasn't, she was right. I couldn't think about Sam. Not now. We had far too much to do. I had promised to take Elina into the West End to do some Christmas shopping; after that we were having dinner with my mother and her boyfriend, Christopher, who were due to leave for Edinburgh the following day. Given that a trip to the West End is a nightmarish experience at the best of times and quite probably beyond hellish just a few days before Christmas, I had suggested leaving Luca with my mother for the day. Elina wasn't having any of it.

'I see him maybe once a year, Beatrice,' she said sternly. 'I am going to spend as much time as I can with him while I'm here. Perhaps if I saw him more often . . .'

'Yes, all right, Elina. We're going to come to Italy soon.'

'Good,' she replied, satisfied. 'Perhaps we can book some tickets today?'

We departed for the tube at ten, the mysterious package left unopened on the bookshelf.

10.45 a.m.
Olivia
The office was almost empty, but Olivia had come in to finish up a couple of pieces for the Valentine's Day issue, the most important of which was the 'Heavenly Scent' spread, the one in which she was to plug the Jakob Roth perfume L'Amour Propre as part of her penance for the salad cream slur.

Writing about perfume was never Olivia's favourite task. Where some writers eulogised about 'sharp citrus with strong undertones of anise' or 'soft orange blossom over buttery iris', Olivia always seemed to come up with 'fruity', 'feminine' or occasionally 'earthy'. She never understood how these people picked out 'hints of tuberose' or 'notes of bergamot'. She supposed she did not have a very good

181

nose. Who, after all, knew off the top of their head what tuberose smelt like anyway?

She was having a tougher time than usual, though, given that she genuinely didn't like the product. And it wasn't one of those situations where you could downplay the bad points about something in order to big up its good qualities: there was nothing about this perfume that she liked, from the name (L'Amour Propre? Self love? Wasn't that a euphemism for masturbation?) to the packaging (a nasty, plastic cerise tube topped with an unidentifiable flower). To Olivia, who liked her perfume classic and restrained (more Chanel No 19, less Paris Hilton), Jakob Roth's new scent was overwhelmingly saccharine. It was the sort of thing a nine-year-old might like, not the sort of thing she ought to be recommending as a Valentine's Day gift. Indeed, she felt that by recommending it as a Valentine's Day gift she might well be throwing many a relationship into jeopardy.

And, let's face it, Valentine's Day was a tricky enough time for couples. Buying the right gifts, getting the right table at the right restaurant, wearing the right underwear: it was an occasion fraught with obstacles. Although, she thought with a smile, it had never been tricky for her. Not with Kieran at any rate.

Not for them the rather awkward dinners in restaurants filled with other couples, roughly a third of whom would be gazing adoringly at each other, a third desperately thinking of something to talk about and the

182

remaining third sniping angrily at each other in harsh whispers.

Their first Valentine's together, Kieran took her away for the weekend. They had only been seeing each other for a couple of months, and it was their first weekend away; Kieran was determined it should be special. He booked a room at a beautiful country house hotel in the Cotswolds, he organised for there to be champagne and flowers on their arrival, and for the pianist in the bar to play 'At Last' at precisely nine o'clock. It was all very sweet and thoughtful and utterly wasted because Kieran forgot to check the weather forecast which predicted heavy snow and which, for once, was right.

They got stuck in a blizzard around junction four on the M40 and ended up spending the night in the Holiday Inn in Cressex Business Park just outside High Wycombe. In fact, it didn't matter where they were, they could have been in a hotel on the moon, because they didn't leave the room once; they barely made it out of bed. It was the perfect weekend, a delicious mix of sex, room service junk food and plenty of cheap Cava.

Since then, the frequenting of unromantic locations had become their Valentine's Day tradition. They'd been to Alton Towers, on a booze cruise to Calais, one year they did a pub crawl the entire length of the Holloway Road. Kieran didn't buy flowers or chocolate for her; she never bought him a card. They always had a brilliant time.

That, Olivia realised, was the thing that was really bothering her about the marriage proposal. For five years she had been in the happiest relationship she had ever known, the only one she'd ever had which never stopped being fun. What if getting married changed that? Everyone told her that marriage felt different, different to simply being together or living together. Olivia didn't want to feel any different. Not about Kieran.

What if the horror stories you heard about married couples were true? What if they found less and less to say to each other? What if they stopped having fun? What if, as so many magazine articles warned, marriage really did kill your sex life? What if, from now on, it was going to be all *l'amour propre*?

11 a.m.
Chloe
Taking Friday off had been a mistake. Not only had it made the walk of shame into the office even more humiliating than it would have been anyway, it also meant that Chloe was behind on her work and in trouble with her boss. Maurice, usually so jovial, so keen to chat and take her out for coffee, was giving her the silent treatment. Aside from a rather snide 'feeling better, are we?' when she'd first arrived in the office, he hadn't said a word to her all morning. That was actually something to be grateful for: it meant she could get on with her work without having to make

chit-chat with him or endure his bad breath, but she knew that it meant trouble.

Trouble landed on her desk just after eleven in the form of an incredibly complex trust which needed setting up 'before the markets close on Christmas Eve'. That gave her five working days to do a good fortnight's work. It would have been uphill struggle at the best of times – and this was not the best of times. Chloe was exhausted from months of not sleeping properly. Last night had been particularly bad, thanks to Michael's visit, the sub-zero temperatures in her flat and the surprisingly un-put-downable *No Fury*. But it wasn't just tiredness that was the problem. She was distracted. The odd thing was that, for the first time in a year, it wasn't thoughts of Michael that were distracting her. It was thoughts of Jack Doyle's grey eyes.

4.30 p.m.
Bea
Shopping in the West End was every bit as harrowing as I'd imagined. The pavements heaved: a toxic mix of irritable Londoners in a hurry and tourists blocking their way to take photographs and point out landmarks to each other. Our little party presented a combination of the two, with the delightful addition of a teething toddler in a buggy.

Our first stop was Fortnum & Mason. For someone so disdainful of English culinary skills, Elina had an impressively lengthy list of items to buy: Earl Grey Tea Jelly, Welsh Chunk Comb Honey, Dark Lime Marmalade, Scottish Shortbread and Ginger & Chilli Biscuits, just to name a few. We went to Liberty to buy fabric for dresses she intended to make for her nieces; and to the London Review Bookshop in Bloomsbury to find a rare illustrated and annotated copy of *The Fairy Tales of the Brothers Grimm* for her youngest daughter who was doing her PhD thesis on eighteenth century German folklore. From there we made our way south to the Victoria & Albert Museum to buy an extraordinarily expensive silver pendant that Elina's best friend had spotted when she'd been over to London for a weekend culture tour, and which she had coveted ever since.

I was thoroughly relieved to get home by mid-afternoon with only three major tantrums under our belts, one of which was from me. Luca had a nap, Elina and I wrapped presents, then we all got bathed and dressed and ready for dinner at my mother's house.

The package, now an increasingly sinister presence in my mind, remained on the bookshelf, unopened.

5.45 p.m.
Olivia

Olivia had three parties to attend that night. First up, Luxe. The upmarket cosmetics firm was holding its drinks party at Blakes in South Kensington: it was bound to be cool, stylish, full of models and no fun at all. Number two was a party thrown by Shine!, a PR agency, which was holding its bash at Shoreditch House. That one was likely to be a bit less glamorous and a lot more drunken. Number three was the Christmas party of an actual friend, Katya, in her house in Islington. It was going to be a long night.

Olivia and Zara got dressed and made up in the ladies' room, fighting for space amongst virtually every other girl in the office, all of whom had parties to go to that night.

'I'll come with you to Luxe, but I'm not sure I'm going to make the Shine! thing,' Zara was saying.

'Oh, please come. I hate going to these things on my own.'

'Liv, you'll know ninety per cent of the people there.'

'So why don't you want to go?'

'Because I'll know ninety per cent of the people there and I don't want to talk to any of them. Plus I've slept with the chief executive. And the head of their fashion division. And they were both rubbish.'

Olivia giggled, which made her smear Chanel Rouge Coco across her cheek. 'Which one was the head of fashion division? Wasn't that Nico?' Zara nodded. 'He was lovely looking. You went out with him for a while, didn't you?'

'Three and a half months. One of my longest relationships ever. He wasn't really rubbish. He was quite good actually. But he was also a pretentious wanker who cheated on me with the art director from *i-D* magazine.'

'Three and a half months is one of your longest relationships ever?'

'I'm exaggerating. When I was twenty-two I went out with someone for almost a year. But I've never found a way to keep it interesting past six months or so.'

'The sex, you mean?'

'No, everything. Once the mystery's gone, once you know all there is to know about each other, favourite books, favourite bands, all that kind of stuff, it all just seems so flat, so pointless. Don't you think?'

Olivia reapplied her lipstick in silence.

6.23 p.m.
Chloe

One of the many plumbing firms with which Chloe had left messages that morning called her back. Yes, they could come round tomorrow, but it was going to cost her.

'To be honest, love, it's probably the electrics. Nothing too complicated. Don't you have a bloke around the house who could take a look at it for you?'

Silently, Chloe seethed. She did not have a bloke, nor did she need one. Most of the time they were useless anyway – it wasn't as if Michael would have been any good fixing the boiler. She refused to be bullied into thinking that having a man was necessary or even particularly desirable. Bouncing from one man to the next was not the answer. It was not the answer to her personal problems, it was not the answer to her domestic difficulties, and it certainly wasn't going to help her draw up a trust fund for some rich guy's daughter. Chloe took Jack's note from the pouch in her purse where she had stashed it, screwed it up and threw it into the bin.

7.15 p.m.
Olivia
They shared a taxi to Blakes with Margie and her PA, Arabella, who was very young, very pretty and almost completely useless. She was also the step-daughter of the man who owned *Style*, and as such could not be fired. Arabella was prattling on about internet dating.

'I've joined a new site,' she was telling Margie. 'Beautifulpeople.com. Apparently it's the largest online network of attractive people in the world.'

'Jesus,' Zara muttered under her breath.

'Honestly, Zara, it's great,' Arabella said. 'Online dating without the ugly people. You should give it a go. You're pretty enough. In the past couple of weeks I've been out with an investment banker, a guy who owns a chain of nightclubs, a ski instructor . . . It's so important, don't you think, to date a wide selection of people before you decide on who you want to be with?'

Olivia gazed out of the window, willing the traffic in front of them to disperse so that she wouldn't have to listen to any more of Arabella's inane drivel.

8.20 p.m.
Chloe

Was blurring vision a symptom of something other than extreme fatigue and the fact that she had been staring either a computer screen or at the fine print of legal documents for twelve hours straight? Chloe got up from her desk and made herself what must have been her eleventh cup of coffee of the day. She put on her coat and nipped outside for a cigarette. Her hands trembled as she lit it. It could just be the cold. Blurred vision and trembling hands. She was sure she'd seen an episode of *House* where the week's victim had exactly those symptoms. She couldn't remember what the diagnosis had been, but it was almost certainly a tumour of some sort. It was always a tumour of some sort. She stubbed out her cigarette and went back inside. She was going to die. She was going to die alone. She was going to die without ever getting her boiler fixed. She ran back to her desk and retrieved Jack's number from the trash.

She rang the number. On the third ring, he picked up. 'Hello?'

She hesitated for a fraction of a second and then hung up. She turned her phone off straight away and shoved it into her desk drawer for good measure.

8.48 p.m.
Olivia

Olivia and Zara lasted forty-five minutes at the Luxe party, then they called a cab to take them to Shoreditch.

190

'I thought you weren't coming,' Olivia said to her friend as they climbed into the back of the taxi.

'Oh, shut up. You know that all you have to do is give me two glasses of champagne and I'll agree to anything.'

'I wouldn't advertise that if I were you. You might give people ideas . . .'

'Just so long as it's the right people.'

'You're such as slapper.'

'Just because I've slept with more than six people, does not make me a slapper, Olivia. It makes me normal.'

'Four people, actually.'

'Four people! Including Kieran?'

'Yes, including Kieran.'

'Jesus Christ, Olivia. Four people?'

'Yes! No need to go mental.'

'Four people?'

10.15 p.m.
Chloe

There was something very creepy about being in the office late at night. The main lights had been turned off, everyone else had left ages ago, but there were still odd noises. Heating systems probably, computers powering down, photocopiers doing whatever photocopiers did when they weren't photocopying. All perfectly explicable sounds which were nonetheless creeping Chloe out. She had no cigarettes left and if she drank another coffee she was pretty sure she'd throw up. It was time to go home.

She rang a taxi (she was allowed to charge them to the company so long as she worked later than ten) and waited downstairs in the lobby with the security guard.

'Long day, miss?' he asked her.

She was about to say something about stating the bloody obvious, but she bit her tongue. 'Certainly has been,' she said.

'No parties to go to tonight then?'

'No,' she said sadly. 'No parties.'

10.21 p.m.
Bea

Dinner was interesting. In honour of her latest boyfriend, Christopher, who hails from Scotland, Mum had decided to cook a dinner with a Celtic flavour. Elina was bemused, to say the least.

Mum and Elina have a complicated relationship. Their initial few meetings, when Marco and I were first going out, were frosty affairs. Mum is, to put it mildly, an extrovert. Elina, while not exactly introverted, can be quite proper, particularly in new company. The first time they met was in France. Marco and I rented a villa in the Languedoc one summer and invited friends to join us for the first week, and family to come for the second. We should have done it the other way around; it would have given us time to recover from the maternal culture clash.

192

Elina was aghast at the way Mum flirted with Marco (this sounds awful, but actually isn't – Mum flirts with everyone, it's really quite harmless and after a while becomes almost endearing; it's her way of making people feel special), she was appalled at my mother's lack of domesticity, in particular her cooking skills, and she clearly felt that Mum's boyfriend (at the time, a rather spivvy cab driver closer in age to me than to my Mum) was an inappropriate choice (I had to agree with her on that point). Mum tried briefly to be friendly to Elina, but finding her a bit frosty gave up, and instead enjoyed herself by being as provocative as possible.

After Marco's death, they bonded. Looking back on it, they coped remarkably well. It would have been easy for them to argue over what was best for me and for the baby, but they didn't. If they had differences of opinion, they kept them to themselves (or at least they must have waited until I was out of the room to express them); they did their best to make everything easier for me. But now that I was back on my feet, old tensions were beginning to resurface.

With my mother hosting the dinner, Kathy running the café solo and the situation with Sam *unresolved*, to put it politely, there was no one I could call on to babysit, so an early dinner was a requirement. We arrived around six. Luca, tired and grumpy from having spent the entire day being dragged around London, was in no mood to play nice. He started to cry the moment I turned off the car ignition. By the time we got to the front door he was wailing and squirming in Elina's arms.

'Oh darling,' my mother cooed as she opened the door. 'Whatever's wrong?' She took him from Elina and bounced him on her hip. He quietened for a moment. Mum grinned triumphantly at us. 'Loves his gaga, doesn't he?'

'May we come in?' Elina asked, giving my mother her iciest smile. 'Only it is quite cold out here.'

Despite my mother's crowing, Luca was only quiet for a few minutes. Before long, he'd started up again.

'He's hungry,' Elina said. She turned to my mother. 'Do you have some food prepared for him?'

'He's probably just knackered,' I said. 'It's been a long day.' I told Mum about our shopping trip.

'What on earth did you take him to the West End for?' she exclaimed. 'Poor thing, no wonder he's exhausted. You should have brought him to me. I could have taken care of him. Couldn't I, darling?'

'He is hungry!' Elina insisted.

'OK, keep your hair on,' Mum said. 'I'll rustle up something for him now.'

Elina opened her mouth to say something – undoubtedly something rude – but thankfully Christopher intervened, ushering her into the living room and offering her a Martini.

I was ridiculously grateful for Christopher's presence. My mother's boyfriend of five months is an affable Scot with a dry wit and a manner that could put a paranoid schizophrenic at ease. He is also what one might call a silver fox. Mum was delighted to bag him – she had to fight off stiff competition from the women in her book group (he is one of only two men in the group and the other is overweight and overbearing, so I'm told). Mum has been through a string of (mostly awful) men since she and my father divorced (messily and bitterly) twelve years ago. Christopher is comfortably the most attractive prospect she's found since.

We sat in the living room enjoying our drinks, trying to ignore the sounds of pots and pans banging and crashing in the kitchen, usually followed by loud expletives from my mother. Eventually, Elina said, 'Perhaps I should go and help out?'

'No!' I cried, a little too loudly, leaping to my feet and at the same time rousing Luca from his slumber. 'I'll go.'

There was, frankly, little I could do to rescue the culinary disaster that Mum had cooked up in the kitchen. All I could do was damage limitation. My hope that the tension between Mum and Elina would start to subside once we'd got Luca down to sleep began to ebb away when we were summoned to dinner. Elina seemed mildly surprised by the soup.

'Cock-a-leekie?' she kept saying. 'What is this cock-a-leekie?' Mum and I got the giggles which didn't help, since she thought we were laughing at *her*, which we weren't really. If anyone says 'cock-a-leekie' enough times it becomes funny. The roast turkey, served with a rather mealy oat and sage stuffing, was received with stoic resignation. It was, as I had warned Elina it might be, cooked to the texture of an old boot.

Elina pushed bits of dried-up bird around her plate. She managed to force down a couple of boiled-to-within-an-inch-of-their-lives Brussels sprouts; she nibbled tentatively on a very sad-looking carrot. To be honest, I wasn't doing much better. Christopher, showing admirable strength of will, almost managed to clear his plate. Mum wolfed hers down. She'll eat anything. Her irritation with our failure to do the same grew as dinner progressed.

'Something wrong with the food, Bea?' She was talking to me but she was looking at Elina.

'Not at all, Mum,' I said, swallowing hard.

'Well, it might not be up to your standards, but then we can't all be domesticated, can we? Chris doesn't mind that I'm no good in the kitchen, do you, love?' Christopher shook his head gamely. 'No, I have . . . other strengths,' she said, giving him a wink. Oh Jesus.

'It's fine, Mum,' I said.

'Fine,' Elina repeated, chewing stoically on a carbonised roast potato. My mother gave her a withering look.

If the first two courses had caused surprise and disappointment, the dessert course, a clootie dumpling, provoked undisguised alarm.

'It's a suet pudding,' Christopher explained to Elina as she peered at the dull brown lump in the middle of the table. 'Better than it looks actually. Here you go,' he said, handing her a bowl. 'Just drown it in custard.'

As Elina gamely tried to eat her dessert, which was as light and airy as a lump of concrete, Mum steered the conversation back to Luca, a subject on which she felt she had superior knowledge and experience, not just with regards to Elina, but me too.

'He's doing ever so well,' she said. 'He can already drink from a cup.'

'Yes, of course,' Elina said. 'I have seen him. But he is still not speaking. Not proper words. All my children were speaking proper words by this age. Marco was speaking proper words at just one year!'

'That's very good,' Mum conceded, before going back on the attack. 'I think one of the problems might be that Bea's got him listening to these tapes, the Italian ones, you know? That's bound to be confusing. One language at a time's enough!'

Elina spluttered; her mouth full of custard, she was unable to reply. I intervened. 'That's not true, Mum. It's much easier for children to learn languages at this age than it is later on. He's doing just fine. He'll speak when he's ready.'

'It is very important that he learns his father's culture, his father's language,' Elina said, her expression a mix of anger and pride.

'Of course it is,' I said, putting my hand on her arm. 'And he will. He'll be just as Italian as he is English.'

'Well,' Mum said doubtfully, 'I'm not so sure about that. He's ever so fond of fish and chips. More so than spaghetti.'

'Actually he isn't any more,' I said, bursting with pride that I actually knew something about Luca that my mother didn't. 'Spag bol's definitely become flavour of the month.' Elina gave a satisfied smile. Mum looked annoyed.

'Let's clear the dishes, shall we?' Christopher said brightly, getting to his feet. I could have kissed him.

Back at the flat, Elina went straight to bed. 'Important day tomorrow,' she said, giving me a kiss on the cheek. 'What time do we need to leave?'

'Whenever suits you,' I replied. I didn't really want to think about it. 'After breakfast?'

Elina agreed and disappeared into Luca's room.

I felt exhausted without being sleepy. I made myself a cup of a cup of fennel tea (I thought my digestive process might need a little help after that meal) and flicked on the television. I tried to watch *Newsnight* but couldn't concentrate on anything; Paxman's hectoring of his interviewees began to give me a headache. I looked over at the bookshelf. There it sat. The Parcel. Unopened.

I got to my feet and retrieved it from the shelf. I weighed it in my hands. A hardback book was my best guess. If Lucy were to buy me a book, what would it be? A self-help book? *How to Survive the Loss of a Loved One*? A story of redemption? The Bible? I wondered whether there would be a note. What would she say to me? What could she say? Had she brought the gift on the day she came to see me? I couldn't remember seeing anything in her hands. Not that I was paying much attention. Perhaps she'd bought it afterwards. Perhaps there would be some sort of rebuke inside, thanks to my refusal to speak to her. Surely she wouldn't have the gall? My heart was racing, I had to know. I held my breath.

I ripped open the parcel. It *was* a bible. A handsome, beautifully bound hardback copy of *The 2010 London Foodie Bible*, 'an insider's guide to the capital's best-kept culinary secrets'. I opened the book. Inside there was a note, handwritten in the same scrawl which had adorned the wrapping paper:

Bea,
See page 48.
Happy Christmas.
With best wishes for the New Year,
Chloe

I exhaled. Wow. That was unexpected. Of all the people I could have imagined might leave me a gift, Chloe would probably not have featured in the top twenty. The girl that just a few days ago I'd labelled an unbelievable bitch had a sentimental side – who knew? I flipped the book open to page 48, as instructed. There it was, number two on the list of the 'Top five delicatessens in north London':

The Honey Pot, Albany Street, N4

Step inside Beatrice Marinelli's deli-slash-coffee shop and feel yourself transported to Italy. In addition to all the traditional Italian basics – a vast range of fresh and dried pastas, cheeses, prosciutto crudo, biscotti and panettone, sundried tomatoes and marinated arti-chokes – the Honey Pot offers delicious homemade daily specials, from creamy risottos to rich pork and porcini stews, via classic favourites such as meatballs in tomato sauce. The Honey Pot stocks 25 different olive oils and specialises in Ligurian pesto. If you're popping in for coffee, make sure you make room for a sweet: the pastries and cakes are a decadent delight.

I could feel myself welling up. Not just with pride, though I was delighted to see us featured so promin-ently. No one had told me about this. I was also incredibly touched that Chloe had thought of me, and felt a little guilty for perhaps being harder on her than I needed to be the first couple of times we'd met. But it wasn't just that, it wasn't just pride, gratitude, guilt. It was disappointment. Some part of me wanted that parcel to be from Lucy. She'd ripped off the Band-Aid now, the wound was open again and someone had chucked a handful of salt on it. I needed to know what she had to say.

10.33 p.m.
Olivia

Olivia and Zara huddled round the heaters on the rooftop of Shoreditch House while Zara smoked a cigarette.

'So, really, four people?'

'Oh, for God's sake, Zara, it's not that extraordinary. I lost my virginity to my high-school boyfriend when I was seventeen. We stayed together until I went to college. At university I met Simon, who I was with for five years. After him I had a brief fling with an awful management consultant called Marcus. Then I met Kieran. There wasn't time for anyone else. I just moved from boyfriend to boyfriend.'

'No drug-fuelled one-night stands, no steamy holiday romances? Never?'

'Never.'

And now she was never going to have them. She was never going to have another first kiss. She'd never again go through the joyful discovery process, when you find out everything there is to know about the other person, when you just can't get enough of them. Never again would she feel the sweet, crazy-making intoxication of falling in love.

'What's up, Liv?' Zara asked her. 'You look like you're about to cry.'

201

'It's nothing. I'm just cold. You don't want another cigarette, do you? Let's go inside and get something else to drink.'

Drink followed drink. Around eleven, Zara disappeared off somewhere with a man who would not have looked out of place in an Abercrombie & Fitch catalogue, and Olivia decided it was probably time to move on. She called a cab and made her drunken way to her third party of the evening.

She called Kieran from the taxi. 'Where are you?' she asked when he picked up. 'It sounds incredibly noisy.'

'We're at the Goat. It's mayhem here, absolutely packed. Seems like half the offices in London are having their Christmas parties tonight.'

'You guys having a good time?'

'Great, yeah. It's really good to hang out with them again.'

There was a moment of silence.

'Liv, you still there? Are you OK?'

She took a deep breath. 'Kieran, how many people have you slept with?'

'What?' She heard him laughing. 'Sorry, I didn't hear that. It sounded like you asked me how many people I'd slept with.'

'That is what I asked you.'

He laughed again. 'Are you pissed? Why are you asking me that now? You always told me you didn't want to know.'

'Forget it.' She was annoyed with him for laughing at her. 'It was something Zara said. Just forget it. I'll talk to you later.' She hung up.

By the time she arrived at Katya's party it was starting to wind down, but there were still a few old friends there, people she knew from university. Ben and Kate, Richard and Anna. And Findlay Westmore, also known as Finn or, to Olivia and her closest friends, the One Who Got Away. His face broke into a wide smile when he saw her.

'Hello, gorgeous,' he said, wrapping his arms around her. 'We were starting to think you weren't going to show.'

'It's been a bit of a marathon night,' she said, speaking into his chest. He was very tall. She'd forgotten how tall he was. 'I wasn't expecting to see you. I thought you were still in Africa or South America or something.'

'Got back a few days ago.' The two of them moved into the candlelit conservatory at the back of the house, now devoid of other guests. 'You look good, Liv. You look great, actually.'

'Not so bad yourself,' Olivia said. Understatement of the year, actually. Finn, who made nature documentaries for the BBC, was tanned and lithe from months spent in the middle of jungles or halfway up mountains.

Finn took her left hand in his. He looked at the ring and gave her a quizzical smile. 'When did this happen?'

'A few days ago,' she said.

'I should've come back a week earlier,' he replied. He was still holding her hand. She pulled it away from him.

Had Olivia been asked to draw up a list of the people she really did not need to bump into that evening, Finn would have topped it. He'd have beaten the Yorkshire Ripper and Osama bin Laden. Not that she didn't want to see him; it was lovely to see him, it was always lovely to see him. She didn't want to be reminded of how lovely it was to see him.

Katya appeared at the door. 'You two OK in there?' she asked. 'Need anything else? Drinks, snacks, a chaperone?' Olivia gave a nervous little laugh. Katya didn't really approve of Finn. More specifically, she didn't approve of the way that Finn treated Olivia. Since the very first time they met, on the second day of Freshers' Week, Finn had, in Katya's opinion, been toying with her. He liked her, he was clearly attracted to her, but never quite enough. She was never the prettiest girl in the room, and Finn was always with the prettiest girl in the room.

'Are you sure?' Finn was holding Olivia's hand again. He pulled her to her feet.

'Am I sure about what?'

'About him. That he's the one?' He was leading her outside, into the garden, and she was letting him.

There was no one else outside. Not surprising, given the freezing temperature. Even the most hardened of smokers were staying inside.

'It's minus three out here, Finn. Let's go back inside,' Olivia said, but she didn't take her hand from his.

'We'll keep each other warm,' he said, a lascivious little grin playing on his lips. He slipped his arms around her waist. 'I missed you, Liv.'

'Finn . . .'

'You didn't answer my question,' he said. He was tracing his forefinger down her neck, across her clavicle.

'Don't do this to me,' she said, making no moves to stop him.

'Answer my question then. Are you sure he's the one?' Then his lips were on hers, his hands in her hair, pulling her closer, and she felt that irresistible tingle of excitement that you only get when you kiss someone you're not supposed to, that frisson that just isn't there when you kiss the man you've been kissing every day for the past five years.

Kieran was out with his brothers. He'd be staying the night at his place, he wouldn't come back to her flat that night, he wouldn't know if she didn't come home. Zara's words came back to her, as clear as if she were saying them right then. *No one-night stands, no steamy holiday romances?*

This was her last chance. She ran her hands down his back, slipping them into the back pockets of his jeans.

Her left hand caught; something snagged. The little diamond on her engagement ring.

'Jesus!' she said, breaking the kiss, pushing him away from her. 'What the bloody hell am I doing?'

'Olivia,' Finn said softly. 'You know this is right. We never got our chance at college, our timing's always been off. This is our chance.'

'No, Finn. We had plenty of chances. You just didn't want to take them because there was always someone better around.' She turned to go back into the house. 'This is so typical of you. This is exactly what you always used to do – you don't want me unless you know that I'm happy with someone else, and then you manipulate me because you think I can't resist you.'

'That's not true, Liv.' He sounded genuinely hurt.

'That's exactly true, so don't make that face at me. You're just pissed off because I can resist you.' She walked away, her stomach knotted up. She felt sick with herself, with her betrayal.

'You still haven't answered my question,' Finn called out. She yanked the back door open and slammed it behind her as hard as she could.

Tuesday 21 December

5.30 a.m.
Bea
I woke very early, took my pills, tried to get back to sleep. No chance. Not today. I turned on the light and tried to read, but I couldn't keep my eyes on the page. Eventually I got up, made myself a cup of coffee and sat down at my desk to write a letter. I wrote the date at the top of the page: 21 December, the shortest day of the year. The darkest day of the year.

Hello again.
It's raining. Always rain in London, never snow.
I've been thinking about the Christmas after we got engaged. Remember, when you decided it would be fun and romantic to rent a cottage in the Scottish Highlands? There would be log fires and walks in the hills and us plus lots of friends, sitting around drinking wine, singing songs? It was going to be just like the Wham! video for 'Last Christmas', only without the skiing and the bad hair. I thought it was

a stupid idea and I told you so. You didn't care, you went ahead and booked it anyway.

We got there a day early, because you wanted to cook for everyone, you wanted there to be a feast on their arrival. Then it snowed. It snowed and snowed and snowed, and none of our friends could make it because we were completely cut off. So it was just you and me (and enough food to feed the five thousand) cut off from the world.

You thought I'd be upset. I'd been proved right; it was a stupid idea. But when, after five days, the snow started to melt and the roads were clear again, I burst into tears because I didn't want to leave. Remember that?

I heard a whimper from Luca's room and went in to get him. 'We're going to visit Daddy today,' I said softly. 'Let's get you some breakfast.'

I did the washing up while Elina got Luca dressed.

'We can walk from here, can't we?' Elina asked me. I glanced outside. It was barely light but at least the rain had stopped.

'We can do; it's not far, a couple of miles, maybe a bit less. But it isn't going to be warm out there.'

'I like to walk,' she said. 'It isn't right to go to a grave site by car. It feels right to walk.'

'We might get soaked.'

'Then we get soaked.'

'Or catch pneumonia.'

'Then we get pneumonia.'

She's determined. Stubborn, even. He got that from her. Luca got it from him. They know what they want, these Marinellis, and they get it.

The three of us, swaddled up like Michelin men, made our way slowly through gloomy streets – down Mount View Road, across to Hornsey Rise, and all the way along Hornsey Lane towards Highgate.

Marco was buried in a far corner of the East Cemetery. It's a rare thing, these days, to be buried at Highgate Cemetery, but we were lucky (if you can call it that) in that the cemetery manager was a regular visitor to the Honey Pot. He was particularly partial to Marco's Tuscan-style breaded mushrooms. When he heard about the accident he contacted me and asked whether I thought Marco would have wanted to rest at Highgate or taken back home in Italy. I imagined that Elina would insist on taking her son home, but she said he would have wanted to stay here, close to me. And, as it turned out, close to his son. At the time, I never thought it would matter to me where his body lay, all that mattered was that he was gone. But now I'm glad he's here, that we have somewhere to go, somewhere to visit, even if we aren't really visiting him.

As I pushed open the iron gates to the cemetery, the sun broke through the clouds for the first time in two days. I could barely bring myself to look at Elina. I knew how smug that would make her.

'You see? He is watching,' she said. She has no truck with my atheism.

We brought gifts, which we laid at the grave site. From Elina, a box of candied flowers from Genoa; from me, a jar of honey. Luca had a red, white and blue scarf, the colours of Sampdoria, but we didn't leave that behind. For starters I didn't think the cemetery caretakers would appreciate it, and in any case Luca would have howled blue murder if I'd tried to get it off him – something his father would have warmly applauded.

Luca and I retreated a little way to a bench across the path, leaving Elina alone for a moment to speak to her son. She stood with one hand resting on his gravestone, chatting animatedly. She'd be telling him what his sisters had been up to, how his nieces and nephews were doing at school. After a while, she stopped speaking and bowed her head to pray.

After a few minutes, Elina came and sat at my side. With the sun shining weakly through the clouds, it wasn't as cold as I had imagined it would be; it was warm enough to stay a while. Elina slipped her arm around my shoulders. I pushed the buggy back and forth, lulling Luca to sleep.

'Do you mind if I join you a while?' An elderly gentleman was standing a couple of feet away. I'd been so lost in thought I hadn't noticed him approach.

'Not at all,' I said as Elina and I shifted along a bit, making space. The man thanked us and sat down next to me.

'Fine boy,' he said, smiling at Luca.

'We like him,' I replied.

'Are you visiting someone?' Elina

'My wife,' he replied. 'She died eig.

'I'm sorry,' I said.

'How about you?'

'My husband,' I replied. 'Two years today.'

We sat in silence. I noticed that there was a woman, in her forties or perhaps her fifties, standing a little way from us along the path. The elderly man noticed me noticing.

'She's my girlfriend,' he said. My face must have registered surprise, or shock, because he laughed. 'You think it's too soon, or just that she's too young for me?'

'No, it's not that . . .' I stammered, lying through my teeth.

'I've no idea what she sees in me,' he said with a grin, 'but I'm glad that she sees it.'

'You have a right to find new happiness,' Elina said pointedly.

'I'm glad you think so,' the man replied. 'My children don't. They think it's all very unseemly. She was ill, my wife, for a very long time. She had Alzheimer's. I lost her in stages. It was very painful.' He looked over at his girlfriend, who was waiting patiently, a cup of coffee in her hand. 'My children were angry when I met her, it was just five months after my wife died. Me, I felt as though I had already been living alone for years.' He wiped a tear from his cheek and

211

ᴶled at me again. 'You, you probably think you have l the time in the world. You may do, you may not. I know that I don't. I may as well take what happiness I can find.'

We watched him go, shuffling back along the pathway towards his girlfriend, who put her arm around him and kissed his cheek when he reached her. Then they left, walking slowly towards the main road, hand in hand.

I could feel Elina's eyes on me.

'Don't even say it,' I said, getting to my feet.

'I'm not saying anything,' she said with a shrug. We walked in silence for a minute or two. Finally, she cracked. 'He spoke a lot of sense, that's all,' she said. 'Who knows, tomorrow maybe you'll be hit by a bus.'

'Charming thought,' I said.

'Maybe, but you'll be gone, and he – that man who is so obviously in love with you – will never know that you loved him back.'

'*I* don't even know if I love him back, Elina,' I said. 'And I don't know that he's in love with me.' I was lying, of course. I hadn't told her about his declaration at the flat the other day. And even though he'd said it, even though he'd stated it bluntly and out loud, I wasn't sure I was quite ready to believe him.

I dropped Elina off at Gatwick at three and drove slowly home; the traffic was hellish, exacerbated by driving rain. Luca and I listened to the radio, I sang along; he fell asleep. It was pitch dark by the time

212

I got home. The shortest, darkest day of the year; his day.

After I'd made dinner and put Luca to bed, I turned on my phone. Four new messages. One was from my mother, asking me how I was doing; one was from Kathy, sending her love and asking if I'd spoken to the man at Hampshire Farms about that ewe's cheese she'd told me about. The last two were from Sam.

Message received today at 12.02: 'Hey Bea, it's me. I know I'm supposed to be leaving you alone, but the thing is, I miss you. Haven't seen you for . . . uh . . . about forty hours and already I miss you. It feels like weeks, like months. Call me back, OK? I really want to talk to you.'

Message received today at 4.15: 'I'm an idiot. I'm so sorry. It's today, isn't it? I'm so sorry for calling before, talking nonsense. I hope you're OK. [Long silence.] You know I'm thinking about you. I hope you're all right. Give Luca a kiss for me. Merry Christmas.'

I turned the phone off again and finished writing my letter.

Your mother thinks it's time I moved on. What do you think? Is two years a long enough period of mourning? I wonder how long you would have mourned me? Longer, I think.

Your mother says you wouldn't want me to be alone. I don't know about that. Would I have wanted you to be alone if I were gone? I can't imagine myself wishing

213

you into the arms of someone else. Maybe she's right,
though, because I can't imagine myself wishing you
anything other than happiness either.
    I love you. You have to know that even if there is
someone else, there won't really ever be anyone else.
It will always be you.
    Always,
    Bea

I put the letter in an envelope and stashed it in the wooden chest which I keep under my bed. Along with another fifteen or twenty letters, this is where I keep the mementos. It's where I keep all the photographs from our holidays and the love letters he sent me in the year we were apart, the ticket stubs from Sampdoria versus Parma and *La Traviata* at the Teatro Carlo Felice, Genoa's opera house. It's where I keep the recipe for the Sicilian aubergine and ricotta sauce, written on a paper napkin from the trattoria on the beach front in San Vito Lo Capo, written in Marco's inimitable scrawl, after he'd managed to convince the lady who owned the place to give it to him. It's where I keep Marco, everything that's left of him. I keep him in a wooden chest, under my bed.

Wednesday 22 December

7.15 a.m.
Olivia

She couldn't believe she had done it. She still couldn't believe she had done it. More than twenty-four hours had passed and she *still* couldn't believe she had done it. The thought of it filled her with shame. Just thinking about it brought a rush of blood to her face, made her nauseous. She was lying in bed, staring at the window, listening for the sound of her future in-laws moving around in the next room. Soon she'd have to get up, she'd have to face them all.

Kieran slipped a hand around her waist. He'd stayed the night before despite the fact that, officially, he was supposed to stay at his place while his parents were around. Just for the sake of decorum.

'You awake?' he whispered in her ear.

'No,' she whispered back. 'I don't feel well,' she said, rolling over to face him. 'I was thinking maybe we should cancel this thing tonight?'

Kieran smiled at her.

'Stop it,' she said.

'Stop what?'

'Smirking like that. Enjoying my pain.'

He laughed and kissed her on the mouth. 'It's funny.'

'It bloody isn't.'

'It's hilarious.'

He thought it was hilarious because he didn't know what she was really upset about. Kieran thought she was upset because, thanks to Zara's incessant goading about Olivia's sexual inexperience, she had returned home after Katya's party, logged on to her Facebook page and typed as her status: 'Olivia Heywood is wondering how many people everyone has slept with? My number is four. Is that too low?'

He thought that she was upset because she had woken, at around midday on Tuesday, to find that she had dozens of replies to her question. Amused replies from her friends, shocked replies from her parents, slightly bemused replies from her co-workers. From her boss. He thought she was upset because she'd had to walk into the kitchen to face Kieran's parents, *who were also her friends on Facebook*, because she'd had to endure a day of ceaseless taunting from Kieran and his brothers. Because her attempts to convince everyone that someone had hacked into her Facebook account had met with hilarity and derision.

If he really knew what she was upset about, he wouldn't have been laughing. If he knew that the reason she was upset was the kiss, that awful, wonderful, soul-stirring, treacherous kiss with Finn, he'd probably be asking for the engagement ring back. Except, knowing Kieran, he wouldn't ask for the engagement ring back. Knowing Kieran, he'd forgive her. And that made her guilt more painful still.

Olivia still blamed Zara for the whole thing. If not for Zara messing with her head, none of this would have happened. Well, that was what she was telling herself, anyway. Burying her face in the pillow, unable to look Kieran in the face, she pleaded, 'Please can we cancel the party?'

'No we can't,' he said, still chuckling, hugging her closer to him. 'You're over-reacting. It's going to be a great night, we're going to have a brilliant time, and I'm going to show off my gorgeous bride-to-be.'

She wanted to cry.

'I love you so much, Kieran,' she said, turning to face him. 'Do you know how much I love you?'

'More than humanly possible,' he replied.

She buried her face in his chest; she couldn't let him see that she actually was starting to cry. 'Can we at least dis-invite Zara?' she asked in a muffled voice.

Fortunately the party was going to be a fairly low-key affair. Olivia had rung around and invited quite a few people, but since it was Christmas party season, most people couldn't make it. So few, in fact, that Olivia got desperate and ended up inviting people she didn't know all that well, like Bea, and people she wasn't entirely sure that she liked all that much, like Chloe.

The decision to invite Chloe was prompted by the discovery, late on Tuesday, that a parcel which she had found on her doorstep on Sunday evening, which she had tossed aside in her hurry to get dinner prepared and herself dressed for said dinner, had come from Chloe. It was a book, a copy of *The Anti-Bride Wedding Planner*, a guide to 'tying the knot outside the box'. Inside there was a note.

Dear Olivia,
Hope this provides some inspiration.
Have a lovely Christmas,
With best wishes,
Chloe

It was really rather sweet. So on Wednesday morning she decided to give Chloe a call to thank her for the book and to invite her over that evening. There was no answer, so she left a message giving details of the party. Then she headed out, destined for the Honey Pot.

Bea was not in the café.

'She's taken a few days off, love,' Kathy, the woman behind the counter, said. 'Family emergency. Can I get you a coffee anyway?'

Olivia, grateful to be in a place where she was unlikely to bump into any Facebook friends, ordered a latte and a pain au chocolat and sat down at a table near the window. Seconds later, the door opened and in strode Chloe, carrying a laptop case. She smiled when she saw Olivia.

'Just got your message,' she said. 'Usually I wouldn't go to a party thrown by someone I barely know, but in this case I'll make an exception. I've got bugger-all else to do.'

Can't imagine why, Olivia thought.

Chloe ordered an espresso and sat down at Olivia's table. 'You don't mind, do you?' she asked, as an after-thought.

'Of course not,' Olivia said. 'Glad of the company. Do you have work to do?' she asked, indicating the computer.

'I always have work to do,' Chloe said. She looked tired. She always looked tired. 'I should be in the office right now. I should have been in the office since seven o'clock this morning, but I just can't be bothered. I rang up and left a message on my boss's voicemail saying I was going to work from home. Which I am going to do. It's not going to stop him going absolutely mental, but somehow I just don't seem to care.'

'Good for you,' Olivia replied, wishing that she could show that sort of fortitude when it came to dealing with Margie. While there was plenty about Chloe she found objectionable, there was also much about her character to admire. Here was a woman who would not let people walk all over her, who would resist completely any attempt to control her – to force her, for example, to bear three children over the next five years.

Chloe was glancing around the room, looking for someone. 'Bea not in today?' she asked Olivia. 'Only I got her a gift too. I left it on her doorstep because there was no answer when I rang. I was just wondering if she got it.'

Olivia shook her head. 'I haven't seen her since we were all in here on Sunday,' she said. 'I'm actually a bit worried about her. Kathy – that's the woman at the counter – says she's had a "family emergency", but I'm not so sure. I think it's something to do with the fight she had with that woman I saw her with last week.'

They were exchanging theories regarding the possible fallout from this altercation when Bea turned up, pushing the baby in his buggy in front of her. She didn't say hello, she walked straight past them, mumbled a few words to Kathy and seemed about to head on upstairs when Kathy tugged at her sleeve and pointed over to Olivia.

10.29 a.m.
Bea

I hadn't even noticed them. I was miles away. I'd taken Luca out to feed the ducks, but – just for a change – rain stopped play, so we, had to come back early. We'd just turned the corner into Albany Street and were about to cross the road when I saw Sam, lugging a bag over his shoulder, Reggie trotting along dutifully behind him. He was headed towards his van, which was parked across the road from his shop. I came to a halt, causing a yelp of consternation from Luca, who likes a brisk pace when we're out walking.

My heart was hammering in my chest. This was ridiculous. This was Sam, the closest thing I had to a best friend. This was the man I made coffee for every morning, the man I counselled about his disastrous love life. This was Sam, the one who could always made me laugh, the one who cheered me up when no amout of recipe recitation could. This was Sam with the devastating smile, the long, lean limbs, the tiny scar above his eyebrow, which somehow always made him look slightly surprised. This was the man who, just a couple of days ago, had told me he was in love with me. And this was the man who, I realised with blinding clarity, made me feel something I hadn't felt since that glorious day in Lerici nine years ago, when a handsome Italian fell into my lap.

And he was leaving. Sam was loading up the van, first with his bag, then his dog. He was going somewhere, going away. Luca was starting to grizzle, annoyed at the hold-up. I still didn't move, I couldn't move, I just stood there watching him. He closed the back of the van. I didn't have much time.

'Sam,' I called out, but he was too far away. He didn't hear me. 'Sam!' I yelled, much louder this time.

I had regained the use of my limbs; I set off at a jog, and then a run, but it was too late. He was getting into the cab of the van.

'Sam!' I called, as loud as I could. His brake lights flickered on, and off, and he pulled away, heading off down the street, away from me. I stood there for ages in the rain, ignoring Luca's protests, a feeling of loss building up in my chest and all the while Elina's words ringing in my ears: *Marco would not want you to live the rest of your life in this kind of pain. That would be the worst thing in the world for him.* I fished my phone out of my pocket and dialled Sam's number. The phone went straight to voicemail. I hung up without leaving a message.

By the time I got back to the café, Luca and I were cold and damp and I was ready to head upstairs, but Kathy told me a girl had been asking after me, and I looked round and there they were. Olivia and Chloe. I was actually really pleased to see them, although I felt a bit awkward about talking to Chloe. I was embarrassed about the gift, and I hadn't had time to get her anything yet. I wasn't even sure whether I was supposed to reciprocate. Still, they had seen me now; there was no getting away from it. I went over to talk to them.

'Sorry,' I said, addressing Olivia. 'Didn't see you there. I'm a bit distracted today. It's been . . . a hectic few days.' I turned to Chloe, who was demurely sipping her coffee. 'Thank you so much for the book,

Chloe,' I said. 'It was very thoughtful of you. I'd no idea we'd been featured, so it really was a great surprise.'

'Pleasure,' she said, and pulled out a seat for me to sit down.

They ordered more coffee, cooed over Luca (well, Olivia did, anyway) and made small talk. Something seemed off. Eventually, Chloe said, 'Apparently you got into a row with your husband's girlfriend on Friday.'

'Chloe!' Olivia put her head in her hands.

'What? You said you'd seen them having an argument on the pavement outside.'

'Sorry, Bea. I did see you, I was just wondering if you were OK. I wanted to say something to you on Sunday, but I wasn't sure it was the right time. I'm not sure now is either, actually,' she said, glaring at Chloe. 'We weren't gossiping, honestly.' She looked mortified.

'It's OK,' I said, not quite sure how I should break the news. A week ago I wouldn't have dreamt of telling them the real story, but now I had told Sam, now my secret was out, it didn't seem so awful to talk about it. I actually *wanted* to talk about it, to talk about him.

'She wasn't my husband's girlfriend,' I said eventually. 'Her name is Lucy. She's the woman who hit him with her car.'

Olivia gasped audibly; she dropped her pastry to

her plate and put her hands over her mouth. There was a horrified silence. Then Chloe said, 'Jesus. Did she kill him?'

'Yes. She did. That was two years ago, and the other day she just turned up on my doorstep, wanting to talk to me. I freaked out. Perfectly understandably if you ask me.'

'Oh my God oh my God oh my God,' Olivia was saying.

'It's OK, Olivia, you weren't to know.'

'Oh my God oh my God,' she said.

'Fuck me,' Chloe said. 'What did you say to her?'

I explained that I hadn't really said anything, I'd just yelled a bit and then run away.

'I don't blame you,' Olivia said. 'What a dreadful thing to do, to turn up on your doorstep like that.'

'Selfish bitch,' Chloe agreed. 'Obviously looking for you to forgive her, just in time for Christmas. That way she can tell Santa she's been a good girl. God, people are stupid.'

'That's what I thought,' I said, 'but now I can't stop thinking about her. Maybe I should have listened to whatever it was she wanted to say. Maybe it would help. And even if it doesn't help me, maybe it will help her.'

'You want to help the woman who killed your husband?' Chloe asked incredulously.

'She made a mistake,' I said. 'A terrible mistake, pretty much the worst mistake you can ever make. She went to prison for it. I've suffered the most awful thing, but I can't help wondering whether her suffering isn't worse in some ways.'

'Do you have a way of contacting her?' Olivia asked.

'She's in the phone book. I looked last night. I even wrote her number down.' I pulled the scrap of paper that was burning a hole in my wallet out for them to see. *Lucy Jenkins 0208 672 3555.*

'You're not seriously considering this, are you?' Chloe said. 'What if she's a complete nutcase? What if a year inside has driven her insane and she has some twisted idea that what's happened to her is your fault? You should stay away from her. Definitely.'

'I take your point,' I said, 'but she didn't seem like a homicidal maniac when she came round the other day. She just seemed unhappy.'

Chloe muttered something inaudible; Olivia placed her hand on top of mine. 'Maybe you should wait a while. Mull it over. Maybe she'll get in touch again.'

'Maybe,' I said, but the thought of her contacting me was actually not much of a comfort. If we did have contact, I wanted it to be at my instigation. I wanted to be in control. 'I thought of writing to Marco about it,' I went on absent-mindedly, 'but, of course, he didn't know her, so he wouldn't be in a very good position to give advice.' It took me a moment to realise that they were both staring at me as though I'd gone mad. 'Oh, sometimes I write to him.' Silence. 'It helps me think things through.' More silence. 'I don't actually expect him to reply.'

'OK,' they replied in unison, exchanging slightly nervous glances.

8.17 p.m.
Olivia

Olivia wore a Day Birger et Mikkelsen sequinned dress with Roberto Cavalli suede heels. It was a bit over the top for a party at home, but after the humiliations she had endured of late, she decided she'd better make an effort.

'Bloody hell,' Kieran said when she emerged from the bathroom, having applied the finishing touches to her make-up. 'You look amazing.' She smiled at him, enjoying the attention, until he said, 'You're not going on the pull, are you? Not trying to bump up that number?' Crossly, she stomped out of the room. It was much, much too early for jokes about that. Fortunately the doorbell rang, so there wasn't time for them to get into an argument.

Olivia was surprised to see that Chloe was the first to arrive. Well, first tied. She had turned up at almost exactly the same time as Zara. When Olivia opened the front door she discovered the pair of them eyeing each other up somewhat icily on the doorstep. Zara presented Olivia with a gift and looked pointedly at Chloe, who was empty-handed

'I've already given her one,' Chloe muttered.

'Come in, both of you,' Olivia said. 'I'm so glad you could both make it.'

'You've forgiven me then?' Zara asked her.

'Not really,' Olivia said.

'Forgiven her for what?' Chloe asked.

'Liv got really drunk and humiliated herself on Monday night and apparently it's all my fault.'

'How's it your fault?'

'It seems she was goaded into the whole drinking and humiliating thing by the fact that I mocked her for only having slept with four people,' Zara said.

'Four people?' Chloe gasped. 'Four?'

'Oh, for Christ's sake,' Olivia said.

Fortunately, Olivia's discomfort was soon to be overshadowed as a topic of interest by the growing tension created as a result of the blindingly obvious fact that Zara had taken an instant liking to Conor while Conor had taken a shine to Chloe. Chloe herself appeared oblivious, concerned mostly with peering at Olivia's family photos, which were on display in various frames around the living room.

'Are these taken in their place in the Bahamas?' she asked Kieran.

'That's right. It's an amazing house. Backs right on to a little river that takes you straight out into the ocean. It's absolutely beautiful.'

'Where does all your money come from?' Chloe asked Olivia, who had arrived with glasses of champagne for the three of them. Kieran did a slight double-take. Olivia had warned him Chloe was blunt, but he hadn't expected this level of directness.

'Um . . . well, my grandfather was a merchant banker,' Olivia explained.

'You know, back in the days when banks actually made money rather than just losing everyone else's,' Kieran added.

'And my dad did very well out of property investments. And my mother – who was a bit of a wild child in her youth – wrote a racy bestseller in her twenties. *Chelsea Girls*, it was called. They made it into a very bad but very lucrative film.'

'You're so lucky,' Chloe said enviously. 'My parents are civil servants, for God's sake.'

'Well, I'm not exactly Paris Hilton,' Olivia huffed. 'I still have to work for a living, you know.' She disappeared off to greet more guests.

'God, I wish I was rich,' Chloe said, turning back to the pictures. As a rule Chloe resented rich people, mostly on the grounds that she'd always felt like the sort of person who ought to have been born into money, but wasn't.

'Can't buy you happiness, though,' Kieran said, wincing slightly at the cliché even as he said it.

Chloe picked up one of the photos, a group shot of Olivia and her family on the lawn of their beautiful house, deep blue sky above, the ocean in the distance. 'They look pretty happy to me,' she said wistfully.

Bea turned up at around nine o'clock. 'I can't stay

long,' she said to Olivia, 'I have the teenage daughter of the bloke across the road watching Luca and she has a party to go to at ten. Also, I'm not entirely comfortable having my child watched by someone with that many piercings. It seems like it could be dangerous. Not for Luca, but for her. He could grab something and rip it out.'

Olivia laughed. 'I'm so glad you could make it, anyway. I thought you might have brought Sam along.'

'I thought about it,' Bea said a little sadly. 'I did drop by his place but he wasn't around. I think he might have gone away.'

Olivia ushered Bea into her living room. A gaudy purple 'Congratulations!' sign now hung over the fireplace, jarring somewhat with Olivia's perfectly tasteful Christmas decorations, which included a tree adorned only with silver and white baubles. Kieran greeted Bea with a kiss and an offer of champagne, which she declined in favour of mineral water.

'Need to keep a clear head,' she said. 'Luca's not been feeling very well.' It was a lie, but confessing to both a dead husband and alcoholism in a single day seemed a bit much.

'Ah, sorry to hear that,' Kieran said. 'He's a lovely little chap, your Luca.'

'It's an unusual name,' Kieran's mum said. She was standing at Kieran's elbow, beaming at the guests as they arrived.

'His father's Italian,' Bea said. She used the present

tense, as she always did. It was simpler, and it kept him closer to her. 'A Sampdoria fan,' she went on. 'He wanted his sons named after the heroes of the *scudetto*-winning season, Gianluca Vialli and Roberto Mancini. So Luca, to give him his full title, is Gianluca Roberto Marinelli. A bit of a mouthful, so we just call him Luca.'

Olivia was only half listening to what Bea was saying. She was eyeing the crowd. 'I'm getting a bit nervous about that lot,' she said, indicating a knot of people in the opposite corner: Zara, flirting outrageously; Conor, slightly bashful in the face of such flagrant attention; Chloe, coolly watching them both, flicking ash from her cigarette out of the window. 'The bloke over there, that's Conor, Kieran's youngest brother.'

'He's a dead ringer.'

'He is, isn't he? In any case, I think there may be some competition for his affections. Zara's set her sights on him but he appears to have eyes only for Chloe. I really don't want my engagement party to degenerate into a catfight.'

'Well, if it does, I'll put a tenner on Chloe.'

'Oh, you don't know Zara. Never bet against Zara. Not when it comes to men.'

'Perhaps we should go over there?' Bea suggested.

'And put ourselves in the line of fire?' Olivia replied. 'I think not.'

They helped themselves to more drinks: Olivia was on the Bellinis; Bea opted for peach juice.

'Have you bought Chloe anything?' she asked Olivia. 'For Christmas, I mean. I need to get her something urgently – I really wasn't expecting a gift from her.'

'Me neither, and no, I haven't got her anything. No idea what to buy.'

'What does one get for the bitch with everything?' Bea wondered.

Olivia giggled. 'She's not that bad, you know. She's just . . .'

'Socially challenged?'

'Yeah. And really lonely, I think. I can't believe she's spending Christmas all alone just because she can't face telling her family that she split up with her boyfriend. I actually invited her to come over here – there's so many of us, one more wouldn't make a difference. But she said, and I quote, she wasn't *that* desperate.'

'She just can't help herself, can she?' Bea said, laughing.

'I don't think she can.'

Olivia did the rounds of the room; she was relieved to have to endure only three jokes about the Facebook debacle. By the time she worked her way around to Chloe's corner, Zara and Conor had disappeared; Bea had taken their place.

'Where did the others go?' Olivia asked.

'Zara dragged Conor into the kitchen,' Chloe replied, 'to get more ice allegedly. More likely to shove her tongue down the poor boy's throat.'

'She can be a little . . . forward sometimes,' Olivia said diplomatically.

'One way of putting it,' Chloe said. 'I think the desperate need to couple always becomes more pronounced around the holidays, doesn't it? People get really hysterical about the idea of being alone.'

'You must be missing Michael,' Olivia said.

'Yes and no. I miss the sex, obviously. We did have very good sex.' Olivia tried hard to pretend that she wasn't embarrassed by this frank admission. 'Of course I miss him. I miss the way he made me feel, but I don't miss the way I felt all the time. I've come to realise, over the past few days, that during our whole relationship I was on this emotional roller-coaster: joyously happy the one moment, sickeningly guilty the next, racked with paranoia about being discovered, tormented with jealousy when he was with her rather than me. It's no way to live, really. But I would like some company. I'm thinking of getting a goldfish.'

'A goldfish?' Bea repeated.

'Yes, they're low maintenance. Why not?'

'I'm just not quite sure I'd classify a goldfish as company, that's all.'

'Well, I would love a dog, but I'm just not sure I'm ready for that kind of commitment.'

'Neither am I,' Olivia said softly.

'You're getting a dog?' Bea asked, but Olivia wasn't listening. She was watching her fiancé.

Kieran was now standing in the middle of the room, tinging his beer glass with a fork. There was a little cheer from the assembled throng. He was about to begin speaking when the kitchen door swung open and Conor, looking a little flustered, came out, Zara hot on his heels. Kieran cleared his throat and launched into his speech.

'I've known Olivia for five years now. It's been a Mills and Boon romance. So I'm told, anyway. I've never read a Mills and Boon but Conor – that's my younger brother there – he tells me they all go the same way. He's a big fan. In the beginning, the heroine can't stand the hero. She thinks he's an arrogant pig, a player. Then she gets a glimpse of his true character and she can't help but fall for him. In our romance, it was the other way round. The first time I met Olivia I saw a beautiful blonde with loads of money who earned her living flogging bum creams to the credulous. It took me, oh, a good twenty-four hours to realise that she was a beautiful blonde with loads of money and the most generous spirit I'd ever encountered. I think I must have known her for about a week when I realised I wanted to marry her. It only took me five years to work up the courage to do so.'

The guests cheered and raised their glasses; Zara demanded a speech from Olivia, who fixed her with a murderous glare. She got to her feet.

'Thank you all so much for coming,' she said. 'I'll keep this short . . .' she said, and then realised that she had absolutely no idea what she wanted to say. Everyone was standing there, looking at her, waiting for her to say something meaningful about marriage, or at the very least tell some touching anecdote about Kieran, and she couldn't think of anything. She couldn't think of a single thing; her mind was a perfect blank slate. She felt her face colour, she felt dizzy. 'I need to sit down,' she said. 'I'm sorry.'

'Liv, are you OK?' Kieran took her arm and led her across to the sofa.

'Sorry, I just . . . felt dizzy. I'm sorry.'

'It's OK, don't worry. It's just champagne and excitement.'

Olivia wished she believed that it was.

Bea left at around ten. Olivia escorted her to the door and thanked her for coming.

'We should get together more often,' Olivia said to her. 'We see each other all the time in the café, it's silly that we don't hang out a bit more.'

'I don't need looking after, Olivia,' Bea said with a smile. 'I'm really OK.'

'I don't want to look after you,' Olivia protested. 'I just want to hang out.'

'I'd like that,' Bea said. 'I really would. I'm not sure how I did it, but I seem to have lost all my girlfriends over the years.'

'I don't know how you manage without them,' Olivia said. 'They're an essential. Even when they do drive you up the wall.' She was thinking of Zara.

'You're right,' Bea said. 'I hadn't realised it until the last few days, spending time, chatting with you. I'd completely forgotten how much better girls can make you feel.'

After Bea left, Olivia stayed on the doorstep for a minute, enjoying the cold, catching her breath. She heard footsteps behind her; it was Chloe, clutching a packet of cigarettes in her hand.

'Apparently it's too cold to have the window open and I'm not allowed to smoke with it closed,' she grumbled.

Actually, Olivia thought, it's a non-smoking house, but never mind. 'I'll keep you company,' she said instead.

'Has Bea gone?'

Olivia nodded. 'She needed to relieve the babysitter, I think.'

They stood in silence for a moment while Chloe smoked.

'I can't believe what happened to her,' Olivia said. 'I can't believe that no one knew. She must have been so lonely.'

Chloe nodded, but didn't say anything.

'I can't imagine what it's like to live like that, to have no one to talk to.'

Chloe bobbed her head again. She was standing with her back to Olivia, looking out into the night. After a while, she said, 'Sometimes it's almost unbearable. Loneliness, I mean. I think it's the worst thing in the world.' She dropped her cigarette butt on the pavement and stamped on it. She turned to face Olivia. 'Thank you for inviting me tonight. It was very kind of you.'

They shut the door and went back upstairs to the party.

Thursday 23 December

8.03 a.m.
Bea

The idea came to me in the middle of the night. I'd come back from the party, sent Danielle the overly pierced babysitter on her way and gone straight to bed (after checking my phone. No messages from Sam. And his lights were out. Maybe Chiara changed her mind?). I fell asleep and had an incredibly weird dream involving Sam, Elina and Danielle – I can't really remember the details of it, but I do know it involved a lot of dogs. I woke up in the early hours and I remembered the flyers that Danielle's father, Terry, had put up in the café a week ago. Something about a dog, wasn't it? Their dog had just had puppies, and he was trying to find homes for them. It was perfect.

I rang Terry, who runs the antiques place across the road, right after breakfast. He only had one left, and he did have one person interested. If I wanted the puppy, he said, I should come and get it sooner rather than later. I rang Olivia.

'Hey,' I said. 'Great party last night.'

'Uh-huh.' She sounded sleepy. I checked my watch. It was just after eight.

'Sorry, I'm a parent. We wake early. I don't even notice how early most of the time. I just wanted to run something by you. Actually, I was hoping we could do this together. I don't suppose you fancy coming round for breakfast, do you?'

I met her downstairs in the café just after nine. I explained about the puppy.

'It's ideal,' I said. 'We both need to get her a present, and she did say she liked dogs.'

'She also said that she wasn't sure about the responsibility,' Olivia said to me, wolfing down her bacon sandwich. 'God, I'm ravenous. Hangovers always make me so hungry.'

'She didn't actually say she wasn't sure about the responsibility, she said she wasn't sure about the commitment. I think that a little bit of commitment might actually do Chloe some good.'

'Ah ha, a present that comes with its very own hectoring tone. I like it.'

The puppy, an eight-week-old Airedale terrier, was adorable. We picked him up from Danielle's dad, placed him in a cardboard box and put the box in Luca's buggy. I carried Luca, Olivia pushed the buggy.

'Have you ever been to her place?' I asked her.

'No, but I have the address. I asked her for it yesterday so that I could send her a card.'

'So we don't actually know if she has a garden?'

'We don't.'

'Do you think we might have been a bit hasty in buying her a dog then?'

In his box, the puppy whined. Luca pointed at him and laughed.

10.14 a.m.
Chloe

Chloe pulled on her brand-new, bright blue Performance running jacket (Stella McCartney for Adidas, an early Christmas present to herself), zipping it all the way up to the top. She strapped on her iPod and stood in the hallway for a few minutes, stretching her hamstrings and quads, trying to shake off the fug of another night without sleep. She was puzzled. The insomnia had started at the same time as her affair with Michael. She'd always assumed it would end with the affair. It hadn't. She still wasn't sleeping. She was still lying awake for hours, wondering about what Michael was doing, what he was thinking, how he was feeling.

Insomnia had its upsides, though. At about four that morning, she'd abandoned trying to sleep and got up to work instead. As a result, she'd been able to email over the documentation that Maurice needed that day by quarter to seven – long before he'd even arrived in the office, so that when he did arrive in the office to discover that she was working from home yet again, he couldn't really give her a hard time. Of course, it didn't stop him calling her to give her a hard time, but it did mean that she didn't feel particularly guilty about not going into the office.

She was just about to leave the house for her run – her hand was literally placed on the door handle – when the doorbell rang, making her jump. She peered through the peep hole. It was Olivia. Olivia, with Bea and her baby. Usually she would have been irritated by the fact that visitors were standing on her doorstep when she was about to go out running. Oddly, though, she wasn't. She was pleased.

She flung the door open. 'Good morning!' she trilled at them. 'This is a surprise.' Bea and Olivia looked a little taken aback by her chirpiness. 'Come in. I was just about to go for a run, but it can wait.' Her visitors looked nervously at each other. 'What's up? It's OK. You can bring the baby in. I'll put some newspaper down on the carpet or something. It'll be fine.'

'We brought you something,' Bea said at last. 'A present. We hope you like it.'

'We hope you like him,' Olivia said.

'You're not giving me the baby, are you?' Chloe asked. 'Because while that is very generous, I just don't think . . .'

'Of course I'm not giving you my baby, you idiot,'

Bea said. She handed Luca to Olivia and picked the little dog up out of the box. 'We brought you this.'

Chloe had never believed in love at first sight. She had always dismissed it as a foolish romantic notion entertained by airheads. But that was until she met Alfie. She didn't know he was called Alfie then, of course, she hadn't come up with the name for him yet, but she did know it was love.

'He's beautiful,' she said, taking the little bundle of fur from Bea. 'He's the most beautiful thing I've ever seen.'

Bea smiled at her. 'So you do have a heart after all.'

Chloe invited them in for tea which they drank in her rather Spartan living room. There was a small black leather sofa, a television in the corner and a desk piled high with papers. Apart from that, the room was bare. There was nothing on the walls, although you could make out, if you looked carefully, the marks left where paintings had once hung. Presumably those of a previous owner.

Bea and Olivia perched on the sofa sipping their tea while Chloe paced the room, holding the puppy in her arms. 'I need to go and buy things,' she announced. 'Bowls, beds, things like that. And dog food.'

'What about your run?' Olivia asked. 'I can stay here with the dog for a bit if you like. Frankly I'd be glad of the peace. It's mayhem at my place.'

'Actually, I don't think I'll bother with the run today,' Chloe said, surprising herself as she said it.

She hadn't missed a run in months. Even when she was working fourteen-hour days she found time to run a few miles at least. 'Where can I buy dog stuff?' she asked, flipping open her laptop to do a search.

Bea and Olivia finished their tea and got up to leave. They were just heading out of the door when Olivia turned to Chloe, a playful little smile on her face. 'I almost forgot,' she said. 'Conor. He asked for your number. I have it, of course, but I didn't think I should give it to him without asking you first.' Chloe cocked her head to one side, considering. 'He seemed really nice. And he's obviously attractive. But I don't actually think I want to start seeing anyone at the moment. Sorry.'

'That's OK,' Olivia replied, 'perfectly understandable.'

Bea and Olivia had reached the end of Chloe's road when they heard a shout from behind them. They turned to see Chloe running after them, the puppy still in her arms. 'Changed my mind,' she yelled.

'I hope she's not going to give the dog back,' Bea muttered.

'Give him my number. Tell him to give me a call.'

11.12 a.m.
Bea

'What are you up to for the rest of the day?' Olivia asked. We were on our way back from Chloe's, basking in the warm glow of our good deed, bathed in relief that it hadn't backfired and left us with an unwanted hound.

'Cooking. I know it's ridiculous to cook a Christmas feast for myself and a toddler, but that's what I'm going to do. And I need to prepare for the waifs and strays party. Which I hope you'll come to, even though you are neither waif nor stray. Bring Kieran. Bring the whole family.'

'We'll drop by, of course,' Olivia said. She didn't sound convincing.

We had reached the café. I was telling Luca to say goodbye to her, trying to get him to wave, but she wasn't listening, she was looking past me, at a family who were approaching. The kids were crying and the parents, weighed down with packages, appeared to be arguing with each other. Everyone looked harassed, exhausted, unhappy. Olivia looked as though she might burst into tears.

'Are you OK?' I asked her. 'Would you like to come in for a bit? You can help me cook.'

'I'm a terrible cook.'

'I'll teach you how to make pumpkin velouté.'

'I have a million things to do today, I really shouldn't,' she said. 'I should go home.'

'OK.'

'I don't want to go home.'

'OK.'

As I opened the front door, Olivia caught me looking

up at Sam's window. 'Why don't you knock? Invite him round for coffee? I can make myself scarce.'

'He isn't there,' I told her. 'Even when the shop's closed up, Reggie – his dog – always sleeps downstairs in the mornings, in the window there, on the armchair. It's his spot; he likes the sun. If he's not there, Sam's not there.'

'You know him so well,' Olivia said, eyebrows raised.

Upstairs, we peeled and chopped pumpkins for the soup. I was going to make loads of it; it would be a nice thing to serve in mugs at the Christmas party, to warm everyone up once they arrived. Funny how not drinking changes you. A year or two ago, I would never have considered serving soup, I'd just have given everyone a stiff drink on arrival. Once alcohol's out of the picture, you have to think differently, about everything.

'I understand why you're cooking up a storm for the party,' Olivia said, 'but why are you doing a whole five-course extravaganza for you and Luca? Will he actually eat any of it?'

'He's pretty good about trying new things,' I told her. 'But it isn't really that. It's symbolic. It may be stupidly symbolic, but it's still a symbol.'

'Of what?'

'Progress.' I took a stick of butter, lopped off a couple of large slices and popped each into a sauté pan. 'Two years ago, I spent Christmas Day at my mother's, drugged up to the eyeballs on sedatives prescribed by my doctor. Last year I spent Christmas here, alone, self-medicating with a delightful combination of bourbon and oxycodone. This year, I will make a lovely meal for myself and my son, and then throw a party for a bunch of strangers. I might not be particularly happy but I'll be sober, and I'll be taking care of my child. Next year, I hope to take him to Italy to spend Christmas with his father's family. Maybe next year I'll be happy as well as sober. It's all about progress.'

Olivia stopped chopping and burst into tears. Carefully, I removed the knife from her hand and slipped my arm around her shoulders. 'What is it? I'm OK, you know. I'm doing OK. You don't need to cry.'

'I'm not crying for you,' she sniffed. 'Well, I suppose I'm partly crying for you. Your situation is very sad. But mostly I'm crying because I should be happy and I'm not, and it's ridiculous, because I have everything and you lost everything, and here you are making the most of it and doing good things for other people and I'm crying. I don't know what's wrong with me.'

We put the cooking on hold for a while and sat down in the living room.

'Why aren't you happy? You seem happy. You're in love with Kieran; he loves you; he wants to marry you. Your job might not be everything you dreamt of but you can change that. You're pretty, healthy, wealthy, in love . . . I don't want to be a bitch or anything but what more do you want?'

Her head in her hands, Olivia mumbled, 'I'm scared.'

'Of what?'

'That it's all going to change. I'm scared that if I marry him, something will change between us and it won't be the same any more. And I'm scared that if I tell him I don't want to marry him, I'll break his heart and it won't be the same between us any more. And I feel so guilty. I feel guilty about my doubts, I feel guilty that I considered sleeping with someone else, I feel guilty that I went blank when I was supposed to be giving a speech at my engagement party—'

'Hang on a minute. Go back to that second one. You considered sleeping with someone else?'

'Only briefly, and I didn't actually want to sleep with him. I was just freaking out because I've never had a one-night stand, and it's one of those things, isn't it? One of those things everyone should experience.'

I started laughing. 'No, it's really not. It's not that I have anything against one-night stands, I've had a few myself, but as far as experiences that you absolutely must have go, I don't think it's one of them. I doubt very much that at the ripe old age of ninety-four, when you're sitting in your rocking chair losing your teeth, you're going to look back and regret that you didn't have any one-night stands. I mean, I'm told that injecting heroin is an amazing experience, too, but I imagine you probably won't regret not doing that either. Assuming, of course, that you haven't already been through your smack phase.' She giggled through her tears. 'I think you should talk to Kieran about it. Tell him you're freaking out. Don't tell him you considered sleeping with someone else. But tell him you're scared. He probably is too.'

I made us both a cup of tea.

'I kissed him,' Olivia announced all of a sudden.

'Kissed who?'

'Finn. The guy I considered sleeping with.'

'It was just a kiss, Olivia.'

'It wasn't just a kiss. It was an amazing kiss. And I hate myself so much for saying that, I hate myself for the fact that my stomach flips every time I think about that kiss.'

I sat down next to Olivia on the sofa. 'Let me tell you something. I got married when I was twenty-eight, which isn't that young, but my friends at the time were dumbfounded. I'd always been this total party girl.'

Olivia laughed.

'Yes, I know. It's difficult to imagine, but I was. Liked my clubs, my drugs, all that kind of stuff. Anyway, then I met Marco and it was game over. My friends were horrified. They couldn't believe I was going to settle down. As far as they were concerned, it was the worst thing in the world.'

Olivia nodded, a glint of recognition in her eye.

'Anyway, I remember having a conversation with one of my girlfriends at the time, who was telling me that she'd met a guy at a party and they'd had this amazing night: they'd sat out in the garden under the stars all night, just talking and talking and kissing and talking some more – you know the kind of thing. Those perfect nights you have when you first meet someone and there's this instant connection and if just feels incredible. And I remember her saying to me, "That is the greatest feeling ever. Aren't you sad, aren't you heartbroken that you'll never ever get that again?"'

'Oh my God, I am. That terrifies me,' Olivia said.

'I know, it terrified me too,' I admitted. 'When she said that to me I just felt crushed . . .'

'Kind of like I do now . . .'

'But wait. I was totally freaked out about it for a couple of days, but then I thought about it. It's not much of a trade-off, is it? How many of those nights do you think you get, if you stay single all your life? Ten, maybe twenty, if you're lucky. OK, maybe more than twenty if you're Scarlett Johansson, but I'm talking about normal people. Actually, you look a bit like Scarlett Johansson, so I'll give you twenty-five. Would you trade twenty-five of those amazing nights for a lifetime with someone you love? I wouldn't. I wouldn't trade twenty-five amazing nights for two years, eight months and fourteen days with the man I loved. I wouldn't hesitate to offer up one thousand of those amazing nights for just one more night with him.'

Olivia burst into tears again, She wrapped her arms around me, squeezing me in a bear hug.

'Olivia,' I gasped. 'Can't breathe . . .' She's stronger than she looks.

'Sorry,' she said. 'It's just . . . I feel ridiculous moaning to you like this. Not just ridiculous but wrong, cruel, evil . . .'

'Evil?'

'Well, after what you've been through, how can I sit here moaning about the man I love wanting to marry me?'

I smiled at her. 'You know what? It's just nice to have a girlfriend to chat to about stuff like this. Particularly as you're not the only one who's been kissing people you shouldn't have . . .'

'What?' The word came out as a shriek.

'Shhhh,' I hushed her. 'Luca.' He was sleeping in the next room.

'Sorry,' she hissed at me, 'but *what*? I can't believe you've been sitting here allowing me to prattle on when you have real, genuine, earth-shattering gossip.'

'Well, I'm not sure about earth-shattering,' I said. 'It's just Sam.'

'Sam, the guy I met in the café? The incredibly hot guy I met in the café? What do you mean, "It's just Sam"?'

'Well . . .' I shrugged. 'He's my friend. And I never used to think about him that way . . .'

'Are you blind?' she asked me. 'How could you not?'

'I don't know,' I said, and my reply was genuine. At that moment I couldn't believe that there had been months and months when I didn't think about Sam like that. As Olivia said, how could I not? 'He's always been there for me, in a strictly friendly way – watching Luca, helping out when I needed things done round the house . . . And, of course, he's never been single. He's always had a woman or two on the go.'

'So is that why you shouldn't be kissing him?' she asked me. 'Because he's got a girlfriend?'

'What do you mean?'

'You said, "You're not the only one who's been kissing people you shouldn't have." So why shouldn't you be kissing Sam?'

'He doesn't have a girlfriend at the moment,' I said, not looking at her directly.

'So what's the problem? Why shouldn't you be kissing him?'

'I don't know . . .' But I did know the answer to that question. It was just hard to answer honestly. I tried anyway. 'Because it feels like a betrayal,' I said. 'He's only been gone two years.'

'Bea . . .' Olivia said, tears welling up in her eyes again. 'That isn't a betrayal. Don't you think you deserve to be happy?'

'I'm not sure I do, actually.'

'Of course you do!' Olivia protested. But what did she know? She didn't know about the drinking, about the terrible start in life that I gave my son, about what I'd put my mother through, what I'd put Elina through.

'I've not always treated people very well,' I told her. I couldn't face going into details. Not yet.

'I don't care what you've done, Bea. I've seen you, the way you chat to your customers, the way you make people feel welcome, the way you love your son, the way you've treated me – helping me out when that cyclist knocked me down, telling me I look like Scarlett Johansson . . . All these things tell me that no matter what you've done in your past, you do deserve happiness.' She squeezed my hand to emphasise her point. 'And you should be kissing Sam. You should definitely be kissing Sam. You should be doing all sorts of things with Sam. Preferably dirty things.'

I laughed. 'Maybe you're right,' I said. 'Because you know the weird thing? That stupid, heady, reckless feeling, the one that my former friend told me I'd never have again? I think I'm feeling it again.'

After Olivia left, I got started on the mini leek, Gruyère and rocket frittatas. Talking to Olivia had made me feel so much better, but now she was gone, my mood turned melancholic. Despite the noises of the kitchen, of chopping and blending and frying, despite Luca's frequent shouts for attention (he was playing in his pen in the living room), the flat seemed uncomfortably quiet. I turned on the radio but the endless medley of Christmas tunes made me want to throw the thing out of the window. I tuned in to Radio 4 and listened to the news, but this was followed by a spectacularly depressing play about spending Christmas in prison. I listened for about five minutes and then turned it off.

Lucy had spent last Christmas in prison. I wondered whether she'd had visitors. I didn't know all that much about her: she was young, just twenty-three at the time of the accident, she was single, she didn't have any children. Her father had been in court for the verdict, I remembered him breaking down after the sentence was passed.

Luca started to cry. I picked him up and cuddled him for a while, then gave him something to eat and put him down for a nap. Then, without really thinking about what I was doing, about what I was going to say, I took the scrap of paper from my wallet, sat down at the kitchen table and dialled the number. It rang and rang, eventually clicking on to a BT messaging service. When the beep came, I held my breath. Eventually, I said:

'This is a message for Lucy Jenkins. It's Beatrice Marinelli here. You came to see me the other day. I was wondering if we could talk.'

I left her my mobile phone number and hoped that I'd got through to the right Lucy Jenkins.

5.25 p.m.
Olivia

Olivia took the long way home. The very, very long way home. She left Bea's place a little after two, intending to just take a quick stroll around Finsbury Park to clear her head before she went back to talk to Kieran. The sun had come out for the first time in days, so she thought she may as well take advantage. It was unlikely to last, after all.

The thing was, everything Bea said had made perfect sense. And yet for some reason she still felt uneasy. Bea was right, what she really needed to do was just sit down with Kieran and tell him how she was feeling. She'd have to put it exactly the right way, though. She didn't want to hurt his feelings.

She walked briskly to the park and looped around it, ending up at the station. Without really thinking where she was going, she hopped on to the tube, getting off again at Highbury & Islington. She wandered along Upper Street, popping in and out of boutiques and shoe shops, resisting the temptation to spend money on herself. 'Tis not the season. Eventually she stopped at Ottolenghi where she ordered a cup of tea and some French toast. She turned off her mobile phone and took her green leather list book out of her bag, opening it to the centre page. At the top of the page she wrote two words: 'Marriage: Against.'

It took her a long time to write a short list. Eventually,

she turned her phone back on. She had three missed calls, all from Kieran. She rang him back.

'Where are you?' he asked, sounding a little exasperated. 'You've been gone all day. Mum's been waiting here for you. You said you'd take her to look at the boutiques on Sloane Street, remember? Did you forget?'

'Shit, Kieran, I'm really sorry. It completely slipped my mind. I'm on Upper Street, I had some last minute Christmas shopping to do.' She was lying again. When was it she'd started lying to Kieran? Oh, that's right – she'd started lying to him right about the time they'd got engaged.

'OK. Well, don't worry about it. I know you're busy. When are you coming back?'

'I'll be there in twenty minutes.'

8.52 p.m.
Chloe

Chloe woke up just before nine. In the evening. She was lying on the sofa; Alfie was curled up beside her, a warm ball of fuzz, gently snoring. She had slept. Not for half an hour, not fitfully, she had really slept. She had started watching a movie on TV at two but she couldn't have seen more than half an hour of it, which meant that she had slept for more than six hours. Six hours!

She sat up, carefully swinging her legs over the dog so as not to wake him. On the floor next to her was an empty pizza box and an empty tub of Haagen-Dazs. She felt a slight pang of guilt, but only a very slight one. So she hadn't run and she had eaten: she might put on a pound or two. Who gave a toss? She went into the bathroom and stepped up on the scales, something she usually did every morning, the moment she got out of bed. One hundred and twenty, the same as yesterday. She was five foot seven and she weighed 120 pounds. Did it really matter if she went up to 122?

She picked up the debris and took it into the kitchen to throw it away. She heard a buzzing sound from her handbag. it was her phone; a new voicemail alert. Two new voicemails, in fact, both from numbers she didn't recognise. She dialled her mailbox.

Voicemail one, received today at three-fifteen: 'Hi, Chloe, it's Conor. Kieran's brother. Olivia's husband's brother. I mean, Olivia's future husband's brother. We met last night. You probably remember. At least I hope you do. I was wondering if you were free for a drink sometime? And when I say sometime I mean within the next seventy-two hours, because after that I'm going home to Dublin. If you're not free within the next seventy-two hours I might possibly be persuaded to come back at another time to take you out. Let me know, anyway.'

Chloe found herself grinning as she listened to him prattle on. Not a bad message at all. He was witty, self-deprecating, a little nervous, obviously, but quite charming. Promising. Apart from the fact that he lived in another country, of course. Then again, she was quite used to dealing with a boyfriend who was mostly unavailable.

Voicemail two, received today at four forty-six: 'Hello. I don't know whose phone this is, but you rang me the other night and then hung up when I answered. It was probably a wrong number, but if it wasn't, if by any chance it happened to be the lovely girl with the sore feet and bad taste in literature, I'd really love to hear from you again.'

Jack's message didn't make her smile. It made her heart race. She played it again. And again. She clicked on his number and stored it into her address book. It was official – she was letting him into her life. She composed herself. What was she going to say to him? How was she going to explain the fact that she'd rung him and then hung up the other day? Her finger hovered over the 'dial' button. And then she noticed that Alfie was pissing on the carpet. She put the phone down and fetched a cloth to clean it up.

9.02 p.m.
Olivia

Olivia was not home within twenty minutes. As ill luck would have it, there was a security alert at Finsbury Park which meant that she was stuck in a train, in a tunnel, for more than an hour. When she finally did get out of the tube, tired, stressed and sweaty, she had no desire to wedge herself on to a jam-packed bus to get home. But thanks to the problems on the tube, there were no taxis to be had.

She rang Kieran and got his voicemail. She explained what had happened. 'I'm just going to go to that Korean place down the road. I'll get something to eat and then come home when it isn't quite so hectic,' she said. 'If you're around, come and join me.'

He didn't come and join her. When she finally did get home, he was alone, sitting at the kitchen table, drinking a beer. It was clearly not his first of the evening.

'Everyone went out,' Kieran said. 'They thought you might appreciate a night off.'

'That wasn't necessary,' Olivia said.

'Wasn't it?' He looked angry.

'I'm really sorry, Kieran, about this afternoon, I just . . .'

'You forgot, I know. It's understandable. You've had a lot on your plate.' The words sounded conciliatory, but his tone said something else entirely. 'You forgot to tell me you'd seen Finn, too,' he said.

'I'm sorry?' Her heart stopped.

'Finn,' Kieran said, getting to his feet and grabbing another beer from the fridge. 'He called a while ago. He wanted to check you'd got home all right the other night. I said you had. Then, about an hour later, he called again. He hung up when I picked up, but it was him again. The same number. Is there something you'd like to tell me?'

257

Olivia felt as though she was going to throw up. She sat down at the table opposite Kieran, stretching out her arms, reaching for his hand. He didn't reciprocate; he leaned back in his chair and pulled his hands away from her. She could tell the truth, hurt his feelings and cause a terrible fight, or she could lie. For the second time that day, she lied.

'I ran into him at Katya's. We talked for a bit, that's all. I didn't really think it was worth mentioning.'

Kieran gave a low, bitter laugh. 'You didn't think it was worth mentioning? Do you think I'm fucking stupid, Olivia?' She jumped. It was completely out of character for him to swear at her. 'Sorry, but you know that I know, don't you? What all your friends call him? Finn, the One Who Got Away. And you didn't think it was worth mentioning that you bumped into him at a party, just before you came home and emailed everyone about how awful it was that you hadn't slept around more.'

Olivia pulled her hand back, folding her arms in front of her, guilt and shame turning to anger. 'How many beers have you had?' she asked him.

'Oh, don't do that,' he snapped. 'Don't you dare do that, turn this back on me. This is not about me having a few beers. This is about the way you've been acting ever since I asked you to marry me. It's like . . . I don't know. It's like you said yes but you meant no.'

'Well, you know women,' she sneered at him, 'always getting our yeses and noes confused.' She got

to her feet and stormed into the bedroom, slamming the door behind her. A minute or two later, she
heard the front door slam as he left.

11.49 p.m.
Bea
It was almost midnight and not just my fridge but the
huge, industrial-sized fridge downstairs in the café
were both pretty much full. I'd made courgette and
herb fritters, baked new potatoes with rosemary and
sea salt, Parmesan, mascarpone and cranberry scones,
blinis with smoked salmon and a beetroot and dill
cream, mini toads in the hole, and a lot of pumpkin
velouté. I'd been cooking all day, almost without a
break, since Olivia left that morning, and I didn't feel
like stopping. I recited my recipes to myself, I wrote
down ideas for dishes I might make the following day,
or the day after that, or sometime next year. I tried
not to keep staring at my phone. I wanted it to ring;
I was terrified of it ringing. If it did ring, and it was
Lucy, I could let her leave a message, I reasoned, I
could gauge her tone before dealing with the living,
breathing her.

Of course, hers was not the only call I was waiting
for. I was waiting for Sam to call me, too. I hadn't left
a message when I'd seen him yesterday morning, but
he would still have seen that he'd missed a call from
me. Where was he? Why wasn't he calling me back?
After checking on Luca, I padded quietly down the

stairs, opened the front door and looked up at his window, just to check. There were no lights on; of course there were no lights on. He was gone. I'd seen him leave.

Where the hell was he?

Friday 24 December

8.16 a.m.
Olivia

'Kieran, it's me. I'm so sorry about yesterday. I handled things badly, I've handled everything badly. I really need to see you. I missed you last night. I hate waking up without you. Will you meet me in the Honey Pot? Say elevenish? I'm going to do a bit of shopping with your mum first, make up for yesterday. I'll see you later, hopefully. I love you.'

9.22 a.m.
Chloe

Chloe overslept, which was surprising given that she had slept almost all the previous day. Given her usual sleep problems, it was nothing less than astounding. Astounding, but welcome. When she did get up, around nine thirty, she dressed to go running. Yesterday's pizza and Häagen Dazs were weighing heavy on her mind, if not her midriff. She clipped a lead on to Alfie's new red leather collar and ventured out into the cold.

She discovered fairly quickly – after a dozen or so metres, in fact – that eight weeks old was a little too young for running. They would have to walk instead. Slowly, and not very far. They could just about make it as far as the Honey Pot. Chloe wondered whether it might be an idea to buy a bicycle. That way she could pop him in the basket and get some exercise.

On their torturous journey to the café, a journey which under normal circumstances took less than ten minutes but today took well over twenty, Chloe noticed a curious phenomenon: she was getting a lot of attention. This in itself wasn't odd – Chloe was actually used to getting a lot of attention from men – but she noticed that the kind of attention she was getting was different. It wasn't lascivious. It was friendly. It was refreshing. Women started smiling at her in the street, too, which initially she found unsettling, but gradually began to enjoy. This, Chloe thought, must be what it's like to have a baby. Only without the unpleasantness of actually having to have a baby. She should have got a puppy years ago.

10.15 a.m.
Bea
Still no messages on my phone.

I hadn't planned to work on Friday, but I was feeling guilty about taking the past few days off with so little notice, so I popped down to help Kathy out for an hour or two. We put Luca in his little bouncy chair behind the counter, but he grizzled and whined – he'd spent all of yesterday watching me cook and he was thoroughly sick of it.

'I'll go next door,' I said to Kathy. 'Maybe Sam's around.'

'Any excuse,' she muttered. 'And there's no point anyway, he isn't there. The shop's shut and that smelly dog isn't in the window.'

My heart sank. This was ridiculous. I knew he wasn't there, but I kept hoping. Maybe he'd come back in the middle of the night? Maybe he'd just been delivering presents to someone? Maybe he'd forgotten his toothbrush?

Luca started to yell. 'I'm going to have to take him upstairs, Kathy,' I said. 'I'm sorry.'

I picked him up, which shut him up instantly, and was about to go upstairs when Chloe arrived, a bundle of fur in her arms. She was beaming. She looked a completely different girl to the bad-tempered bitch I'd met ten days ago.

'Thought I'd just drop by to introduce you to Alfie,' she said proudly. 'I know you've already met, but he wasn't Alfie then.'

'You're getting along OK then?' I asked her.

'Like a house on fire. We have to get the peeing under control, but aside from that, he's perfect.' Chloe's mobile rang. She took it out of her coat pocket and looked at the screen, then clicked 'Ignore' and slipped it into her handbag. 'Nothing important, just the boss,' she said with a grin.

'Shouldn't you speak to him?'

Chloe shrugged her shoulders. 'No mobile phone policy, remember?' I laughed. 'Honestly, though. I really can't thank you enough – for Alfie, for being so forgiving, especially after the way I was when we first met . . .'

'Ancient history now,' I said. 'Fancy a coffee?'

'Actually I fancy a slice of that almond cheesecake. A large slice, preferably.'

Chloe, Alfie, Luca and I sat at the corner table, the one at which Chloe had been sitting the first day I noticed her. She wolfed down her cheesecake, and when she'd finished, she asked for a second slice.

'Ravenous,' she said to me through a mouthful of creamy, buttery goo. 'Haven't eaten like this in years, but for some reason I suddenly just don't give a fuck.' Glancing across at Luca, she pulled a face. 'Sorry. Shouldn't swear in front of him. It'd be a bit embarrassing if his first word was "fuck", wouldn't it? Oh fuck, now I've said it again.'

I laughed. 'Now you've said it three times, and he's about to due to say a real word. If anything, he's a bit late. He does Mama and Gaga – that's his grandmother – and a few other things. Not Dada, of course.' Chloe looked stricken. 'Sorry, didn't mean to be maudlin. He hasn't spoken a real word yet.'

'An-ti-dis-es-tab-lish-men-tar-i-a-nism,' Chloe said to Luca, enunciating slowly and clearly. He looked at her coyly, tugging gently on one of Alfie's ears.

'You have a way with children, don't you?' I said.

We were on to our second cup of coffee when Olivia arrived. She didn't come in straight away, she just stood there, on the pavement, looking left and right, at her watch and then down the street. She seemed agitated. I rapped on the window and motioned for her to come in. She smiled, a little stiffly, and mouthed, 'In a minute,' at us. A moment or two later, Kieran turned up. He kissed her, more a peck than a real kiss, and they came into the café, hand in hand yet somehow miles apart.

'If it isn't the happy couple,' Chloe said to me, her voice low, eyebrow raised. 'They seem perfect together, don't they, and yet something seems a bit off to me.'

'I think they *are* perfect together, it's just that someone, a blonde someone, has slight commitment issues,' I replied.

We stopped gossiping when they came to sit down. After a moment of awkward silence, I asked Kieran where the rest of his family was.

'Everyone's doing their own thing today,' he replied. 'Last-minute Christmas shopping, mostly. Though I've a nasty feeling my parents are going to Madame Tussauds.'

'Are you going shopping too?'

'God, no,' Kieran said. 'Thankfully Livvie got everything done by the end of last week.' He smiled at her, playing with the hair at the nape of her neck.

'Must be great to have a wife,' Chloe said. 'Someone to pick out the presents and fetch the dry cleaning, make the dinner, get everything organised. I'd like to have a wife.' Olivia gave her a sharp look. 'Oh, I didn't mean . . . Well, I know that's not what being a wife is about, it's just—'

'I know exactly what you meant,' Olivia snapped. For once, Chloe looked genuinely contrite. Kieran pulled his hand away and stared glumly into his coffee cup. It was one of the very few occasions when it was truly wonderful to have both a baby and a puppy around – the awkwardness was dispelled as everyone turned their attention to the cute things in our midst. Interestingly, Olivia reached for Alfie, while Kieran asked if he could hold Luca. After a few minutes, they made their excuses and left. As they walked out of the café, Olivia reached for Kieran's hand. He held hers for a moment or two, but then he dropped it.

12.32 p.m.
Olivia
'Shall we just go home?' Kieran asked Olivia as they headed away from the café.

'Is that what you want to do?' she asked. He shrugged. They stood at the end of the road, not sure which way to turn. Olivia had a horrible feeling, a desperate feeling, that she had led them somewhere they didn't want to go, to a point at which they had to make a choice they didn't want to make.

'No, not home. Let's go out somewhere. We can have lunch.'

'We just had breakfast,' Kieran pointed out.

266

'Are you calling me fat?' she asked, hand on hip, a parody of anger. They both started to laugh. 'Come on,' Olivia said, 'I've got an idea.'

They went to All the Way, José, a truly awful Tex-Mex place near Covent Garden which was heaving with tourists.

'Remember this place?' Olivia asked, dragging him through the door.

'How could I ever forget? I'm all for walks down memory lane, Liv, but don't you think this is a bit extreme? Last time you came here you spent the next twenty-four hours throwing up.'

'Maybe it's improved,' she said.

He glanced around the room, surveying the throng of tourists, teenagers and out-of-towners. 'Somehow I doubt it.'

The last time they had come here had been five years earlier. A colleague of Kieran's had decided, for reasons that were never quite established, to hold a birthday party here. Kieran's party of twelve was seated at a table in the corner; at the table immediately beside them sat two women, one of whom was drinking tequila shots. The other, the beautiful blonde wearing very expensive shoes, was sipping a mineral water, looking pissed off.

Kieran had been sitting at the end of the table, closest to the girls. The conversation amongst his party was pretty inane, and he found himself eavesdropping.

'One drink, Zara,' the blonde was saying, 'one drink

and then I'm out of here. God, this place is vile.' There was something slightly haughty about her manner, which Kieran immediately found annoying. He found it hard to look away, though; she really was gorgeous.

'Oh relax, Olivia,' her friend said to her. 'Here, have a quesadilla.'

'That looks repulsive.'

'It's surprisingly good, actually.'

The blonde, 'Olivia', took a bite of a quesadilla that, Kieran had to admit, did not look appetising. She grimaced. 'Oh my God, that's revolting. How can you eat this crap?'

'It might have something to do with the fact I've had three tequilas,' Zara replied. 'Pretty much anything would taste good to me right now.'

Olivia rolled her eyes. 'Couldn't you develop a crush on a barman at a better class of bar? The Met Bar or Asia de Cuba or something?' she muttered crossly. 'I mean, this place really is beyond the pale.'

At the next table, Kieran laughed. Olivia looked over at him; it was clear that he was laughing at her, or at the very least at something she'd said.

'Can I help you?' she asked, her cheeks turning pink.

'No, sorry, I just couldn't help overhearing—'

'You probably could help it,' Olivia said, turning away from him. 'You just chose not to.'

'Jeez, Liv. Give him a break,' Zara said, adding in a whisper, 'He's really fucking hot.' Olivia rolled her eyes again.

The pair of them had by this time been noticed by a few others on Kieran's (mostly male) table.

'Would you ladies like to join us?' asked one.

'Love to,' Zara replied, just as Olivia was saying, 'No thanks.' She ended up sitting at the end of the table, squeezed in between Kieran and a loud Australian with the build of a rugby player, a seemingly endless repertoire of sexist jokes and a body odour issue. Kieran was clearly the better conversational choice.

'So,' Olivia asked brightly. 'What is it you do?'

'I work for a medical charity,' Kieran said. 'Organising vaccines for children in developing countries.'

'Wow. That sounds interesting. Very . . . worthwhile. Do you get to travel much?'

'Quite a bit. I was in Mozambique last week actually.'

'Really? I went to Mozambique last year. Stayed at a fabulous place. The Azura, on Benguerra Island – do you know it?'

Kieran smiled. 'I've heard of it. Rooms are about three hundred quid a night, aren't they? It's not really the kind of place charity staff tend to stay.'

'Well, no, I suppose not,' Olivia said, a bit miffed. 'It *is* a carbon neutral resort, though,' she muttered.

'Ah, well, I didn't know that. Perhaps I should tell my employers. Still not entirely sure they'd be happy putting us up at a place where the bill for a couple of days' stay is fractionally higher than the average annual wage, but there you go.'

'He's a sanctimonious git,' Olivia complained to Zara in the ladies, room a while later.

'A drop-dead-gorgeous sanctimonious git though, you have to agree.'

'That's beside the point,' Olivia said. She peered at herself in the mirror. 'God, I look green. I really don't feel well either. I think I'm going to go home.'

'You look fine,' Zara said, swaying slightly as she tried to reapply her lipstick.

'Zara, you've had six tequila shots. You can't even tell which one of me we're talking about.'

'OK then, but you go. I'm going to hang around. That Australian guy's really quite charming, don't you think?'

Kieran watched Olivia leave with a surprising sense of disappointment. Why did he care if she didn't come back? They clearly had nothing in common. But he did care. He followed her outside where he found her at the corner of the street, throwing up into the gutter.

'Jesus, are you OK?' he asked her, putting an arm around her shoulders.

'Do I look OK?' she asked, in between heaves.

'It's just . . . you didn't seem drunk in there.'

'I'm not drunk, you idiot,' she gasped. 'I haven't had a drink all night. It must have been that bloody awful food.'

Kieran eventually managed to find a taxi driver who could be persuaded to let a puking girl into the back of his cab and escorted Olivia home. He helped her out of the car and to the front door.

270

'Will you be all right?' he asked as she fumbled with her keys to get the door open.

'I'll be fine.'

'Is there someone at home to look after you?'

'I'll be fine,' she insisted stiffly. 'Thank you for your assistance.' Her attempts at retaining her dignity were really quite endearing. She opened the door, took a couple of steps inside and fainted.

Kieran paid the taxi driver and told him to leave.

He helped her to her feet and up the stairs; he sat with her on the bathroom floor, holding her long blonde hair away from her face as she threw up into the loo. He ignored her pleas to leave her alone, bringing her glasses of water and cups of herbal tea. Eventually, he helped her into bed and spent the night sitting on an armchair in the corner of her bedroom, while she slept fitfully, every now and again getting up to vomit copiously.

'One bite,' she kept moaning, 'one bloody bite.'

Now, five years later, the two of them found themselves sitting in exactly the same spot that Olivia and Zara had been that fateful night. They ordered drinks.

'Do you want to tell me what's going on, Liv?'

Tentatively, Olivia reached into her handbag. She pulled out the little green book, opened it to the centre page and handed it to Kieran.

At the top of the page he read the words: 'Marriage: Against'. Beneath it was a list.

- Half of marriages end in divorce
- How many end in death? Look at Bea
- I don't want to become a bridezilla
- I don't want to become the little woman
- I'm not sure four people is enough
- I don't think I want to have three children in quick succession
- If I weigh 138 pounds now, how much will I weigh after three children in quick succession?
- I'm not religious and I'm not sure I want my children to be religious
- But what choice will I have faced with his mother?
- I don't want us to change

He looked at her, his face stony. 'You should have told me,' he said, closing the book. 'You should have told me that this wasn't what you wanted.'

Olivia placed her hand on top of his, holding the book open. 'Wait,' she said, 'we're not done. Next page.'

Angrily, he wiped a tear from his eye. 'There's more? I'm really not sure I can stand any more.'

'Turn the page, Kieran. Please.'

The page, headed 'Marriage: For', was almost blank. There were just two entries.

- He's very good in bed
- Hard as I try, I can't imagine that I will ever love anyone remotely as much as I love Kieran

Kieran closed the book and put it back on the table. He smiled at her. 'That's it? I'm good in bed?'

'And I love you.'

'You're an idiot, you know that? You really are. Let's have a look now.' He reopened the book to the 'Against' page. 'So, "half of all marriages end in divorce". One: I'm not sure that statistic is correct. I think it's just under half.'

'Oh, well then, that's OK.'

'And two: so what? So some marriages don't work out. Some jobs don't work out. Sometimes you'll buy a house because you think it's amazing and then five years later you find that you have subsidence and the place is about to fall down. If you don't do something because it might go wrong, you'll never do anything.'

'I suppose . . .'

'And death? Seriously? You don't want to get married in case I die? Would it be better if we didn't get married and I died then?'

'Of course not, but . . .'

'Well, honestly. You don't want to become a bridezilla? Don't become one. It's pretty bloody easy. We have a small, simple wedding, organised by us. Or we hand the whole thing over to our respective mothers and let the chips fall where they may. You might end up walking down the aisle in the biggest taffeta meringue known to man, but so what? It's the marriage I'm concerned with, not the wedding day. And little woman? Really? The little woman who doesn't cook, doesn't clean and takes everything to the dry cleaners because she can't be arsed to use an iron? Some little woman you'll be.'

The waiter arrived and brought them more drinks.

'And now,' said Kieran with a grin, 'we get down to the nitty gritty. Four people.'

'Oh God,' Olivia moaned, her head in her hands. 'Can we just ignore that one? It isn't what I really feel anyway. I don't want to sleep with anyone else.'

'Because I'm so great in bed?'

'Exactly.'

Kieran laughed. 'OK, I won't torture you with that one. Although there is something I need to know, Liv,' he said, his tone becoming more serious.

'What?' she asked.

'This thing with Finn. I don't want to know what happened at the party. I know you had a thing for him for a while – for a long time. It doesn't matter, so long as it's over. So long as it's out of your system now.'

'Kieran, I honestly wouldn't care if I never saw him again. I promise you. I did have feelings for him, you're right, but they were never based on anything real, and they're gone now.' She shuffled her chair over, closer to his, and kissed him on the mouth.

'OK then,' he said, looking at her carefully, searching her face for clues. 'So long as you're sure?'

'Never been surer.'

'Right. Moving on: children. You've always said you *did* want to have children . . .'

'I do, but maybe not three, and maybe not now.'

'Well then, that's fine. I was joking about the three-children thing, you know I was. We could have one, we could have three, we could have seventeen. I don't actually mind how many we have. I wouldn't mind if we decided to adopt.'

'You really are the most easy-going man on the planet,' Olivia said, reaching out to take his hand.

'Can we put that in the 'For' column then?'

A large, noisy group of people arrived; they were seated at the next table. They looked like a family, at least three generations, babbling away in a language Olivia didn't understand – Portuguese, possibly. An elderly woman, the head of the family, the matriarch, sat at the head of the table, holding forth. Olivia eyed them nervously. Kieran followed her gaze and started to laugh.

'That's not going to be us, you know,' he said. 'My mother lives in a different country and she really isn't that scary. As for the religion thing, Liv – you have realised I'm an atheist, haven't you? Yes, we'll probably have to make compromises along the way – of course my mother will want our kids to be baptised – but is that really such a bad thing? It's a ceremony, it's a family occasion. It doesn't have to mean anything more than that.'

Kieran reached out, stroking her cheek with the back of his fingers. 'So, is that it? Is there anything else you're freaking out about? Anything else about the prospect of walking up the aisle with me that terrifies you?'

Olivia drew a deep breath. 'Oh God, Kieran, what if it changes the way we are? I don't want us to change. This is the best relationship I've ever had, the happiest, most fulfilling relationship I could imagine. It's not that I don't want to get married, it's just that I'm terrified that things won't be the same any more. I don't want to change what we have, I want to protect it.'

'I do too, Liv. That's all I want to do. And somebody incredibly wise – or possibly a writer for a cheesy American television programme – once said that the thing about marriage is that it isn't a commitment you make once. You make it over and over again, every day. I think that's the perfect way to protect something great.'

The waiter brought over their quesadillas.

'Do we have to eat those?' Olivia asked, her stomach turning at the thought.

'This was your idea.'

'I know, but do we really want to spend all of Christmas Day throwing up?'

'They'll be offended now if we don't eat them.'

'Kieran, our waiter is a seventeen-year-old Albanian working for sub-minimum wage. He doesn't give a crap
if we eat them or not, provided we leave him a tip.'

Kieran got to his feet. 'Still, I don't want him to feel

276

that we didn't like them. I'll tell him we've been called away. An emergency.'

He really was the sweetest man ever.

4.15 p.m.
Chloe

After coffee and much cheesecake at the Honey Pot, Chloe carried a sleeping Alfie home. On the way, she picked up a carton of Cookies 'n' Cream ice cream and a *Guardian*. At home, she worked for a couple of hours, going through the papers Maurice had faxed over, then she turned off the phone, flung herself on to the sofa and spent the day reading the paper, finishing off *No Fury* and getting started on *The Shipping News*. She couldn't remember the last time she'd felt so relaxed.

It wasn't until late afternoon, once darkness had fallen and she'd been forced to rouse herself from the sofa to clean up a puddle of pee in the kitchen, that she noticed it was snowing. And not just a couple of flakes either, it was snowing heavily, proper snow, the sort you almost never see in London, certainly not at Christmas anyway. Something about it, the stillness of it, the light of the almost-full moon reflecting off the white carpet in her tiny back garden, made her feel terribly lonely.

She located her Venice guide book, gathered Alfie up in her arms and rang her parents.

'I'm having a wonderful time,' she said to her mother. 'Venice is beautiful. We went to the Palazzo Ducale

277

this afternoon. It was amazing. Snowing? No, not here. Is it snowing there? That sounds lovely.' She chatted to her father, who spent five minutes complaining bitterly about the performance of England's batsmen in the Ashes, and had a quick word with each of her sisters, neither of whom were remotely interested in what she was up to, which was a relief since she was having to make it all up.

Talking to them did little for her sense of isolation, however; if anything, it exacerbated it. She could picture them now, all six of them, her parents and her well-adjusted sisters and their respectable husbands, the boys sitting around the living room, drinking a decent bottle of red, the girls in the kitchen preparing the evening meal. All right, so it was a tableau which in part made her want to hurl, but at least none of them was lonely. They all had someone.

Hadn't she been saying, just the other day, that it wasn't such a bad thing to be alone? She liked being alone. She liked her own company. Her own company was frequently preferable to that of others. She was intelligent and thoughtful; other people rarely were.

'I'm fine on my own,' she said out loud. Alfie whimpered. 'Sorry, Alfie. I'm not on my own, am I? I have you. And I'm fine with that.' She took him into the kitchen and gave him a bowl of Claude's Kitchen Organic Homestyle Chicken and Turkey Casserole for Puppies. Only the best for Alfie. She sat down at the kitchen table, watching him eat.

She wasn't fine. She didn't feel fine at all. She felt like a Dorothy Parker poem. How did it go?

> *I shudder at the thought of men . . .*
> *I'm due to fall in love again.*

She helped herself to a bowl of Cookies 'n' Cream and picked up her mobile. She opened her address book and scrolled down to Jack's name. Then she scrolled back up to Conor's. And back to Jack's.

The thing was, she knew it made more sense to call Jack than to call Conor. Jack, after all, was the one who made her heart race, the one who passed the butterfly test. But, given that she had just got out of a year-long and emotionally devastating relationship with a man who passed the butterfly test with flying colours, perhaps Conor was the safer option. After all, she wasn't *really* due to fall in love again. She was just due to have a bit of fun.

She scrolled back to Conor's number and pressed dial. He answered on the second ring. She could hardly hear him over all the background noise.

'Sorry!' he yelled at her once he'd finally established who she was. 'Hang on a minute . . . That's better. I'm in the kitchen now. It's mayhem in there – we're having a family SingStar contest. My nieces are doing "Love Machine" by Girls Aloud. It's a bit disturbing actually. You don't really want to see quite that much pelvic thrusting from nine-year-olds.'

'Quite,' Chloe replied.

'Anyway, thank you for calling me back. It's great to hear from you.'

'I know it's late notice,' Chloe said, 'but I also know that you don't have much time, so I was wondering if you wanted to go for a quick drink this evening? Assuming you're permitted to duck out of the family festivities?'

'No problem at all,' Conor said. 'To be honest, we've had enough festive fun over the past few days to last us a bloody lifetime, and we haven't even got to Christmas yet. Since I asked you out, I really should be suggesting the venue, but I don't actually know anywhere. Can you help me out?'

They agreed to meet at the Fox, the pub just around the corner from the Honey Pot, at six thirty, giving Chloe a hour or so to decide what to wear.

'Definitely something casual,' she told Alfie as she pulled various pairs of jeans and tops out of her wardrobe. Alfie, sitting in the middle of the bed, chewed thoughtfully on a printed McQueen T-shirt with a low neckline. 'Oh, good choice, boy,' Chloe said, carefully removing the shirt from his mouth. 'That would have been perfect if it hadn't been covered by dog slobber. Perhaps you'd better watch from the armchair.' After several costume changes she decided on a simple jeans, boots and sexy-but-not-overtly-sexy top.

She had calculated the exact time she needed to leave if she was going to arrive twelve minutes late (ten wasn't really late at all, fifteen was too late), she had her coat on, she was ready to head out the door, and then she decided to phone Jack. The thing was, if she didn't call him now, she wouldn't be able to talk to him until Sunday at the very earliest – it wouldn't do to call on Christmas Day. Was it polite to call on Boxing Day? She wasn't sure. So she probably shouldn't call until Monday. And she wanted to talk to him before Monday. She grabbed her phone and rang his number.

It went straight to voicemail. She left a message.

'Hi, Jack, this is Chloe. You left a message on my phone the other day. And I think you may have left a dinner invitation in the book I bought from you, though I can't be absolutely sure about that. Maybe someone else left it there as a bookmark. If it was a dinner invitation, I'd like to go. Give me a call.'

5.32 p.m.
Olivia

Olivia and Kieran returned home to find his parents delivering a heartfelt rendition of Abba's 'Fernando' (they had enjoyed *Mamma Mia* way too much) to a rapt audience in Olivia's living room.

'Where have you two been?' Richard demanded. 'You've missed your first turn. So far, you have *nul points*, as they say in Eurovision, so your first performance better be a good one.'

After some deliberation, Kieran and Olivia chose

'This Old Heart of Mine' by the Isley Brothers. They massacred it. It was truly, truly awful, but Olivia didn't care. She realised, amid the howls of delight and derision from her in-laws-to-be, that she felt completely relaxed for the first time in ages, for the first time since Kieran had popped the question. Everything was going to be all right. All she had to do was let go.

After the SingStar sing-off, they sat down to dinner, an Irish stew prepared by Richard and Brendon.

'What happened to Conor?' Kieran asked his parents. 'I thought he was supposed to be providing dessert.'

'He was,' Sheila, Kieran's mum, said, 'but he had to go out for a bit . . . I think he's met a girl.'

Kieran and Olivia exchanged glances. 'Zara or Chloe, I wonder?' Kieran murmured.

'I do hope it's that Zara,' Sheila said. 'Chloe was awfully pretty, but she seemed a bit . . . frosty. And much too thin.'

'A man likes a bit of meat to hold on to,' Daniel added. 'Curves. That's what we want. Like you, Olivia.'

Olivia smiled sweetly. Just let it go, she thought to herself, let it go.

Over dessert (ice cream, thanks to Conor's dereliction of duty), the conversation turned, yet again, to wedding plans. Sheila was lobbying for a ceremony in Ireland.

'It doesn't have to be Dublin if you'd rather something rural,' she said. 'I'm originally from Roscommon, you know? It's a lovely part of the world. There's the most beautiful church there, the Sacred Heart. It would be such a beautiful place for a wedding.'

Kieran cleared his throat loudly. 'Mum, let's not get ahead of ourselves,' he said. 'We haven't even set a date yet, let alone started thinking about venues. We have Olivia's family to think of, remember? We need to hold the ceremony in a place which is convenient for them too, and for our friends.'

'Oh, but Olivia's family's so wealthy,' Sheila said. 'They can go anywhere.'

Kieran rolled his eyes at his mother. Under the table, Olivia slipped her hand into his and gave it a squeeze. 'That does sound lovely, Sheila, but we'll not make any decisions for a while, I shouldn't think. We're haven't decided where the wedding will be, or what sort of ceremony we're going to have. You know I'm not Catholic, don't you?'

There was a loud clatter as Sheila dropped her spoon.

7.38 p.m.
Bea
Luca was asleep. I sat at the window of his bedroom, watching the snow fall for a while. It was amazing – an actual white Christmas! When was the last time that had happened in London? The streets were quiet; most of London seemed to have packed up and gone

away for the festive season; there were just a few revellers out and about, tottering along the pavements. Every now and again a brief snowball skirmish would break out.

I made myself a cup of herbal tea and ran a bath. Years ago I would have done this with candles and a glass of red wine, but now the only candles in the house were birthday candles, and the red wine was obviously a no-no. I turned off the light anyway and lay there in the dark, enjoying the silence.

I had almost slipped off to sleep when I heard my phone ringing in my bedroom. I let it ring. It stopped, and then started again. Anxious that Luca shouldn't wake, I hopped out of the bath, wrapped myself in a towel and, my teeth chattering, went to get the phone.

I picked up without checking who was calling. 'Hello?'

'Beatrice?'

A woman's voice. It was her. For a moment or two I couldn't speak. Eventually, I answered. 'Yes, this is Bea.'

'It's Lucy Jenkins here.'

I sat down on the bed in the dark. My heart was racing, my breathing shallow. I was conscious of a trickle of water dripping from my hair down the nape of my neck. I shivered. I didn't say anything.

'Beatrice?' she said again. 'I'm returning your call.'

Still, I was finding it hard to speak.

'I wanted to ask you', I said at last, 'why you came the other day. I didn't give you a chance to speak, I was upset.' I was going to say that I was sorry, but I couldn't quite bring myself to apologise to her.

'I shouldn't have just turned up like that, I should have called you first.'

I didn't argue with her.

'You had a child with you,' she said.

'My son, Luca.'

'His son?' Her voice broke; she started to cry.

'Yes, Marco's son. We didn't know I was pregnant ... He didn't know I was pregnant when he died.'

She started to sob. 'I'm so sorry, I'm so sorry.'

I let her cry. I didn't know what to say. I didn't know how to comfort her. I wasn't sure that I wanted to. For what seemed like a very long time, but was probably just a minute or two, neither of us spoke. Eventually, I asked her, 'Is it forgiveness you're after?'

'I just wanted ... to know that you were all right.'

Another long silence.

'I am all right,' I said at last. 'I wasn't for a long time, but I am now. I have my son, and my business. I will be all right. Will you?'

'I don't know.'

I was about to hang up, there wasn't really anything more I had to say, or that I needed to hear. But then it struck me that Marco wouldn't have left things like this. 'He would forgive you,' I told her. 'Marco would have forgiven you.'

Chloe

By the time they ordered their third drink of the evening, Chloe had learned that Conor was twenty-five years old and studying architecture at Trinity College Dublin. He supported Liverpool Football Club and, to a lesser extent, Celtic; and his favourite place in the whole world (apart from Anfield) was Tarifa on the Costa de la Luz in Spain.

They didn't have a lot in common. Chloe was not particularly interested in architecture, she hated sports in general and football in particular and she had always preferred France and Italy to Spain. But that aside, there was no denying that Conor was good-looking, funny and charming. He was also young enough not to be interested in a serious relationship. She had no doubt that, given another drink or two, she could be persuaded to go to bed with him.

Then her mobile rang.

'Sorry,' she said, taking the phone from her bag and checking the screen. It was Jack Doyle. 'Do you mind? I have to take this.'

She took the phone outside, lit a cigarette and took a long drag. 'Jack?' she said. 'Thanks for calling.'

'Pleasure. Hope I didn't interrupt your Christmas Eve festivities.'

'Not at all. I'm just having a drink with . . . some friends. What are you up to?

'Stuck in London, would you believe. I was supposed

to be heading up to Yorkshire to spend Christmas with my dad and my brother, but they've had a blizzard up there and the trains aren't running.'

'Oh God, are you on your own for Christmas then?'

'Looks that way. My own fault for leaving it so late. I was supposed to get the train yesterday but I ended up getting horribly drunk with my best mate and his wife and never got to the station.'

'Well . . . since you're all alone . . .'

'Hey, you don't have to ask me to spend Christmas with you. I wasn't angling for an invite.'

'I know you weren't. It's just there's this party that I'm going to tomorrow evening which might be fun. The food will be good in any case.'

'If you're sure, that sounds great. At the moment I'm looking at beans on toast and a couple of cans of beer.'

'It's a date, then. I'll text you the details.'

She dropped her cigarette butt into the snow and went back inside. Conor was just finishing up his third pint. 'Everything OK?' he asked. 'Fancy another?'

She hesitated for a moment. One or two more drinks and she could probably be persuaded . . .

'Actually, I really ought to get going. I don't want to leave the puppy on his own for too long. Not unless I want to be cleaning up dog pee all night.'

They walked home though the snow. Despite Chloe's protests that she didn't need him to escort her to her door, Conor was insistent. When they got there, they lingered on the doorstep for a moment. He wanted her to invite him in.

'Thanks for the drink, Conor. I had a really good time.'

'Me too,' he said, a note of disappointment in his voice. He leaned in and kissed her on the mouth; he slipped his hand around her waist and pulled her closer. The snow was starting to fall more heavily now, swirling around them as the wind got up.

'You should go,' Chloe said, pulling away from him. 'Maybe I'll see you again before you go back to Dublin?'

'Sure,' he said, turning to leave. She watched him walk along the road, his shoulders hunched against the wind. He cut a rather sad figure and she was tempted to call him back, but she knew she'd regret it when she woke up next to him in the morning. She went inside and mopped up three puddles of pee in the kitchen.

11.56 p.m.
Bea

I'd intended to get an early night, I had plenty to do on Christmas Day. So after I finished the call with Lucy, I put on a sweatshirt and leggings and went to bed with a book. I found my mind wandering, I couldn't focus on the page, so I just turned out the light and closed my eyes. The conversation I'd had with Lucy went round and round in my head. I'd thought that talking to her would bring some sort of

288

closure; it hadn't, but I was still glad that we had spoken. Maybe in a few months' time I would call her again. I had no intention of becoming her friend, but there was a chance that by helping her I could help myself.

Unable to sleep, I got up and made hot chocolate. I checked on Luca, who was sleeping soundly, and returned to my seat by the window to watch the snow. It was falling thickly now; there were at least a couple of inches coating the bare branches of the elm outside. It was beautiful.

The street was deserted, and must have been for a while now, since there were barely any footsteps in the carpet of white. Carefully and quietly, I opened the window and leaned out, taking a long deep breath of cold air. I glanced downwards. I was wrong. There were some footprints down there. There was one distinct set of prints coming from my right, leading from a snow-covered van directly to Sam's front door.

I pulled the window closed, checked Luca again, pulled on a pair of boots and, without even brushing my hair or putting on some lipstick, went downstairs. I opened the front door and took a couple of steps out into the snow. There was a light on upstairs. I rang the doorbell.

Like mine, Sam's intercom doesn't work, so you have to wait for someone to come to the door to let you in. No one came. I stood there, shivering, wishing I'd had the good sense to put a coat on before I ventured out.

It struck me that he might have looked out of the window and seen that it was me and decided not to come down. It struck me that it might have been a better idea to phone him. I took a step back, took one last look up at the window and went back inside. I'd just got to the top of the stairs when my doorbell rang.

I turned and ran back down as fast as I could, flinging the door open when I got to the bottom of the stairs. There he was, standing in the snow, a bright red beanie on his head, grinning at me.

'Was that you a second ago?' he asked me. I flung my arms around his neck and kissed him.

When he'd finally disentangled himself from my embrace he suggested we go upstairs. I made more hot chocolate, to which he added a nip of whisky (to his mug, not mine) from a silver hip flask, which he pulled out of his coat pocket. We were standing in the kitchen, me leaning against the oven, him against the counter, opposite each other.

'So . . .' he said.

'Where have you been?' I asked him. 'I called you. You didn't call back.'

'I needed some time to think,' he said, 'so I drove down to Bristol for a couple of days, to catch up with some old mates.'

'I thought . . . I don't know what I thought. I thought you were gone. I watched you go, and it felt . . . agonising.'

'You watched me go?'

'I called out to you, ran after you, but you didn't hear me,' I told him. 'At least I hope you didn't hear me.'

He crossed the room and put his arms around my waist. 'I didn't hear you. I'm sorry. But I did need to get away. And', he said, pulling me closer, kissing me lightly on my neck, 'it looks like my absence might have made your heart grow a little fonder, which is exactly what I hoped might happen.'

'Oh, so it was all a plan, an evil scheme designed to ensure I'd fall in love with you?' I asked.

'Designed to make you realise you already *were* in love with me,' he said, grinning.

'Oh really?'

'It worked, didn't it?'

'Yes,' I said, kissing him on the mouth. 'It did.'

Christmas Day

6.42 a.m.
Bea

Something was different. I looked up at the window. It was still dark but there was a pale luminosity about the sky. A reflection of the snow.

Something was different. The arm hooked around my waist. His arm. Sam. I waited to feel guilty, to feel the shame of my betrayal. Nothing. I didn't feel guilty, I didn't feel ashamed. This wasn't a betrayal.

There was a whimper from the room next door: Luca starting to stir. Gently I started to pull my body away from his, but he tightened his grip, pulling me back.

'Where do you think you're going?' he asked sleepily. I allowed him to pull my body back to fit his.

I'd imagined, when I thought about it, which admittedly wasn't very often, that the first time I slept with another man it would feel strange. Maybe not the sex, but this bit, the morning-after bit. It didn't. It felt comfortable. I felt happy.

I rolled over and kissed him. 'Luca's waking up,' I said. 'I'm going to go and get him.'

'He can sleep another few minutes,' Sam said, his eyes still closed, tightening his arms around me again.

'It's Christmas, Sam!'

He opened his eyes. 'Oh yeah. Forgot about that. Off you go then.'

I slipped out of bed and pulled my robe around me. Sam was smiling sleepily at me.

'What?' I said.

'Best Christmas ever,' he replied.

I went into Luca's room and pulled the blinds open. It was still snowing, much more gently now. Outside the streets were white and pristine, unsullied by human footprints; there were only a few tiny tracks: cats or foxes, disturbing the perfection. Gently, I picked Luca up out of his cot and gave him a kiss.

'Happy Christmas, my boy,' I whispered, nuzzling his warm neck.

'Ma ma ma ma MA!' he replied, giving me a huge grin.

I gave him a bath and dressed him in a fleece body-suit and a pair of dungarees. The two of us went into the kitchen where Sam, dressed in jeans and nothing else, was making coffee.

'Happy Christmas, my man!' he said, holding out his arms to Luca.

'Sam!' Luca said, loudly and clearly. Sam and I stopped moving, gawping at each other for a moment.

'He said your name!'

'He did, didn't he?'

I hitched Luca up on my hip and pointed to the handsome, shirtless man standing in my kitchen. 'Sam?' I said.

'Sam,' he replied.

We had smoked salmon and scrambled eggs with wholewheat toast for breakfast before opening our presents. We opened Luca's gift from his gaga: a tractor and trailer set, which I approved of, and a 'my first mobile phone' which was lurid green and made a hideous noise, of which I did not approve at all. Elina, his *nonna*, had got him a beautifully bound and illustrated book of fairy tales (in Italian), which was much too old for him, but which I would treasure. She'd also bought him some lovely clothes and, best of all, a fantastic wooden train set which he was immediately fascinated by. It was, in fact, the only present which held his attention longer than the wrapping paper.

'I think that's probably enough presents for now,' I said to Sam. 'Do you fancy a walk in the snow?'

'Yeah, great. I think there's time for one more present, though, don't you? He picked up a small round gift and held it out. 'What about this one? Is this also for Luca?'

'Yes it is. In fact, everything under the tree's for Luca. There might be one thing for me from Elina. Mum didn't bother this year, she got me gift vouchers from John Lewis.'

'Can I give him this one then?'

I hesitated a moment, but Sam was already reading the card. '"To Luca, love Daddy x".'

'It's not actually from his father, obviously,' I said, taking the gift from him. 'I just thought it would be nice to give him something anyway. It's a bit ridiculous really.' I felt stupid and awkward.

'Not at all, he should have something from his father.' He took the gift back and waved it under Luca's nose. 'Let's see what you've got here.'

Together they unwrapped a mini football, which Sam then spent the next ten minutes kicking to Luca's feet in an attempt to get him to kick it back. He didn't. He did pick it up and throw it, though.

'Basketball player, clearly,' Sam said kindly.

8.06 a.m.
Olivia

Olivia propped herself up against her pillows and reached for her green leather notebook. Beside her, Kieran was sound asleep. They'd decided to forgo the pretence of separate beds for Christmas Eve. And not just for Christmas Eve if Olivia was to have her way. She'd decided that in addition to Letting Things Go, she was also going to Reclaim Her Life – from Kieran's family, from Margie, from everyone else who seemed to be sticking an oar in. She wasn't sure whether these twin goals – LTG and RHL – were complimentary, or whether they were compatible at all in fact, but she was going to give it a go.

In the meantime, she was making a list. Or rather, she was making two lists: a simple, chronological plan for Christmas Day, and a Wedding list – just a few preliminary thoughts about the big day.

Christmas Day, to do:

9.15 Call Conor to make sure he's up [Very important, since he'd failed to make it to midnight mass the previous evening. If he missed breakfast, there'd be hell to pay.]
9.30 Make coffee, squeeze orange juice
10.15 Breakfast [Made to order by Kieran, Olivia was in charge of the Bucks Fizz only.]
10.45 Turkey
11.00 Present opening – part one

Olivia liked Christmas presents to be opened in an orderly manner. She did not approve of gift free-for-alls. She accepted that there were stockings to be rummaged through as soon as you woke up, and that the kids would want to open one or two presents earlier, but thereafter, things should be well organised. You waited until everyone was in the room and had a drink in their hand, and then the youngest children would select presents at random from beneath the tree, read the card and message aloud for everyone to hear, and present the gift to the appropriate person. As a result, present opening could take a while.

   1.15 Baste turkeys, prepare vegetables
   1.35 Call family
   1.50 Put potatoes and parsnips in oven
   2.15 Sprouts and carrots
   2.30 Lunch
   4.00 Present opening – part two
   5.30 Cake and champagne
   7.00 To the Honey Pot with all those who want
   to join

Olivia had a feeling – she hoped at least – that it might just be her and Kieran, and probably Conor, who would go to the party at Bea's. This was, after all, a waifs and strays party. Turning up with one's entire extended family was probably against the rules.

Having completed the day's 'To Do' list, she turned to her 'Preliminary Wedding Thoughts' list. This one was going to be much more interesting.

9.03 a.m.
Bea
Our walk didn't take us far. Sam popped next door to fetch his dog, Reggie, who's an elderly hound and did not appear terribly enthusiastic about running around in the freezing cold. In any case, the snow was so deep that pushing the buggy through it would have

been a trial, so Sam was holding Luca in his arms.
The sun had come out, the clouds almost cleared; it
was still bitterly cold, but so beautiful! I couldn't
remember London ever looking so beautiful, all the
dirt and the litter hidden from view under the thick,
white blanket.

Luca seemed baffled by it all, his eyes so wide they
looked as though they were about to pop out of his
head.

'It's snow, Luca,' Sam was explaining to him, carefully handing him tiny handfuls of it, which he of course
immediately shoved into his mouth, only to looked
completely shocked by how cold it was.

'No,' Luca said.

'Snow.'

'No.'

'He'll get there,' I said.

Sam slipped his hand into mine and we walked to
the end of the road. The snow and the sun and the
fact that it was Christmas Day brought out the best
in our neighbours; even the more unsavoury of the
local youth smiled and said hello as we went by. I
thought of what we must look like to them, to everyone
we passed: the perfect little family, the handsome dad
with a couple of days' stubble on his chin, holding
the perfect brown-eyed boy in his arms, walking hand
in hand with happy, relaxed mum, their faithful dog
trotting along a few paces behind them. It's what I
should have had with Marco but didn't. It's what was

snatched from me so cruelly two years ago. And now here I was, getting a second chance.

12.45 p.m.
Chloe

A plaintive whimper woke her up. She opened her eyes and looked straight into those of Alfie, who was sitting on her pillow a couple of inches from her face, looking worried. Chloe glanced over at her alarm clock. 'Fuck, it's late,' she mumbled. 'Sorry, Alfie. Catching up on my sleep. You must be starving.'

In the kitchen Chloe grabbed a bottle of champagne from the fridge, opened it and poured herself a glass. Yes, she was alone, but it was Christmas after all. And yes, technically it was breakfast, but it was after midday, which lessened the depravity of it, and in any case champagne is a perfectly legitimate breakfast drink (along with vodka, Chloe considered champagne to be the only acceptable breakfast alcohol).

She put out a bowl of organic puppy food for Alfie, but then felt a bit guilty. How was he to know it was Christmas if he didn't get a treat? In the fridge she found a block of pâté that she'd received as part of a Christmas hamper from a grateful client and cut off a large chunk, which she popped into Alfie's bowl. He wolfed it down appreciatively and looked up at her in expectation.

'More?' she asked. 'You'll get fat.' But she cut him another lump anyway. She couldn't eat pâté now without thinking of that foie gras at the Christmas party. The very thought made her feel ill. She topped up her champagne glass and took it into the living room, where she flicked on the TV and checked her phone.

Two new messages received that morning. She dialled into her voicemail.

Message received at 9.44 a.m.: 'Darling, it's Mum. I know we spoke yesterday but I wanted to ring and say Merry Christmas anyway. I do hope you're having fun. We're having a marvellous time here, it's so lovely to have your sisters home. Talk soon, bye.'

Message received at 11.15 a.m.: 'Chloe, it's me.'

She hit 'Pause'. It was Michael. She put the phone down on the table and took a slug of champagne. Then she picked it up again and resumed the message.

'I wanted to say Happy Christmas, babe.' He was speaking just above a whisper. He must be at home. 'I miss you, Chloe. God, I miss you so much. I can't stop thinking about you. I know you said that you wanted this to be over, but . . . I just can't believe it. Do you miss me? I think you must do. I'm sure you do. Listen, I can get away tomorrow, for an hour or two. I'm going to come and see you. Around three. OK?'

3.44 p.m.
Olivia

They sat down to lunch at 2.37, almost on schedule. Olivia was very pleased with herself. And the food was not half bad; they'd gone traditional: turkey with all the trimmings, roast potatoes, parsnips, sprouts. The usual. Afterwards there was Christmas pud (provided by Sheila) and highly intoxicating brandy butter (made by Olivia). They pulled crackers; the boys started reminiscing about the Christmases of their childhood; everyone drank a lot of wine. Sitting at the head of the table, Olivia sat back and surveyed them all. She missed her family, that was true, she missed playing croquet on the lawn in the sunshine, but this could be good, too. She could happily alternate, a Kinsella Christmas, in rainy Dublin or freezing London, then a Heywood Christmas in the sun. It would work. They'd make it work.

The kids, who had sat patiently through the majority of the Christmas stories, were starting to get restless. 'More presents,' came the cry, but Olivia insisted they stick to schedule.

'Go and play on the Play Station for a bit,' she offered, pouring more wine for Kieran's dad. 'We'll come through in a bit.'

The younger children happily scampered off into the living room, but Shannon, Richard and Diane's eldest, who was eleven but considered herself to be very grown up, opted to help clear plates. She pottered backwards and forwards from the living room to the kitchen, carefully carrying crockery and glasses, until eventually she came back to the table with Olivia's green notebook in her hand.

'This was in the kitchen,' she announced. 'Whose is it?'

'Oh, that's mine,' Olivia said, reaching for the book slightly anxiously.

Shannon did not relinquish it. She flicked through the pages.

'Shannon,' Sheila admonished her, 'give Olivia her book.'

But Shannon had started to read. '"Pre-lim-in-ary wedding thoughts,"' she pronounced slowly.

Sheila shut up. She was interested now. They all were.

'"The wedding should be: small, not too formal, non . . ."' I can't read this word. Mum?' Shannon showed the book to her mother.

'". . . denominational,"' Diane read out.

'What does that mean?'

'It means it won't be Catholic,' Kieran said. The rest of the family exchanged anxious glances.

'You are going to get married in a church though, aren't you?' Sheila asked anxiously. 'It's not going to be one of those register office jobs, where everyone stands around on some high street outside the town hall for the photos. I couldn't bear it. That's not what you want, is it?'

'I promise it won't be like that,' Olivia said, giving Kieran's mum her most reassuring smile. 'Perhaps that's enough for now, Shannon?'

'She's a very good reader,' Diane said. Shannon took this as encouragement.

'"No wedding dress,"' she read out, to gasps of

astonishment from the rest of the table. '"I will be wearing . . . cow-chure." What's cow-chure?'

'"Couture",' Olivia corrected her. 'It means I am *thinking* of just getting a great dress from a great designer. Not one that is specifically made for a wedding. And these are only preliminary thoughts, you know. I hadn't really intended for them to be shared with anyone,' she said pointedly, fixing Shannon and her mother with a steely glare.

'"Honeymoon somewhere we've never been before,"' Shannon continued, either oblivious to Olivia's ire or simply not caring.

'I'm definitely up for that,' Kieran said, delighted to hear something non-controversial. 'Uruguay, maybe. Or Suriname. Or Cambodia. Or somewhere in central Africa, maybe?'

Olivia smiled at him, slipping her hand into his. 'Anywhere you like, darling. So long as it's not in a war zone.'

'"No wedding list,"' Shannon went on.

'Olivia, you have to have a wedding list,' Suzie protested. 'People expect it. They'll want to give you gifts.'

'They're welcome to give us gifts,' Olivia replied. 'But I'm not about to tell them what to buy us. Plus, it's not like we need a new toaster or a new set of dinner plates. We have all that stuff already.'

'You could ask for cash,' Brendon suggested.

'Tacky,' Olivia countered.

'Or contributions to a charity,' Kieran offered.

'That's a bit worthy, Kieran. And in any case, that's what you do at funerals.'

'Can we open more presents now?' Oscar yelled from the living room.

'Absolutely,' Olivia called back, relieved. 'Let's go through to the living room.' She politely but firmly removed her notebook from Shannon's grasp. 'Thank you, sweetheart,' she said with a venomous smile.

4.12 p.m.
Chloe

After cleaning up the third batch of puppy poo that day, Chloe decided to get pro-active. She clearly wasn't a sufficiently strict mother. But she had no idea how to discipline her wayward puppy. What was one supposed to do? Rub their noses in it? That seemed cruel and undignified. And also unhygienic. She needed help. She opened her laptop and did a search for obedience schools. She needed somewhere that wasn't going to be too strict, too authoritarian. She wondered if there was a Montessori equivalent for dogs?

She made a shortlist of three likely-looking places, and then moved on to dog-sitting services. She hadn't really thought about what she was going to do with him when she went to work. The thought of leaving him all alone brought a sharp pang to her chest: this is what motherhood must feel like. Only there was no maternity leave for puppy owners. It really was most unfair.

She found a number of pet sitters, including some that combined obedience training with taking care of the hounds. That would be perfect, but it wasn't going to be cheap. It was expensive, this dog-owning business. And, no doubt, not tax-deductible. Still, when she looked at her little cherub curled up in his hand-crafted wicker basket, she knew it was all worthwhile.

Dealing with Alfie's needs wasn't just a practical thing, it was also a welcome distraction from the Michael problem. Her first instinct, when she'd got his message, was to call him back and tell him to sod off. But she hadn't. Some masochistic part of her wanted to see him, to hear what he had to say. Perhaps, she reasoned, letting him come round and say his piece was the best thing: it would give them closure. She knew, though, that she was rationalising. The chances were, if she allowed to him to come round, if she allowed him to hope, he would end up talking her into bed. She knew that she should trust her first instinct: the wise thing to do, the safe thing to do, would be to call now and tell him not to come.

She didn't call. Instead, she found herself a new distraction by deciding what to wear to Bea's party.

5.35 p.m.
Bea

When I thought about Christmas Day, when I was planning it, I thought about making the food and throwing the party, making sure it was a good day for Luca. That was it, really. I didn't have any expectations about how it would really be. And it turned out so much lovelier than I'd imagined.

After we'd had our walk, we went back to the flat. I put the guinea fowl in the oven to roast and got started on the side dishes (onions stuffed with pancetta, porcini and chestnuts, caramelised radicchio with pine nuts), while Sam read Luca a story and put him down for nap. Then he poured himself a glass of wine and helped (sporadically and, if I'm honest, not particularly effectively) in the kitchen, while I cooked, and we both swapped Christmas stories from childhood. It felt incredibly relaxed; it felt comfortable. Marco and I had never actually spent Christmas in this flat, so there were no jarring moments, no incidents when I thought to myself, that's what *he* did that year, no comparisons to be made. It just felt new, and exciting.

And though I adore my son more than anything on earth, I have to say that I had forgotten how much of a pleasure it is to slave over a hot stove for someone who actually appreciates your food, who devours it with gusto, with delight, someone who can express their appreciation in fully formed sentences. For months I'd been insisting, to my mother, to Elina, to anyone who asked me, that this Christmas should be about me and Luca, no one else. But somehow having Sam there felt perfect – we were already so close, the three of us. We immediately felt like a family.

When the eating and the crackers were done, we moved on to more presents. Sam fetched an enormous box from underneath the tree, which he began to unwrap with Luca. It was a wonderful silver retro racing car for Luca, big enough for him to sit on.

'Sam, that must have cost a fortune,' I said, 'you shouldn't have done that.' But Luca's shrieks of excitement as Sam pushed him around the living room on his new car suggested otherwise. Then it was my turn. I hunted under the tree for the little box I'd wrapped weeks and weeks ago, when I'd spotted a 1940s Longines watch in the antiques shop across the road.

Watching someone you care about opening the first present you've ever bought them is a nerve-racking experience, but I could tell from the moment he opened it, from the smile on his face, that he liked it.

'That's a beauty,' he said to me, giving me a kiss. Then he said, 'There's nothing under the tree for you, I'm afraid.' I laughed. 'No, I'm not joking,' he said. 'Honestly. I couldn't wrap your present. I tried, but it just ended in disaster. So it's still next door.'

'OK . . .' I said, intrigued.

'So, what I need you to do is stay here, leave the front door open, close your eyes and don't open them until I tell you. OK? No matter what you hear?'

I sat there for a minute or two, my eyes closed. I started to feel ridiculous. I decided to defy his instructions and got up to clear the table. I went backwards and forwards to the kitchen, carrying plates and dishes, closely followed by Reggie, who was hankering after more leftovers. Eventually I heard a noise, some banging and crashing, the sound of something being manoeuvred, followed by quiet cursing.

'Are your eyes closed?' a voice called out.

'Yes,' I lied, retaking my seat.

There was more banging and crashing, and a good deal of huffing and puffing, even some half-hearted barking from Reggie.

'Is everything all right?' I called out, starting to feel slightly anxious.

'Just you keep 'em closed,' Sam replied.

Thirty seconds or so later, I was instructed to open them.

On my kitchen windowsill, the sunniest spot in the room, Sam had placed a terracotta trough, which ran the length of the sill, and in it there were herbs. There was trailing thyme, parsley, sage and basil, coriander, tarragon, even some creeping rosemary. It looked beautiful. It smelt divine.

'A herb garden!' I cried out, delighted. 'You made me a herb garden!'

'You like it?' he asked. 'I've been working on it for a while. We had a slight scare when the tarragon seemed to be failing a few weeks back, but I think it's on the mend now.'

'It's perfect, Sam. It's the perfect present. I love it.'

Sam stayed upstairs with Luca and Reggie while I went downstairs to get everything ready for the party.

I hadn't had this luxury, of having another adult around the place to help out with childcare, not since Mum had moved out. Over the past few days I'd been spoiled. First with Elina, then with Sam. I could really get used to the extra help. It did make life so much easier.

The doors were opening at six, but I didn't really expect anyone to turn up much before seven. Having initially feared there would be too many people and not enough food, I was now worried that the snow-fall might deter people from leaving the house at all. I pictured a rather sad gathering of five or six of us, sitting around surrounded by canapés, trying our best to appear festive.

Kathy and her daughter, Elsie, turned up early to help with the set-up.

'You didn't have to come, you know,' I told them. 'It's not like you're without family.'

'Bloody glad to get away from them,' Kathy replied. 'My other half and my dad have been arguing poli-tics solidly since the Queen's speech.'

'Not solidly,' Elsie pointed out. 'There was that brief interlude when they argued over who they hated most, Chelsea or Arsenal.'

'Yeah, and that was the highlight of the afternoon.'

We set out the canapés and heated up the soup, while Elsie prepared two sorts of punch: alcoholic and non, her mother keeping a beady eye on how much vodka she poured into the alcoholic one. Just before six, Sam came round with Luca, who was fast asleep in his buggy. He said hello to Kathy and Elsie before giving me a long, slow kiss on the mouth.

'Oh, finally got it together then, have you?' Kathy muttered grumpily. 'Longest running "will-they won't-they" saga since Mulder and Scully.'

I blushed furiously and busied myself with re-arranging blinis on a tray.

6.45 p.m.
Chloe

For someone who regarded herself as both fashion-able and quite cool, Chloe had an uncomfortable habit of arriving very promptly at social events and finding herself the first one there. She had intended to arrive no earlier than seven thirty, but having told Jack that the party started at six, she suddenly panicked, fearing he might get there on time, think she'd stood him up and leave.

When she arrived at the Honey Pot there was just a handful of people there: Bea, Sam (holding Bea's little boy in his arms), a couple of women, one of whom worked in the Honey Pot, and a tall, burly Scot whom she recognised as the landlord of the Fox. They said their hellos and Bea made introductions; she offered Chloe a mug of soup, which she declined, and a glass of punch, which she accepted.

'How many people are you expecting?' Chloe asked.

'Anyone's guess,' Bea replied. She looked a little

nervous. 'Have you had a good Christmas Day?' she asked.

'Uneventful,' Chloe replied. 'I didn't get up until midday.'

'I think I saw you in the pub last night, didn't I?' Alec, the owner of the Fox, asked. 'With a chap?'

'A friend, yes,' Chloe said, ignoring Bea's enquiring looks. The door swung open and a small group of people entered, none of whom Chloe knew. There was a heavily pierced young woman, accompanied by an older man, a very tall, very thin man dressed in a black suit with a hat, and the homeless, possibly paranoid schizophrenic bloke who hung out on the corner outside the bookshop most days.

She helped herself to a Parmesan, mascarpone and cranberry scone and a second glass of punch and withdrew to the corner of the room. Surveying the rather odd collection of party guests, she was regretting inviting Jack along. What would he think? That she had no real friends and so had to hang out with a collection of weirdos and virtual strangers? This was of course true, but not really something she wished to advertise.

Sam, who had handed Luca to Bea, came to join her in the corner of the café. 'Bea tells me you've got a new puppy,' he said.

'Alfie,' Chloe replied. 'Bea and Olivia bought him for me for Christmas. He's adorable. An Airedale terrier.'

'You should bring him round to meet Reggie, my

lurcher. He's getting on a bit now – I think he must be well over a hundred in human terms – but he does like a bit of company.'

Chloe kept one eye on the door while making small talk, or rather dog-talk, with Sam. It was hardly the most scintillating conversation, but she was relieved to have someone to talk to. If Jack could arrive now, while she was standing in the corner talking to a hand-some man, that would be ideal. Unfortunately, Sam abandoned her to go to chat to the next group of people who came through the door. He was replaced by the heavily pierced girl, who introduced herself as Danielle. Danielle, it turned out, was the owner of Alfie's mother and without gainful employment.

'I'm thinking of going to art school next year,' she told Chloe. 'But I haven't decided whether I want to do that here or in New York. Y'know?'

'So what are you doing in the meantime?' Chloe asked, though she wasn't particularly interested in the answer.

'Anything. Helping my dad out in the shop. I've done some telesales stuff – which I don't recommend, by the way.'

'I'll bear that in mind.'

'I do some babysitting, walk people's dogs. You know the sort of thing.'

Chloe didn't know, but she was suddenly interested. 'You wouldn't want to take care of Alfie, would you? While I'm at work?'

They were just sorting out the details (Chloe, delighted

to discover that Danielle had no idea how much money some people charged for those sorts of services, was on the verge of securing an extremely favourable deal) when Olivia arrived. With Kieran and Conor in tow. And immediately behind them, following so closely that Conor actually held the door open for him, was Jack Doyle.

7.42 p.m.
Olivia

The Honey Pot was buzzing by the time they arrived; there was barely room to push through the door. Bea came over to give her a welcoming hug and pass round glasses of punch. There were a handful of people whom Olivia recognised from the neighbourhood – the bloke who owned the antiques store and a tall man in a hat whom she'd seen at Highgate Cemetery – but most of the people there were strangers. Apart, of course, from Chloe, who was standing at the opposite end of the room, looking anxiously over the heads of the crowd in Olivia's direction.

Olivia squeezed through the throng, grabbing a couple more glasses of punch on the way over to meet Chloe.

'You OK there?' she said when she finally reached her, assuming that the arrival of a friend would put Chloe at her ease. Chloe, however, barely seemed to notice her.

'Happy Christmas,' she said distractedly. 'Lovely to

see you.' But she wasn't even looking at Olivia, she was standing on tiptoes, trying to get a good look at something that was happening on the other side of the room. 'Oh, this is a nightmare,' she said all of a sudden, taking the glass of punch from Olivia's hand and swigging it back. 'This is a disaster.'

'What's going on?' Olivia asked, trying to see whatever it was that Chloe was looking at, but failing. She was about six inches too short.

'What the hell are they talking about?' Chloe hissed.

'What are who talking about?

'Conor and Jack. They're standing over there having a conversation, chatting away as though they're best friends. This is a nightmare,' she said again.

'Who the hell is Jack?' Olivia asked.

Chloe gave Olivia a brief recap of the past few days, the encounter at the bookshop, the telephone messages, drinks with Conor the night before.

'I know he's your soon-to-be brother-in-law,' Chloe said, sounding almost apologetic, 'and he is really lovely, but I'm just not . . . feeling it. I probably shouldn't have gone out with him. I didn't want to get his hopes up . . .'

'Oh, sod that,' Olivia said, dismissing Chloe's concerns with wave of her hand. 'You did nothing wrong. First of all, Conor's just come out of a long relationship, so he probably wasn't looking for anything serious, and secondly, Kieran says he's been a bit of a player in the past, so I really wouldn't worry about it.'

They were joined at the back of the room by Bea, who was carrying a tray of Roquefort shortbreads.

'Good crowd,' Olivia said, popping one of the biscuits into her mouth.

'Not bad at all. I was a bit worried the weather was going to put people off.'

'God, these are delicious,' Chloe said, polishing off one shortbread and helping herself to a couple more. 'If I could cook like you do I'd be the size of a house.'

'That reminds me,' Olivia said. 'I never got round to asking you if you cater weddings.'

Bea had never catered a wedding. 'I'm really not sure I could, Olivia. I suppose it would depend how many people you were inviting, what sort of food you wanted . . . My staff is tiny, you know. There's really only me and Kathy and a few casuals who help us out . . .'

Kathy, who was standing just a few feet away, overheard her name and came over to join them.

'Olivia's getting married,' Bea explained. 'She was asking if we could cater her wedding. I was just saying that we just don't have the staff—'

'Rubbish!' Kathy cut in. "Course we could do it. We simply hire a few extra people. It's a brilliant idea. We need to expand our business, get some new revenue streams . . .'

'Mum got this book, *Embrace Your Inner Entrepreneur*, for Christmas,' Elsie said apologetically. 'She's been reading it all afternoon.'

'Ambition, Beatrice,' Kathy said. 'That's what it's all

about.' She turned to Olivia. 'So how many people are you thinking of inviting to this wedding?'

While Olivia and Bea talked catering, Chloe had climbed up a few steps at the back of the café in order to give herself a better view of what was going on elsewhere. Across the room, Jack and Conor were still chatting. The conversation looked amicable enough. Then, all of a sudden, they both turned round to look at her. Conor smiled; he looked genuinely pleased to see her. Jack's expression was harder to read.

'Oh fuck,' Chloe muttered under her breath.

8.12 p.m.
Chloe
They were approaching. Conor in front, Jack a couple of paces behind him, they worked their way through the crowd. It probably took less than thirty seconds for them to get to her, but to Chloe it felt like for ever. When Conor reached her, he kissed her on the cheek. 'Merry Christmas,' he said. 'Great to see you again.'

She mumbled something incoherent and turned to look at Jack. 'Hi,' she said. 'Glad you could make it.'

'Happy Christmas,' he said. He didn't kiss her.

The three of them stood there, an awkward silence descending over their group.

'So,' Jack said eventually, 'which pub were you two drinking in last night? Somewhere local, I take it?'

'Have you met Bea?' Chloe asked, ignoring his question in the vain hope that he might forget about it.

317

'She owns this place. Makes all the food. Here, have a toad in the hole. They're very good.'

Jack took one and popped it into his mouth, the faintest hint of a smile playing on his lips.

'I'm enjoying the book very much, by the way,' Chloe said.

'*No Fury*?'

'No, the other one. But now you mention it I did enjoy *No Fury* too.'

'There's no accounting for taste,' Jack said.

Chloe introduced Jack to Bea, Olivia and Kieran, who were debating the pros and cons of autumn versus spring weddings. Olivia was leaning towards autumnal, Kieran preferred spring.

'The weather's better, everyone's in a good mood, looking forward to summer,' Kieran argued.

'Why not just have it in summer then?' Bea asked.

'Too hot,' they agreed in unison.

'And everyone gets married in summer,' Olivia pointed out. 'People get really sick of going to weddings. Whereas an autumn wedding is unexpected. What do you think, Chloe?'

Chloe swallowed her quail's egg in one gulp. 'Christ, I don't know. All weddings are essentially the same, aren't they? All your friends come along, they sit through the really boring bit – the ceremony – then they get to have some drinks, then they sit through another boring bit – the speeches – and then they have more drinks and dance. I don't really see why

318

anyone makes such a fuss over when or where you have these things.' She realised that everyone was looking at her oddly. 'What?' she said. 'It's the truth, isn't it?'

The evening was not going particularly well, Chloe felt. She hadn't been able to have a proper conversation with Jack at all. First Conor was there; then she'd made that speech about weddings, which apparently no one agreed with; and now Jack was being monopolised by Bea, who was talking to him about classic Italian recipe books. The crowd was beginning to thin out a little. Chloe took the opportunity to grab her coat and nip outside for a cigarette.

Her phone beeped in her pocket. She'd missed a call. Michael. She checked the time; it was just before nine. She needed to make a decision. She rang him back.

'I was starting to think you weren't going to call,' he said, speaking in a whisper. 'Hang on a moment, I'll just—' He broke off. She heard him call out that he was going outside to smoke a cigarette. 'Sorry,' he said, speaking in a normal voice now. 'Happy Christmas, baby.'

'Michael, why are you calling me? We've said everything there is to say, we've talked about this. I don't want to see you any more, OK? I don't miss you,' Chloe said bluntly. And she meant it. In that moment, she really did. 'I'm sorry, but it's the truth. I don't miss you. I actually feel better since we broke up, I feel better about myself. I'm sleeping now, you know that? I sleep. For hours on end.' Behind her, the door banged shut as more revellers left the party.

'Chloe, we just need to give it a bit more time,' Michael was saying. 'After New Year, things will be different, I promise you—'

'Oh my God, will you please stop promising me things?' Chloe said. 'You're always promising. Things won't be different next year, they'll be exactly the same; we'll all just be a bit older and a bit more exhausted by it all. You'll still love being with me, but you'll still love your wife and your children and you won't want to leave them. And I don't want you to leave them either, Michael. It's time you stopped using me as an excuse for avoiding everything and started working on your marriage. Either that or just leave them, but not for me.'

'Chloe, I want to be with you, I do, please . . .' He was pleading with her.

'You're too late, Michael. I've met someone.' She needed to put an end to this, once and for all.

'You're lying.'

'I'm not lying,' Chloe said, flicking her cigarette away, watching the sparks fly into the snow. 'I have met someone. Nothing's happened yet, we haven't even been on a date, but I think we will. And I really like him . . .'

'You're saying this to upset me.'

'Michael, I'm really not. I'm sorry you're upset, but

I'm not making this up. I have met someone, I met him the other day, in a bookshop. It was totally unexpected, I wasn't looking—'

'What's his name then?'

'Jack. His name's Jack Doyle.'

She ended the call and slipped the phone back into her pocket; she took a deep breath and turned to go back into the party and there he was, standing just behind her. She jumped.

'God, you gave me a fright,' she said. 'You shouldn't creep up on people like that.' She was blushing a deep red. How long had he been standing there?

'Met someone, have you?' he asked her with a smile. Long enough, apparently. 'And his name's Jack Doyle? Are you sure it's not Conor?'

'I'm very sure,' Chloe said, as he leaned in to kiss her.

10.15 p.m.
Olivia

Conor managed to persuade Alec, the landlord of the pub, to open up for a couple of hours. He and a handful of other party-goers decided to see out the night there. Chloe and Jack had disappeared a little while ago, Chloe saying she needed to get home to Alfie. Olivia and Kieran stayed until everyone, bar Sam, had gone home. They offered to help with the clear-up, but Bea wasn't having any of it.

'We'll do it all in the morning,' she insisted.

'Thanks for a really great night,' Olivia said to her.

'And I'll come in and see you in a couple of days so we can talk some more about wedding food.'

They walked home in the snow, Olivia holding tightly on to Kieran's arm.

'I told you not to wear those heels,' he said, laughing as she skidded dangerously across the icy pavements for the third time in a hundred yards. It was a clear night, the moon a perfect crescent in a cloudless sky. They were walking slowly now, deliberately picking their way through the snow, arms wrapped around each other.

'OK, I'll give you an autumn wedding if you'll give me honeymoon in Iran – how does that sound?' Kieran suggested. They were making wedding bargains.

'No war zones, Kieran.'

'Iran's not a war zone. The Iranians are not at war with anyone.'

Olivia rolled her eyes. 'They might be by the time we get married.'

'Charming. OK, how about Uzbekistan then? It's supposed to be incredible.'

'Don't they torture people there?'

'They torture people in lots of places, Olivia. They torture people in America. That's never stopped you going shopping for shoes in New York.'

'They do not torture people in America.'

'Guantanamo Bay.'

'Guantanamo Bay is not part of America. It's a

US army base in Cuba. And they're closing down Camp Delta now anyway.'

'You're being pedantic.'

'You're being ridiculous.'

Planning this wedding was going to be fun.

11.15 p.m.

Bea

Luca was sound asleep in his buggy behind the counter by the time the last of our waifs and strays – Olivia and Kieran – left the café. Predictably, however, by the time we'd closed up and gone upstairs, he'd woken up and was ready to party.

'Maybe if I give him something comforting to eat he'll go down,' I said to Sam, who was doing me no favours by dancing around the room to the radio ('I Wish It Could Be Christmas Everyday', of course), flinging a delighted Luca up into the air.

'That's really not helping,' I said as I opened the fridge. There was some of the bread and butter pudding left over from lunch.

'But Bea, it's Christmas,' Sam said plaintively. 'If he can't stay up late at Christmas, when can he stay up?'

I popped the pudding into the oven to warm it up. 'If you're going to stick around,' I said, 'we're going to need a bit more discipline in this house.'

He grinned at me. 'I'm definitely sticking around.' He stopped throwing Luca about and brought him over to me.

I took my son from his arms. 'Would you like some panettone, Luca?' I asked him.

'Panettone,' Luca said.

'What did you say?'

'Panettone,' he said again with a giggle.

'Bloody hell,' Sam whispered, 'he really is Italian.'

For some ridiculous reason, I started to cry. Sam put his arms around me and Luca, hugging us both.

'Oh my God,' I sniffed, 'when I tell Elina this, we'll never hear the end of it. And my mother will be *furious*.'

The three of us ate dessert together, all repeating the word 'panettone' *ad nauseam*. Then I put Luca to bed and sat with him until he fell asleep. Sam was in the kitchen, washing up. I went up behind him and slipped my hands around his waist.

'You don't need to do that,' I murmured into the space between his shoulder blades.

'I know I don't,' he replied, carrying on.

'Did you mean what you said?' I asked him. 'About sticking around? Because it's not exactly your modus operandi, is it? In the time I've known you I don't think I've ever seen you stay with the same person for more than a couple of weeks.'

'Bea—'

'No, let me finish. It's not that it's a big deal for me—'

'Oh, thanks!'

'No, I mean it is a big deal for me, but that's not what worries me. Luca's already so attached to you,

324

he adores you, you know? So, even if this doesn't work out, you can't disappear from my life. Even if we hate each other—'

'We're never going to hate each other,' he said, drying his hands and turning to face me. He pushed the hair back from my face and kissed me. 'Have you ever wondered why none of the other women lasted?'

'Because someone better turned up?'

'No, you idiot, because I was waiting for someone better, for the one someone better, the only person I was actually interested in, to notice that I was there, that I was interested.'

'I hope we're talking about me?'

He kissed me again. 'Of course, you fool.' And he took my hand and led me to bed.

I woke in the early hours. I slipped out from under Sam's protective arm, pulled on my robe and walked quietly into Luca's room. He was fast asleep, breathing as deep and slow as only a baby can. I sat in my seat at the window. The blind was open – I had forgotten to close it when I went to bed. The snow had stopped and the rain had started again, turning the white blanket into much uglier slush. It wasn't sad to me, though. It didn't feel like the end of something. It felt like the beginning.

ALSO AVAILABLE IN ARROW

Confetti Confidential

Holly McQueen

Isabel Bookbinder dreams of pearly white weddings, happy brides, handsome grooms. And champagne towers that don't topple over. She dreams of the perfect wedding. But not for herself . . . For her clients.

It's all about bride management as far as Isabel's concerned. Even when she misplaces a couple of brides and loses her job working for wedding guru Pippa Everitt, Isabel isn't disheartened. She throws herself straight into launching *Isabel Bookbinder, Individual Weddings*, and with a pop starlet and a millionaire as her first clients, business is looking rosy.

Unfortunately for Isabel, nothing ever goes quite according to plan. . .

Praise for Holly McQueen

'If you like Sophie Kinsella's *Shopaholic* books and you miss Bridget Jones, then meet Isabel' Louise Bagshawe, *Mail on Sunday*

'Marvellously funny' *Jilly Cooper*

'I think Isabel and I were twins separated at birth. I love her!' *Katie Fforde*

'I quite fell in love with Isabel. Funny, charming and accident-prone, she is the perfect heroine for today' Penny Vincenzi

arrow books

ALSO AVAILABLE IN ARROW

Confessions of a Reluctant Recessionista

Amy Silver

It's crunch time for this spendaholic

Cassie Cavanagh has never minded being 'just a PA'. In fact she's quite content with her lot. She has a city job she kind of enjoys – after all she is indispensable, you know. She has a boyfriend who showers her with gifts – what more could a girl want? And she earns enough to (just about) finance the luxuries she's become accustomed to.

But Cassie hadn't banked on being made redundant. Nor had she pictured her boyfriend leaving her for an older woman! Nor had she ever imagined having to take financial advice from her student flatmate.

Reluctant to embrace the art of being thrifty, if Cassie's going to survive the recession in style, she's got a lot to learn about budgeting. And even more to learn about herself . . .

arrow books

ALSO AVAILABLE IN ARROW

A Funny Thing About Love

Rebecca Farnworth

The funny thing about love is that just when you think you've got it sorted, it turns round and bites you. Which is exactly what's happened to Carmen Miller.

Her ex-husband's girlfriend is pregnant, her career as a comedy agent is going down the pan, she's made a fool of herself with fellow agent Will Hunter, a man she's fancied for ages, and to cap it all she has to move out of her flat. Surely things can't get any worse.

Moving down to Brighton to write the TV comedy series that she's always dreamed about, Carmen meets the divine Daniel. A man so gorgeous, she doesn't even mind that he's got long hair. It seems that Carmen's life is on the up again. Until, that is . . . love bites again. Looks like Carmen's back where she started.

But could it be that love isn't the problem? Maybe she's just been choosing the wrong men.

arrow books